THE INTERROGATION OF
ASHALA
WOLF

D0263923

THE INTERROGATION OF
ASHALA WOLF

AMBELIN KWAYMULLINA

**WALKER
BOOKS**

This is a work of fiction. Names, characters, places and incidents
are either the product of the author's imagination or, if real, used
fictitiously. All statements, activities, stunts, descriptions, information
and material of any other kind contained herein are included for
entertainment purposes only and should not be relied on for
accuracy or replicated as they may result in injury.

First published in Great Britain 2014 by Walker Books Ltd
87 Vauxhall Walk, London SE11 5HJ

2 4 6 8 10 9 7 5 3 1

Text © 2012 Ambelin Kwaymullina
Cover image © Mircea Bezergheanu / Shutterstock.com

The right of Ambelin Kwaymullina to be identified as author of this
work has been asserted by her in accordance with the
Copyright, Designs and Patents Act 1988

This book has been typeset in Garamond

Printed and bound in Great Britain by Clays Ltd, St Ives plc

British Library Cataloguing in Publication Data:
a catalogue record for this book is available from the British Library

ISBN 978-1-4063-5339-6

www.walker.co.uk

This is for Blaze, because it was his
idea in the first place; and for the towering tuarts,
with all my love.

THE HALLWAY

He was taking me to the machine.

I'd known they were going to start the interrogation today as soon as a smiling Doctor Wentworth had pronounced me "much better". She'd sounded pleased. Proud of her work, I guessed. I suppose she had a right to be, because I'd been in bad shape when I arrived – barely conscious, and bleeding from the hole in my stomach where the blade had gone in. I'd caused that wound myself, by flinging my body onto one of their short, sharp swords when I realized I was caught. My desperate escape attempt had almost succeeded, too. I'd come close to death. *Just not quite close enough.*

I still couldn't believe that Wentworth, of all people, could work in a detention centre. Because, like me, the doctor had an ability. She was a Mender, and a powerful one, at that. Otherwise, she'd never have been able to make my gaping flesh knit back together so impossibly fast, leaving me with barely a scar. Only, unlike me, Wentworth had a tattoo on the inside of her wrist: the regular Gull City Citizenship mark of a seagull in a circle, but with a line through the middle. That tattoo meant Wentworth's ability was considered harmless enough for her to be given an Exemption from the Citizenship Accords. Wentworth still wasn't quite a Citizen, but she wasn't technically an Illegal any more either. She was an Exempt, and that meant she could use her ability without fear of being hauled off by enforcers. Perhaps she even believed, as most Citizens did, that locking Illegals like me away was a good thing, or at least a necessary thing. Only surely she *had* to realize that Detention Centre 3 wasn't the same as the other centres, not if the whispers about Neville Rose and Miriam Grey were true. And I knew better than to hope that they weren't. There was no way I was going to be that lucky.

I turned my attention to my surroundings, tuning in

to the feel of the dry air on my skin and the sound of two very different sets of footsteps along the corridor. My feet seemed to be making a muddled, shuffling sort of noise: a pathetic contrast to the clear, measured pace of the guard beside me. I wished, not for the first time, that I had access to my ability, but my Sleepwalking power was blocked. Reaching upwards, I slid my hand along the stone band that circled my throat, my fingers lingering over the metal pad at the front that was set with nine tiny numbered buttons. I had no idea what the combination to the lock was, and for as long as the rhondarite was touching my skin, I wouldn't be able to Sleepwalk. And even if I did manage to get rid of the collar, my troublesome ability wouldn't be much help. It took time and preparation and, oh yes, actually falling *asleep* to be able to Sleepwalk. Plus, using my ability took a lot more energy than I had right now, or was likely to have anytime soon. I was only going to get steadily weaker in this place. Especially once I got to wherever I was being taken, and the questions began.

We'd been walking through long white hallways for a while, so we had to be getting closer to our destination, but I didn't know how close. This entire sprawling complex was made out of composite, a super-tough

9

building material churned out by the recyclers. Every wall, floor and ceiling was the same – smooth, pale and embedded with tiny flecks of colour that caught the light. I'd always thought composite was kind of pretty, but being surrounded by so much of it made me feel lost. It was difficult to tell exactly where in the detention centre I was. Worse still, I wasn't even sure I knew *who* I was any more.

This morning I'd smiled at a fellow prisoner, a dark-haired, brown-skinned girl dressed in white detainee shirt and pants. She'd seemed so frail, so defeated, that I'd wanted to cheer her up. Then I'd realized I was looking in a mirror. It had been a dreadful shock. How could I have changed so much? They'd only caught me yesterday! Surely I wasn't, surely I couldn't be that sad-eyed girl – at least, not where it counted, not on the inside. Because she'd seemed terrifyingly vulnerable. As if she was the kind of girl that might tell secrets to the government. The kind who could be broken by the machine.

I stumbled, tripping over my own feet. My guard put out a hand to steady me, and I jerked away. He let his hand fall, and I gazed at him resentfully, thinking that he was every bit the ideal enforcer – dark hair brushed precisely into place, black uniform perfectly fitted to his lean, muscled body and a rhondarite sword in a sheath at his hip. Ever since the two of us had left the hospital, I'd been half-expecting him to say something, but he'd remained utterly, emotionlessly silent. *Justin Connor, coldly perfect, and perfectly cold.* Georgie had been more right than she knew when she had compared him to those old world sculptures that flanked the entrance to the Gull City Museum.

But even as I thought that, unwelcome memories crowded into my mind, of times when Connor had been something very different from the aloof stranger who walked beside me now. I suddenly felt like crying, and with what was no doubt an enforcer's instinct for weakness, he chose that exact second to glance down at me. *If he notices I'm upset, I really will die.* Taking a breath, I blurted out the first thing that came into my head: "Georgie thinks you look like an angel."

One eyebrow soared upwards. "A *what*?"

"An angel," I repeated. My voice, to my relief, was steady, and I concentrated on pouring as much scorn as I could into it. "A human with wings, like the old world statues. Only you're not. In fact, there's barely anything human about you."

"They're not real."

I glared at him. "What's not real?"

"Angels."

"Then why," I demanded, "does Hoffman say they walked the earth during the Reckoning?"

"I didn't think you'd read Hoffman's *Histories of the Reckoning*."

"Every word of the entire fifteen volumes." Or at least, I'd had bits of the fifteen volumes recited to me by Ember, which was virtually the same thing.

"Well," Connor said dryly, "those angels were supposed to be messengers of some kind of god. Since a lot of people thought the Reckoning was a holy judgement on humanity, it's likely they imagined the angels. Because even if there were any gods, they didn't cause the Reckoning. Everyone knows it was humanity's abuse of the environment that made the life-sustaining systems of the earth collapse."

I fell silent, wondering if he was lying about the angels. If they did still exist, the Bureau of Citizenship probably had them locked up somewhere, since the government wouldn't be any keener on humans with wings than they were on humans with abilities. On the other hand, it had been over three hundred years since the Reckoning, so maybe the angels had died out long ago. Or maybe they cut off their wings so they could blend in and survive. Connor would do something like that. Connor would do whatever was necessary, I knew that from personal experience. He'd been so clever and convincing, first exploiting a childhood friendship with one of my Tribe members to make contact with us, and then telling endless lies, the biggest of all being that he was an administrator, a simple clerk. I should have demanded more proof that he was what he claimed to be, and I was miserably conscious of the reason why I hadn't. Right from the start, there'd been an odd connection between Connor and me, an inexplicable bond that I couldn't deny or explain. In secret, fanciful moments, lying beneath the night sky with the rest of the Tribe snoozing around me, I'd foolishly imagined that Connor and I might be like those binary constellations Ember had once told me about, two stars orbiting each other. It seemed ridiculous now, and it *was* ridiculous. Only I'd felt so strongly that I'd known him – that, even though he was a Citizen, the patterns of his thoughts and emotions were akin to my own. But the truth was that he was nothing like me, and I'd never known who he was.

"So," I sneered, "I suppose you believe in everything the government says about Illegals? That rubbish about putting the Balance in jeopardy?"

"You don't think we need to preserve the inherent harmony between all life?"

Now he's just trying to provoke me. "You know I believe in the Balance. What I don't believe is that having an ability makes me or anyone else a threat to it. How exactly is someone like Georgie supposed to be dangerous? All she can do is predict the weather!"

"Which is why," he replied calmly, "she probably would have received an Exemption, had she not run off to join your Tribe."

"Yeah, and spent her whole life having to apologize for being born with an ability. She's better off with us."

"Will you still say that when she is so busy staring at the sky that she wanders off the edge of a cliff?"

Inwardly, I flinched. I *did* worry about Georgie, who could be a little odd. But there was no way I was going to admit that to Connor. "Georgie's fine. The Tribe watches over our own. Not that I'd expect you to understand, since it's obvious the only person you care about is yourself."

His blue eyes flicked to me. "You might be surprised by the people I care about."

"Are you going to tell me that you've got a family somewhere? Like your Illegal cousin, for example? The one you wanted to bring to the Tribe?"

He shook his head. "As I'm sure you've realized, there is no such cousin. It was a ruse."

"You mean a lie. Like telling me you were an administrator was a lie. Connor the clerk, who hated the way enforcers pushed Illegals around and was so sympathetic to our cause. What was the point of all that pretending anyway?"

"What do you think, Ashala?"

"I don't know, *Connor*!"

Except I did know. He'd been gathering information about the Tribe, trying to find a way to detain us. *To detain me.* Which, in the end, was exactly what he had done.

The frustrating thing was, I'd known for the past week that he wasn't what he seemed. Seven days ago, Daniel, who had been spying on the centre from the grasslands, had spotted Connor walking out of the gates dressed in enforcer black instead of administrator beige. But before I'd had the chance to do something about it, a piece of spectacularly bad luck put me and an enforcer troop in the same place at the same time. It had been sheer, terrible coincidence that they made an unscheduled supply run into the bustling farming town of Cambergull on the exact same morning I was there to attend a clandestine meeting. They hadn't even been searching for me, and I might have bluffed my way past them too, if the troop hadn't included the one enforcer who could identify me on sight.

"I guess you'll be getting a big promotion out of this," I said bitterly.

"I expect I will, yes."

"You're awfully smug for someone who caught me by accident."

"And you are not very grateful."

I was so astonished, it took me a second to be able to speak. *"Grateful?"*

"I probably saved your life in Cambergull. Or weren't you conscious enough to remember?"

"No," I lied. "All I remember is a bunch of enforcers standing around uselessly, while I bled to death." Which was what the rest of them had done. Every one of them had frozen in horror when they'd realized their valuable prisoner was badly hurt. Not Connor,

16

though. He'd taken charge, putting pressure on the wound, sending someone running for a doctor, and finally rushing me to Wentworth once it was clear ordinary medicine wasn't going to be enough. *If he's waiting to be thanked, he'll be waiting a very long time.* It seemed the last and cruellest betrayal, that he would fight so hard to save me for interrogation instead of allowing me to slip quietly into the safety of oblivion.

"If you had any decency in you," I said tiredly, "you'd have let me die."

His face was completely devoid of expression. "That would have defeated the purpose of capturing you."

Because dead people couldn't be subjected to the machine.

For a perilous instant I was on the verge of saying, *Don't you care at all?* I could feel the words rising up, fighting to be spoken, and before they could escape me, I changed them into something else. "You've *never* asked the Question?"

"The what?"

"You know, Connor. The Question. The one that Friends of Detainees keeps writing in red paint across the front of Bureau of Citizenship offices." The posing of a simple, ten-word question was one of the

17

strategies of the growing reform movement, a loose alliance of groups and individuals who were pushing to have the Citizenship Accords dismantled altogether. Enunciating every word distinctly, I put the Question to Connor: "'Does a person with an ability belong to the Balance?'"

He shrugged dismissively. "I have never asked that."

"You genuinely believe we're outside the natural order? That you can treat us however you like without causing disharmony, because we're simply not part of the Balance in the first place?"

He nodded, and I knew I should leave it alone. But it still seemed unreal to me that he could be this person, that there was no trace left of the Connor I'd thought I'd known. "I guess that explains how you sleep at night," I snarled. "Because I honestly don't know how you could live with yourself otherwise."

"I will do what I must, in order to preserve my world."

"I'm one Illegal trying to live free! You *really* think that capturing me, putting a collar around my neck and interrogating me is necessary to save your world?"

"Yes."

There was an unmistakable ring of truth in his voice. He truly thought I was some kind of unnatural thing,

18

and it hurt, more than I'd expected it to. Focusing on the floor, I tried to breathe past the sudden pain around my heart. Then Connor spoke again. "You're not 'one Illegal'."

"What?"

"You are the Tribe, Ashala." I frowned, and he continued. "You were the leader, the glue that held them together. Now you're gone, it won't be long before they start squabbling with each other, and leave the safety of the Firstwood. We think it shouldn't be more than six months until they're detained. The enforcers here are taking bets on it."

I inhaled sharply, furious, and not only because of what he'd said. The consuming rage I'd felt at discovering his betrayal rose up, and I wanted to make him feel some of the pain he'd caused me. *If I had a sword, or a knife, or a big heavy bit of wood...* But I didn't. All I had to strike him with were words. "The Tribe is bigger than me. They'll go on, and grow stronger with every Illegal that joins them. Until the day they march on your centres, enforcer."

"Is that supposed to be a threat, Ashala?"

I bared my teeth at him. "There will come a day when a thousand Illegals descend on your detention centres. Boomers will breach the walls. Skychangers will send lightning to strike you all down from above, and Rumblers will open the earth to swallow you up from below. There will be nowhere to hide, nowhere to run, and no way to stop them from freeing every single Illegal in this centre. And when that day comes, Justin Connor, think of me."

He stopped dead, and swivelled around. I hoped I'd finally got to him, that he was annoyed, infuriated even. Only whatever emotion was illuminating his features wasn't anger. I wasn't sure I could even have described it, except to say it was powerful and deeply felt, transforming him from a distant marble angel to a flesh-and-blood human being. He was so impossibly gorgeous that I almost instinctively reached out to touch his face, seeking confirmation that such living perfection could be real. Then, to my astonishment, he pressed his fist to his heart in an enforcer's salute, a silent gesture of respect.

I staggered backwards. *He's mocking me.* I waited for him to laugh, or make some sarcastic comment, but he just stood there, arm across his chest, body slightly bent towards me, blue eyes intent upon mine. *What is this, some kind of weird enforcer acknowledgement of a worthy opponent or something?* It didn't feel like that, though. It felt like he was offering me his allegiance, which was nonsensical. He was an enforcer, a Citizen, and I was a detainee, an Illegal. He was the betrayer, and I the betrayed. But, for the space of a few unsettling seconds, something seemed to pass between us that ignored everything we were, and formed our relationship anew. Until he resumed his stride down the hallway, and the moment was lost.

Troubled, I fell in beside him. *What was that?* I couldn't afford to be so shaken, not in this place where all I could rely on was myself. I stole a glance at him under my lashes, and found that he was once again an unreachable statue. *What did you think, Ashala?* I asked myself jeeringly. *That he was going to tell you it was all part of some elaborate plan, and he didn't betray you?* Somewhere deep inside, a small, defiant part of me answered, *Yes*. Right on top of that, I heard a familiar voice saying, "Trust your heart, Ash."

Georgie? Wide-eyed, I scanned the hallway. But she wasn't here, and I realized the voice had been in my head. *I've been captured, I've almost been killed and now I'm losing my mind?* It was crazy to hear voices in your head, and crazier still to be comforted by what they told you. I choked back a hysterical giggle, and stifled the hope that, despite everything, had flared to life within me. *You are tired,* I told myself, *and injured.* My mind was playing tricks, and all my heart would do was betray me. Again.

Connor stopped suddenly, and I stumbled to an awkward halt, realizing to my dismay that we were standing in front of a door. It was white, like every other door in this place, but I knew what was behind it.

We had reached the machine.

DAY ONE

THE ADMINISTRATOR

But I found no machine waiting for me. Just a man dressed in administrator robes sitting behind a large white desk with an empty chair in front of it. Then I noticed another door on the far side of the room. Behind that door, I had no doubt, was the machine.

Connor waved me towards the administrator, before stepping away to take up a position against the wall at my back. I sensed his watchful gaze upon me as I moved forwards, obviously ready to intervene if I took it into my head to make some futile escape attempt. I ignored him, focusing instead on the elderly man behind the desk. He had a nice face – brown eyes that twinkled out from

23

behind wire-rimmed glasses, a long, inquisitive nose and a mouth that seemed to curve up at the corners, as if he smiled a lot. I felt ever-so-slightly reassured. Until I reached the chair, and he said, "Hello, Ashala. My name is Neville Rose. You can call me Neville, if you like."

I sat down heavily. *It's him.* I should have realized. Not that I'd ever met the man before, but I'd heard the stories that had circulated about Neville Rose during the six years he'd run Detention Centre 1; tales that he and a doctor named Miriam Grey had secretly experimented on Illegals and developed some kind of interrogation machine. I'd known too that he'd been put in charge of this place, the government's brand-new detention centre for Illegal orphans. So it made perfect sense that he'd be waiting here to ask me questions. I just hadn't expected him to seem so … sweet. Grandfatherly. Harmless.

He wasn't harmless. Not at all.

I swallowed nervously. Neville continued speaking, in that same pleasant tone. "I'm the Chief Administrator here at Detention Centre 3, and I would like it if the two of us could be friends. I almost feel like I know you already." He reached down to open one of the drawers of the desk and pulled out a thin file. There wasn't a name on it, just a number, but I knew this had to be *my* file, my very own entry in the detailed records the government kept on all Illegals and runaways.

It hadn't taken them long to figure out who I was, or rather, who I'd been, before I ran. Then again, I guessed Connor had been feeding them information about me for weeks now. I comforted myself that I knew a little about Neville too, and he wouldn't even realize it. I'd never told Connor that some of the Tribe made runs into the towns and Gull City, picking up gossip where they could. It was surprising how much could be learned by hanging around a Friends of Detainees rally.

Neville tapped the cover with one long finger, and said cheerfully, "According to this, Ashala Jane Ambrose, you're sixteen years old, and were born in Gull City. Although you call yourself Ashala Wolf now, don't you? Why wolf, can I ask?"

He peered at me over the top of his glasses. I stared back, wondering if he truly expected to lure me into handing over information about myself with the friendly grandpa routine.

Finally, he spoke again. "All right, Ashala. If you

don't want to talk about your name, let me ask you something else. How do you think you ended up here?"

What is that, some kind of trick question? "I was captured in Cambergull, and this is the closest detention centre. Where else would they bring me?"

"That's not quite what I meant. It's your choices that brought you here, Ashala. You see that, don't you?"

"No," I said flatly. "I don't."

"Let me put it this way. You could have entered this place like any other detainee and lived peacefully among others of your kind. Instead, you've come here as a law-breaker, no longer entitled to the same privileges as the others." He shook his head at me. "You were twelve when you ran away from Gull City. Old enough to know you were required to undergo a Citizenship Assessment after you reached the age of fourteen. And that you should have asked for an assessment earlier if you suspected you had an ability. You did suspect, didn't you?"

Oh yes. Ever since I was eight, when I'd had an intense, vivid dream that I was flying over the city, and I'd woken up on the roof. After a couple more incidents like that, it hadn't taken a genius to figure out I had some kind of power that occasionally let me do

26

the things I was dreaming about. "Yeah, I suspected. That's why I ran away."

"So you *chose* to ignore the Citizenship Accords. What's more, by living in the Firstwood, you encourage others to do the same, and it's not even adults you're influencing. It's innocent children."

I opened my mouth to tell him that the kids I knew could think for themselves better than most adults could, and then decided against it. I didn't want to confirm there were no adults in the Tribe, although there weren't. Most Illegals ran away before they were assessed at age fourteen, and anyone who didn't was either put in detention, or given an Exempt tattoo. Or even a Citizenship tattoo, if they were able to fool an assessor. It wasn't like the whole system was completely foolproof – I knew that some adult Illegals must escape detention, or get tired of living as an Exempt, because I'd heard there were other groups of Illegals hiding out in the countryside that had people of all ages in them. But no adult had ever tried to join the Tribe, yet.

I had no reason to share any of that with Neville, though, so I shrugged and said, "I don't *make* anyone do anything. If people choose to run, it's because they want to live free."

The Chief Administrator spread his hands outwards in a pleading gesture, giving me a good view of the Gull City seagull on the inside of his wrist. "Can't you see how irresponsible you're being? Detention is necessary, Ashala." He quoted softly, "'There is an inherent Balance between all life, and the only way to preserve it is to live in harmony with ourselves, with each other, and with the earth.' Do you know who wrote those words?"

"Alexander Hoffman. It's from *Letter to Those Who Survive.*"

He was obviously surprised that I knew that. "Ah … yes. Do you know why he wrote the Letter?"

"He was trying to tell anyone who lived through the Reckoning how to make sure it never happened again. But he never said anything about people with abilities being a threat to the Balance. Not in the *Letter*, not in the *Histories*, and not anywhere else."

I could see he hadn't expected me to know that, either. A lot of people didn't. Ember said it was a common misconception that it was Hoffman who'd come up with the idea for the Citizenship Accords, when really it was the government, or more specifically, the Council of Primes. I considered telling that to

Neville in a superior tone of voice, but he started speaking again before I could get a word in.

"Hoffman was writing during the Reckoning. People didn't begin to manifest abilities until the end of it, and there were very few who had them. He could not have known what a danger you Illegals would become. We know now, though, don't we? How many cities are there, Ashala?"

I frowned, realizing where he was going with this. "Seven."

"That's right. Seven great cities, as sophisticated as anything in the old world, except without the pollution, the overcrowding and the terrible disparity between rich and poor. But in the beginning, there weren't seven cities. There were eight."

It always annoyed me when people tried to use a two-hundred-and-fifty-eight-year-old tragedy to justify the Citizenship Accords. "All that Skychanger was trying to do was make rain. She couldn't have known what would happen!"

"One young girl threw the world so far out of Balance that Vale City now lies beneath the waters of Lake Remembrance. Was the Council of Primes wrong to be afraid?"

I'd been taught all about this back in school, and I hadn't found it a very convincing argument for the detention of Illegals then either. "The reason there was such torrential rain was because it happened about forty years after the Reckoning ended, when the weather was still a bit wild. But the ecosystem stabilized two hundred and thirty years ago. A Skychanger couldn't cause a flood that big any more."

"And are you going to tell me that a Rumbler couldn't cause an earthquake? Or that a Firestarter couldn't start an inferno?" He leaned towards me, his brown eyes drilling into mine. "After what happened to your own family, Ashala?" Reaching into the file, he drew out a photograph and tossed it across the desk.

I gasped at the sight of the familiar faces, snatching up the image and scanning it greedily. *I can't believe they found this! I thought all the photos burned.* My gaze skimmed over the freckled, red-haired woman; the tall, brown-skinned man; and a younger version of myself, to focus on the fourth person in the picture – a plump, happy child with brown curls. *Cassie.* She must have been about five years old. She hadn't grown much older.

"Your parents were the ones who called in the assessor," Neville said gently. "For your sister, though, not for you. They never knew you had an ability too, did they?"

"No," I whispered. "They didn't." I hadn't even said goodbye to Cassie when I'd left for school that morning, and I should have known, *somehow* I should have known that Mum and Dad had guessed she was a Firestarter.

Neville pulled out another photograph – a picture of the scorched earth that was all that had remained of my house – and laid it flat on the desk. "We can never be sure what happened. Clearly, though, your sister's assessment was badly handled."

"Badly handled?" I hissed. "Cassie was murdered."

He sighed. "I think you know that her death must have been an accident. I realize you have some misguided notions about the government, but I can assure you we do not set out to slay children. Besides, you must know that no one would ever deliberately kill a Firestarter."

I gazed down at Cassie's picture, acknowledging sourly that he did have a point with that last bit. A person would have to be insane or suicidal to murder a Firestarter, because when they died, their bodies released an inferno. It was just such a blaze that had killed my parents, the assessor and his two enforcer guards. But not Cassie. She had to have been dead before then. Firestarters didn't burn, not while they were alive.

I'd learned over the years that it did me no good to wonder exactly how Cassie had died. It wasn't like there was any way I could ever find out for certain. Except now I couldn't seem to prevent my mind from crowding with all the questions I'd tried to shut out. *Did she run away from them, and fall and hit her head? Did she do something that made one of the enforcers panic and strike out at her? Was she afraid? Was it quick?* And the one that really tormented me: *Did she call out for her big sister?*

Something splashed on the photograph; to my deep embarrassment, it was a teardrop. I had a sudden, odd awareness of Connor, almost as if he'd moved closer, but a quick glance backwards told me he was standing exactly where he had been before. I rubbed at my eyes angrily, furious with myself for showing weakness. *Get a grip, Ashala!* Neville pushed a handkerchief across the desk, and I picked it up, wiping at my face. *I'm tougher than this. I am.* Only I didn't feel tough. I felt vulnerable and raw, as if someone had gone digging around inside me and left all my old wounds exposed.

"I can see," Neville told me sympathetically, "why you ran, Ashala. You were grief-stricken and confused. But you're not twelve years old any more. You can understand now that our entire society is built on the need to preserve the Balance. That's why we have Accords in the first place. The Necessities-of-Life Accords, that require the governments of the seven cities to provide food, clothing, medicine and shelter for all. The Benign Technology Accords, to ensure that we never develop the harmful technology that had such disastrous consequences for the old world, like nuclear power, or genetically modified crops. And the Citizenship Accords, to prevent Illegals from upsetting the Balance."

I wanted to argue, only I still felt teary. So I settled for scowling at him as he continued. "Our society strives to ensure that human existence never again puts the earth in jeopardy. Don't you think a world like that is worth protecting?"

"Of course I do!" I answered huskily. "I have no problem with the Benign Technology Accords and the Necessities-of-Life Accords. Or the Advanced Weaponry Accords or the Collective Transportation Accords or any of the others. But the Citizenship Accords are *wrong*.

People with abilities are not a threat to the Balance."

"I'm afraid you are. You bring forces into being that are too powerful and unstable to be allowed to exist unchecked. It isn't your fault, and I don't blame you for it. I genuinely care about you, Ashala." Nodding at Cassie's picture, he added, "I know you miss your sister. Perhaps you'd like to keep that photo?"

I was so muddled with grief that for a brief second I almost said yes, without even thinking about why he'd made the offer. Then I realized what he was doing, and I felt cold all over. *He wants to trade for the picture.* Despite everything I knew about Neville Rose, I'd almost let myself be taken in by his act. Only I was starting to think that the reason he was so convincing was because it wasn't an act, not to him. Inside his mind, where Neville kept the story of himself, I was certain he believed he was a good man, who'd been forced to do a few bad things for the sake of the Balance.

And it was horrifying how tempted I was to make a deal.

I quashed the wounded and exhausted part of myself that was desperate enough to trade a scrap of information for a scrap of kindness, and said, "You say that you care, but you don't. You don't care enough, and you don't care the *same*."

"The same as what, Ashala?"

"The same as you would about one of your own." The smiling face of my lost little sister beamed up at me from the photo, and I rubbed my thumb across her cheek. "If some ordinary kid had died the way Cassie did, there would've been an outcry and an investigation. There wasn't, though, not for a girl killed during an assessment. You set us apart, and you tell yourself it's for the good of the Balance."

"It *is* for the good of the Balance."

"How can it be," I demanded, "when Illegals are part of the Balance?"

He stiffened, recognizing where those words came from. "You shouldn't let yourself be taken in by the ravings of a few dissidents. I know you'd like to believe otherwise, but I'm afraid the answer to the Question is no."

He seemed a bit nettled, and it occurred to me that the growing strength of the reform movement must get to people like Neville Rose. When I'd left Gull City, there'd been barely a handful of people at each Friends of Detainees rally. Now there were hundreds.

"What makes you so sure Illegals aren't part of the Balance? A two-hundred-and-fifty-eight-year-old flood?"

"That flood was a warning. It was a demonstration of the unnatural effect abilities can have on the harmony of the world—"

"That flood," I interrupted, "was an accident, and one that could never even happen again." I looked away from him to gaze at Cassie one last time. Then, gathering up every ounce of willpower I possessed, I tossed the photo casually onto the desk, and the handkerchief after it. "The answer to the Question is *yes*. Which means it isn't going to be people like me that will cause the end of the world, Neville. It'll be people like you."

His lips tightened in the first hostile reaction I'd seen from him. *Anger*. It wasn't my words or my actions he was responding to – it was the fact that I was smiling. He probably thought I was laughing at him. In truth, I wasn't thinking about him at all. In my mind, I was in another place entirely.

About a year ago, Ember and I had sat together on a hillside on a sunny day. We'd just heard that Neville Rose had been appointed as the Chief Administrator of the new detention centre that was being built far too close to the Firstwood for my liking. Ember had been running over everything we'd ever heard about Neville – or at least, she'd started out that way, but had rapidly detoured into imparting deep thoughts about the nature of humanity. I guess it was hard to stay on track when you had an ability that effectively made you a walking library. Finally, though, she'd come back to Neville again. "There's a word," she told me, her pale face serious, "to describe people who believe so fervently that Illegals are a threat to the Balance that they can do the kinds of appalling things to us Neville is supposed to have done."

"There're two words," I said. "Nasty. Bastards."

She smiled and shook her head. "No. Mad." Her strange eyes – one brown and one blue – grew shadowed. "It's even a *necessary* insanity, for a society like ours. They couldn't keep the detention system going without it."

I shrugged, wiping clean a patch of ground and drawing on it with a stick. "Here, tell me what you think of this." It was my latest idea for how we could attack the new centre.

Ember groaned. "Not this again! Firstly, we don't

have enough Illegals with the right kinds of abilities for something like this. Secondly, even if we did, you know as well as I do that very few of them could control their abilities enough to pull this off. Thirdly, even if you *did* have your imaginary army, I can still see a dozen problems that you haven't thought of."

"So tell me what they are, and I'll solve them."

She rubbed out the drawing with her foot, her expression a familiar mixture of affection and exasperation. "It wouldn't matter if you did solve them, Ash. What do you think would happen to the Tribe if we attacked a detention centre? The government would throw every enforcer it had at us. When will you understand? We can't change the world with violence. Only with ideas."

I lifted my face up to the sun. "I can't see how ideas are much use against armed enforcers. Tell you what, though – if Neville Rose ever gets hold of me, I'll talk your philosophy to him."

And Ember had laughed, the pleasant, silvery sound echoing down the hill and through the trees of our forest home.

Neville's voice brought me back to the present. "Take her through." For a second, I couldn't make sense of his words, until I realized he was speaking to Connor.

Rising to my feet, I looked down at the grey-haired man behind the desk, and said, "I'll tell you, if you still want to know."

He glanced up, his pleasant expression firmly back in place. "Tell me what, Ashala?"

"Why I chose the name Wolf." I smiled a wide, joyful smile left over from that sunny day on the hillside. "It's because I always travel in a pack."

I could feel his puzzled stare following me as Connor escorted me towards the door on the far wall. It was highly unlikely that I was ever going to leave Detention Centre 3. So Ember would never know that I'd done what I'd told her I would. But the thought of her and the Tribe filled me with a sense of warmth and love and family that I knew Neville Rose could never understand or touch.

I walk among my enemies. But I carry my friends with me.

THE MACHINE

I stepped through the door and found myself facing a long white chair, one that was fitted with restraints, which were clearly supposed to go around someone's ankles, wrists and neck. I took a shuddering breath and gazed around the rest of the room. There was a screen mounted on the wall behind the scary chair, and to my far right, a woman in red medical robes stood at a table, pushing buttons on a shiny black box. She had to be Miriam Grey and, like Neville, she didn't look very intimidating. Grey was short and plump, with pretty green eyes and dark hair streaked with silver. Her entire attention seemed focused on the mysterious box, and

I studied it nervously, puzzling over what it did. Two cords ran out of it, one leading to the screen on the wall, the other to an adjustable silver hoop that rested on the table. Everything suddenly came together, and I realized, *This is all the machine.* The chair was to confine me, the hoop went on my head, the box was its heart and the screen was for… I didn't know, but *something* bad.

Miriam Grey stopped pushing buttons and peered at a display on her spooky box, studying a pattern of blinking lights. Then she gave the thing an approving pat and picked up a tiny metal case from the table, hurrying over to where Connor and I were waiting. She stood in front of me, shifting awkwardly on her feet, before finally deciding to smile. At least, she curved her lips in a way that would have been a smile on anybody else. On her it seemed somehow wrong, as if she was copying something she'd seen other people doing without understanding the reason for it. "Hello, Ashala. It's good to meet you."

I almost winced at the grating sound of her high, shrill voice. Everything about her seemed slightly off. And her eyes – there was something missing from those moss-green eyes, or from the mind behind them. I watched as she opened the case and pulled out a vial of colourless liquid. *Be brave, Ash!* But when she held it out to me, I couldn't keep myself from taking a step back, almost colliding with Connor. He put a hand on my shoulder, pressing it slightly in a clear warning not to run. It was a gesture I should have found threatening. Instead, warmth flowed from his fingers into my shaking body, and I pulled away, more disturbed by my reaction to him than I was by anything else in the room.

Grey spoke impatiently. "This is to keep you awake, so you can't Sleepwalk."

My heartbeat slowed as I put together the meaning of her words. Rhondarite could interfere with electronic devices, so they were going to have to remove the collar to be sure the machine would work properly. They didn't need to be concerned about me using my ability, since I was too weak and, ironically, too tired. But I hadn't shared many details with Connor about Sleepwalking, and since it seemed to be a rare talent – I'd certainly never heard of anyone else who could do it – they'd have no other way of knowing what my limits were.

Flicking off the stopper, I forced myself to toss the liquid down my throat. Almost immediately, I felt better. Everything became brighter and sharper, and my whole body buzzed with a dizzy kind of energy. I handed the vial back to Grey, doing my best to stare defiantly into those empty eyes.

She gave me another skewed smile, and went back to her box. "I'd like you to take your place in the chair, please."

I took a reluctant step forwards, and another. There was a sudden noise behind me, and I jumped, looking back to find Connor had let the door swing closed. *Guess Neville Rose isn't going to follow us in.* No surprise there – he would want to be able to pretend to me, and maybe even to himself, that he wasn't a part of what happened in this room.

Grey began humming, the sound mixing with the low drone of the box to create an unpleasant cacophony. My thoughts scattered, seeming to break and run from the horrors before me, and I found myself remembering an old world tale about a man who had been thrown into a den of beasts called lions by the government. I didn't know what lions were, but I figured they were probably a bit like saurs, huge reptiles with claws and razor-sharp teeth. One of the winged humans that Connor didn't believe in – an angel – had saved the man, although I couldn't quite recall how. My vision

44

blurred, and for an instant it seemed as if I was moving past a terrible green-eyed monster, while a black-haired angel stood silent and shining at my shoulder. I blinked, and the strange images vanished. *What a stupid thing to imagine.* The doctor was no lion, and Connor was definitely no angel come to save me. And even if he was, I thought dazedly, he couldn't fly me away. *He's given up his wings…*

Reaching for the chair, I slid into it. Connor tightened the restraints around my wrists and ankles, before entering the sequence that undid the lock on the collar. He took it away and put it on a shelf beside the door, giving me time to take a few deep, happy breaths before he returned to clip the final restraint around my neck. He was so close that I could see the pulse beating at his throat, and I suddenly wanted to speak to him, to whisper … I don't know, something heart-rending and brilliant. Ember had told me once that she'd known a girl who wanted to die, until someone had spoken six words to her that made her decide to live instead. I'd asked what the magic words were, and she said it didn't matter, the point was that no one ever knows when something they say will cause a profound change in somebody else.

I'd tested that theory on Wentworth in the hospital this morning, hissing at her as she checked my wound, "They're going to torture me unless you help me escape." Her young, cheerful face had grown shocked and a little worried, but she hadn't helped. *What would Connor do if I asked him to save me?* Laugh, probably. Except whether it was due to some weird effect of the stuff in the vial or an insane desire to torment myself, the urge to say the words was almost overwhelming. I bit down on my tongue, forcing myself to sit absolutely still and totally silent as he finished with the restraint. He retrieved the silver hoop, fitting it around my head before stepping back to stand by the door. I had a clear view of his face, and it was so completely devoid of warmth or feeling that I was glad that I'd been able to stop myself from speaking.

Miriam Grey's unpleasant voice filled the room. "I need to ask you some questions, Ashala. How many people are there in the Tribe?"

Thirty-eight, I thought automatically, and waited for her to get annoyed by my lack of response. Only she was strangely quiet. The hoop heated up, though, and sent tendrils of energy burrowing into my skull. They seemed to poke at me, digging around as if they were searching for something.

Grey began firing off one question after another: "How do runaways get to the Firstwood?" "Do any of them have help?" "How many of the Tribe have abilities that can be used offensively?" "What are those abilities?"

The digging sensation intensified, like wormy fingers were rifling through my mind, and fear surged through me. *It's trying to read my thoughts!* I tried not to think of the answers to her questions, but it was impossible to keep my head from filling with images. Firstly of the Tribe members with relatives who'd helped them escape – *Daniel, Briony, Anika, Keiko, Lia and Micah.* Then the practice sessions, where we all tried to perfect our abilities – *Trix making the earth rumble beneath us; Daniel moving so fast he was a blur in the air; Leo lifting a boulder that was three times his own weight.*

The energy worms came streaking hotly towards those precious memories. Panicked, I imagined a protective wall springing up around my thoughts. A towering, unbreakable wall. The zooming tendrils slammed into it, falling down to nothingness, and the machine made a plaintive beeping noise.

Ha! Take that!

I was feeling pretty happy with myself, until Grey spoke again, sounding creepily pleased. "Quite the strong one, aren't you? I think I'll have to set the level higher than I thought. I'll make the adjustment, and we can get started."

Get started? Hadn't we already started? I tried to see what she was doing. The restraint around my neck wouldn't let me move my head far enough, but I could hear her pushing buttons on the box. She was setting the level? The questions she'd been asking must have been a trial run, a way to work out how high she needed to set the machine to break into my mind. *This isn't over.* I gripped the arms of the chair, steeling myself in anticipation of what was to come. The hoop around my head warmed, then flashed white-hot. And the world exploded into shards of light.

When my vision cleared I found myself alone, and elsewhere. I was outside, standing on one of a number of rocky hills that rose up out of a rolling grassy plain. A *familiar* plain, with a familiar forest in the distance. Was I home? I couldn't be home! Yet this was my grasslands, my Firstwood, my bright blue sky. *Wait, what's that sound?* I concentrated on the far-off thumping noise.

Footsteps. Something large, approaching at speed. A saur? Seemed a bit loud, even for one of them.

In a sharp moment of clarity, I knew what was happening. I wasn't home. My body was still strapped into a chair in Detention Centre 3, and my mind was – where? *Here.* I was *in* my mind, and the thing that was coming was the machine.

A giant, red-eyed beast came pounding over the horizon. It looked like an oversized hound, complete with a shiny collar that was blinking with bright lights. Only while most of the beast was furry flesh, its legs and tail were made from glinting black metal. When it saw me it paused, jaws opening to display rows of gleaming teeth. I couldn't understand why it didn't come for me, until I realized what it was waiting for.

This was a hunt, and it wanted me to run.

I skidded down the hill, knowing I would never outpace the beast but that I had to try anyway. I stumbled into the long, yellowy grass and pelted forwards, making a dash for the trees. Behind me, the thumping of metallic paws grew nearer, and nearer. *I'm never going to reach the Firstwood before it reaches me.* I could feel the heat of its panting breath, and I knew the only reason it hadn't grabbed me already was because it was enjoying the chase. Still I kept going, running until my legs were burning and my chest was tight. The trees were tantalizingly close, but not close enough.

Someone shouted, "Over here!"

There was a girl standing by the tree line. A chubby, pale figure with a mop of short red curls. *Ember?* She held up a giant meaty bone dripping with blood. The smell of it wafted over the grasslands, a rotting aroma that made my eyes sting. The beast made a happy noise and swerved away from me, towards Ember.

"Watch out!" I screamed.

Ember grinned and threw the bone. It went flying up into the air, spinning in circles before it began to descend. For some reason, it seemed to be falling very slowly. The huge hound took off after it, and Ember yelled, "Ash! Get to the trees and climb."

I sprinted, barely pausing even when I reached the forest. Scrambling and clawing, I grabbed for the low branches of a peppermint tree, and swung myself up its twisting brown limbs before leaping across to one of the giant grey tuarts. I climbed even higher, not stopping until I was sitting, gasping and near-exhausted, on a sturdy branch a long way above the ground. A voice spoke in my ear. "Hi, Ash."

I jumped. "How did you get here?"

Ember rolled her eyes. "I'm in your head. Part of your subconscious."

"Part of my *what*?"

"I belong to the portion of your mind that exists beneath your conscious awareness. Except I'm showing myself to you as a friend, so you can interact with the deeper levels of your understanding. You see—"

"That's OK," I interrupted hastily. "You're a piece of me, come to help. I get it."

She seemed a bit put out at not being able to finish her explanation. *Exactly like the real Ember.* It was weird, and yet comforting too, as if one of my best friends actually was here.

"Ash, have you figured it out yet? The machine – it gets in your head and hunts memories."

"It's going to take my memories?"

"Not take them. It's going to display them, for other people to see."

"On that big screen?" I clutched at her arm. "Em, can they see us now? *Are we on the screen?*"

"No, the screen is blank, promise." She nodded at where the hound was still chasing after the bone as it continued its too-slow journey across the sky. "The bone is a memory. Once the dog gets hold of it, that memory is what they'll see, and that's *all* that they'll see."

"How can you even know that when *I* don't know that?"

"But you do know," she replied patiently, "because I'm you, and the machine is interacting with the whole of your mind so, at some level, you understand it. Only, Ash, I'm afraid this thing is on the hunt for painful memories. Either ones that hurt, or ones that it hurts to give up."

I tried to make sense of that. "Memories that hurt – I guess they'd be significant to a person. While memories that hurt to give up…"

"Are the ones that betray. Exposing something about yourself, or others."

I choked in dismay. "The bone – I mean, the memory – it isn't one that gives away any secrets about the Tribe, is it? Or about the Serpent? If they find out what he's planning…"

"Don't worry, Ash. It won't tell them anything they don't already know."

We both looked out at where the bone was getting closer and closer to the ground. The beast, sensing the prize was almost within reach, had started to leap upwards, with its long pink tongue lolling goofily out of its mouth.

Ember spoke quickly. "I haven't got much time left, and I need you to understand how dangerous Neville is. Did you notice the windows?"

"What windows?"

"That's what I mean. There weren't any. Not in the machine room, and not in the room where you met Neville. Think about it. Why weren't there any windows?"

The answer was obvious. "So no one can see in." The Tribe had heard lots of rumours about the machine, but never any hard facts, and now I knew why. The only ones who ever saw that machine were helpless detainees, or people who were completely loyal to Neville, like Connor. "Neville's hiding the machine, even from people who work at the centre."

"Yeah. You've got to be careful, Ash." She gave me a hug, and whispered, "I'm afraid I had to give them a memory that hurts." And she was gone.

I moved closer to the trunk of the tree, pressing my face to the grey bark and breathing in the eucalyptus scent of the leaves. It felt so real that for a few wonderful seconds it was easy to forget that this wasn't one of my beloved tuart trees. I tried to lose myself in it, to forget where I really was, and almost succeeded. Until the *crunch!* of the dog biting down on the bone echoed over the grasslands.

The sound cracked powerfully across my skull, making me feel like my head was splitting open, and I found myself oddly suspended between two places, at once sitting in the tuart and strapped to the chair in the room. An image began to form on the screen above the chair, a picture of a young boy walking through the Firstwood. I could see him clearly enough to make out all the places where his Gull City blue clothing had been mended, and I knew I was strolling along beside him, although I couldn't see myself. This was *my* memory, being played out from my perspective, and from somewhere in the room Connor and Grey were watching it too.

The boy scampered along with quick, impatient movements. His small, nimble frame made him seem about eight years old, even though he was nearly ten. *I know which day this is.* I shut my eyes tight, hoping to see only darkness.

Instead, I was pulled into the memory.

DAY ONE

THE MEMORY

Jaz had been chattering since we left the camp, flitting from one subject to another and then back again. I couldn't keep up with what he was saying, but that was all right, because he never stopped talking long enough for me to respond anyway. So I let him run on, focusing on his behaviour. He was fidgety, jumpy, brimming with energy. In anyone else it might have meant they were nervous. Not Jaz, though. He was himself, which meant he'd believed me when I'd said the thing with the saurs was all sorted out. He had no idea what was coming.

I examined the forest, checking we were alone.

We'd travelled some distance from the Tribe's territory. The caves where we made winter camp, and the vegetable and fruit gardens that were lovingly tended by the Leafers, were far behind us now. I listened hard, but the only sounds were those of birds chirping, animals scurrying through the undergrowth and the wind blowing sorrowfully through the tapering, glossy green leaves of the tuarts. I really had expected someone to follow. Maybe Briony, who'd screamed at me that I didn't have to do this. She thought everything would be OK if we apologized to the saurs on Jaz's behalf. That was Bry all over, always thinking she could get out of a difficult situation with a few nice words and a pretty smile. Andreas, our only Scaly, had told her it wouldn't work. The saurs were difficult to communicate with, even for a reptile speaker, but Andreas could talk to them well enough to know they weren't interested in an apology. They wanted something else entirely.

They wanted Jaz.

I watched as he ran ahead of me, trying to savour every last second with the brown-haired boy who'd always been my secret favourite among the youngsters. At first I'd loved him for being a Firestarter like Cassie, but I'd soon come to adore him for himself alone, unable to resist the irrepressible, brightly burning ball of energy that was Jaz. He'd come creeping into my heart, filling part of the void Cassie had left. Now he was in terrible trouble, because he'd broken the Pact with the saurs. It was the thing that kept us all safe, and not just because it meant that the lizards let us live here. The saurs were our protection against the government. Their presence alone was a deterrent to enforcers ever seriously trying to cross the grasslands, even if anyone did figure out a way to find us in the vast forest that we knew better than anybody.

Unfortunately, the threat of being eaten by saurs hadn't quite been enough to prevent two idiot enforcers from wandering onto the grasslands with those new energy weapons that everyone was calling streakers. They must've been crazy to take such a risk. But they'd got away with it, and Jaz was going to pay for their actions. Because he'd been the one who'd found the rabbit they killed, and he'd eaten it. *How could he have been so stupid?* Only I knew it wasn't stupidity. It was sheer thoughtlessness, and a reckless disregard for consequences was so much a part of Jaz's nature that it was hard to be mad at him for it. Anyway, I didn't have time to be angry. There was no time left for anything any more. Except for this journey that ended in death.

Jaz's cheerful voice interrupted my grim thoughts. "Ash, how about here?" He'd stopped a few paces in front of me and was pointing to a small patch of ground that ran beside a stream. "I think this is an excellent place to practise my ability. There's water and everything!"

I considered it. There didn't seem to be anyone else around, and we were near the fringes of the Firstwood too, which was good. I could do what had to be done here, and then go to the grasslands where the saurs would be waiting.

"OK, Jaz, let's practise," I said in a bright tone that I hoped didn't sound too fake. "Remember the rules, though. You need to sit down and focus."

He dropped to the ground next to the stream, and I sat opposite him. After a moment a tiny flame flickered into being between us. Then another, and another. I held my breath, hoping he wouldn't lose control as he had so often before. *Let him have a good day. Please, let him have a good day.*

And he did. The flames continued to appear until

they'd built themselves into a small fire that burned steady and perfect.

"Jaz!" I exclaimed. "You did it."

He grinned in delight. "I didn't set your boots on fire or anything!"

"Great job, Jaz." I reached around the fire to ruffle his spiky hair. "Tell you what, let's have a toast to celebrate."

He watched me as I pulled out my water bottle, his small face uncharacteristically serious. For an anxious second I thought he'd realized what I was doing. Until he said, "Ash? I want you to know I'm sorry. About the rabbit, I mean."

I shrugged. "Don't worry about it."

"I just thought *someone* should eat it since it was already dead. Those stupid enforcers didn't even want it, they were only seeing how far their streakers would shoot."

"I know, Jaz. Like I said, it's OK." I held up my flask, watching as he pulled out his. "A toast, yes? To the fire!"

"The fire!"

We clinked our bottles together and drank. I made sure I took a long, deep draught to encourage him to do the same. Although he probably wouldn't need to drink much. The herb that Ember had mixed into his water was strong. I used it myself when I wanted a proper heavy slumber without dreams or Sleepwalking. It should make Jaz sleep for hours, certainly long enough for me to carry out my plan.

The two of us sat in silence for a while, sipping our water and watching the fire die. I noticed that he didn't seem very tired. *Maybe I should have used more of the herb?* I went to lift my flask to propose yet another toast, but found my arm strangely heavy. I stared down at it, puzzled. Why couldn't I move?

"That herb is pretty powerful stuff," Jaz said.

My heart froze in my chest. "Jaz, what have you done?"

"Switched the flasks. Also put in more herb, since you're bigger than me." He sighed. "How stupid do you think I am, Ash?"

I tried to reach out to him, but found my limbs sluggish, unwilling to obey me. "You don't understand, Jaz."

"Yes, I do." His gaze, when it met mine, was steady. Determined. *Completely unlike Jaz.* "I understand that the reason we can live in the Firstwood without the saurs chasing us out or gobbling us up is because you made a Pact with them. None of us is supposed to eat the flesh of animals. I thought it'd be OK, since I didn't kill that rabbit myself, but it's not. Now you have to give me to the saurs. That's the way it is."

The herb was working fast. I could no longer support myself, and I began to topple to one side. Jaz jumped up and put his small hands on my shoulders, lowering me to the ground. "You know," he said, "I never did have much of a home before. Almost didn't here either. Remember how everyone wanted to throw me out for stealing when I first got here? That was before you made me promise not to do it any more. Only every time something went missing after that, everybody blamed me. Until you went around and found their things, and said they'd misplaced them. And everyone was *very* sorry that they'd been mean to me." He gave me sidelong glance. "Except you and I both know that I did take their stuff, even though I'd promised not to. I've never been able to figure out how you found my stash."

"Jashhh..." It was getting harder to form words. "Run. You have to runnnn..."

He shook his head. "If I run, they'll take you. But that was what you wanted all along, wasn't it?" I blinked in surprise, and he laughed. "See? I *do* understand. You were going to wait until I was asleep, and give yourself to the saurs instead of me. Only you didn't tell the others that, because you're the leader of the Tribe, and they wouldn't let you do it. Well, guess what? I won't let you either." He rested his hand on mine, and squeezed it. "You're more of a mum to me than my own mum ever was, Ash."

I tried to grab hold of him to keep him with me, but my stupid body wouldn't respond. He bent to press a kiss on my cheek. "Don't feel too bad, Ash. Maybe the saurs won't eat me. I'm too little to be much of a meal, and too tough to be tasty. Besides, they might be won over by my endearing personality." He gave me a classic Jaz grin, brimming with reckless mischief. Then he bounded away, leaving me to watch helplessly as his small feet disappeared into the forest. I tried to crawl after him. But the herb took me, plunging me into a sleep from which I couldn't wake and in which I couldn't Walk. I could say nothing, do nothing. *Save no one…*

I woke hours later to find the air was cold and the sky was growing dark. "Jaz," I yelled, "Jaz!" He didn't answer, and I staggered in the direction he'd taken, following the marks of his footprints to the edge of the Firstwood. When I reached the grasslands I found his water bottle sitting upright, as though he'd left it there for me. No, not his water flask. He'd switched them. This flask was mine.

I fell to my knees beside it, my chest so tight that I had to gasp for air. Scanning the earth around me, I read the grim story told by the tracks in the soil. The passage of the saurs was marked by flattened grass, and I could picture how the big lizards must have looked as they came pounding across the grasslands, their dark, scaled bodies so much larger than Jaz's tiny frame. And Jaz, my brave, stupid Jaz, had come out of the forest to meet them.

I checked for signs of a Firestarter death inferno – flames or scorched earth or smoke – but there was nothing. The saurs understood what Jaz was, and they wouldn't have risked damaging their hunting grounds by killing him where the grass would burn. *They'll have taken him to water, and then...*

Gruesome pictures filled my mind, and I couldn't

make them go away. *I should have known what he was planning.* Somehow, some way, I should have known. I'd lost another Firestarter. And it was all my fault.

I pressed my face into the ground that Jaz had walked, and wept useless tears into the small imprints of his footsteps.

The memory stopped, freezing on that moment of wrenching grief.

Everything dissolved into nothingness, before reforming around me in a new shape. I was back in the tree, holding tight to the trunk of the tuart and looking out to where the distant dog-beast was squatting on his haunches. The monster stared at me across the long stretch of earth between us, his red gaze seeming oddly sympathetic. Throwing back his head, he howled, a deep, mournful cry which echoed across the grasslands and shook the trees of the Firstwood.

Yes, I thought. *That's how I feel.*

The world of the machine started to fade, but the hound's howl stayed with me. It was still lingering in my ears when I found myself back in the white room, my body soaked with sweat and my face wet with tears. I closed my eyes, unable to process another image, another emotion, another thought. My mind curled in on itself, hunching into a tight ball, and I felt myself slipping gratefully into unconsciousness.

The last thing I was aware of before darkness claimed me was an angel, come to lift me into his arms and carry me out of the lion's den.

DAY TWO

THE CELL

I woke in an unfamiliar room. Blinking groggily, I tried to work out where I was. White ceiling above me. Uncomfortable mattress beneath me. Small barred window in the wall in front of me. *Some kind of cell?*

I sat up, and instantly regretted it when my head seemed to explode into a million pieces. *Guess it's no surprise that I have a headache.* Groaning, I collapsed back onto the bed, and closed my eyes against the bright glow of the morning sunlight. I could feel the smooth coldness of rhondarite against my neck, so at some point Connor must have put the collar back on me. He'd probably replaced it pretty quickly when I'd passed out – either Grey's stay-awake drug had worn off or my desire for unconsciousness had been stronger than whatever was in the vial. I tried to remember how I'd got here, and realized Connor must have carried me. *Wonderful.* As if I hadn't been humiliated enough.

I reviewed the rest of yesterday's events, trying to work out exactly what information I'd revealed. *Jaz.* They knew he'd been one of us. Since he was gone, though, that didn't really matter. No one could hurt him any more. And I'd told them about the Pact. But Ember had thought that it was possible the rabbit killing had been an attempt to mess with the Pact, which meant news of our agreement with the lizards had already leaked. It wasn't the kind of thing anyone would have made a special effort to keep secret, because we hadn't believed it could be used to hurt us, and it *shouldn't* have. Contrary to what the government had assumed, the presence of a few dead animals wouldn't have been enough to make the lizards think we'd betrayed them. If only Jaz hadn't eaten the rabbit!

I tried sitting up again, more slowly this time. I still didn't want to move, but my bladder was insisting I did, so I staggered across the room to use the toilet on the far wall. I was washing my hands in the basin beside it when there was a high-pitched wailing sound from outside. My pulse quickened in excitement. *An alarm?*

Pushing down the toilet lid, I climbed on top so I could reach the window. I couldn't see much – a patch of ground, the smooth composite walls of surrounding buildings and some administrators, strolling calmly along. Disappointingly, they didn't seem concerned about the wailing noise. Whatever was happening, it wasn't any kind of emergency.

I examined the window more closely, testing the strength of the bars and wishing I could access my ability. I'd have no trouble escaping if I could manage to Sleepwalk. When I Walked, I moved through the world in an unconscious state, seeing everything as part of a super-intense dream. The cell might appear to me as some kind of wily monster, holding me in jaws filled with long teeth like the bars on the window. All I'd have to do was smash those teeth in my dream and my fist would shatter the bars, setting me free. Only I had no chance of Sleepwalking with rhondarite around my neck.

I made my way back to the narrow bed, resting my pounding head in my hands and trying to regain some strength. I'd been sitting there for what seemed like ages – and not feeling any better, either – when the cell door swung open, and familiar voice said, "You're awake."

Connor stood in front of me, carrying a flask in one hand and a small rectangular package in the other. He scanned my face, and something jagged and wild flashed across his eyes, like lightning in a clear sky. *Anger?* But I could see no reason for him to be mad.

He held out the silver flask. "Drink this."

"What is it?"

"Medicine from Doctor Wentworth."

To keep me strong enough to continue the interrogation. I took the flask wearily, and edged back on the bed so I could lean against the wall. A spark of rage flared up inside me, as if I'd been infected by Connor's bad mood. I didn't have the energy to be truly angry, but it was enough to inspire me with a certain obstinate defiance. Moving with deliberate slowness, I drank some of the medicine, and counted to thirty before I took another swallow. Then sixty, before drinking again. Then ninety. I'd got all the way up to one hundred and fifty seconds between sips when Connor finally spoke. "You have to drink all of it, Ashala."

"Make me."

He looked exasperated. "You don't want me to do that."

That was true enough. The petty satisfaction I was getting out of annoying him wasn't worth having the medicine forced down my throat. Besides, even the small amount I'd had was doing wonders for the ache in my head. I took a few decent swigs. "So what's bothering you this morning?" I asked. "Don't tell me you didn't get that big promotion after all!"

"There is nothing bothering me."

Is too. I studied him intently as I continued to drink, noticing he seemed tired. "Having trouble sleeping? You should see Wentworth about that. Although I doubt she's got anything for a guilty conscience."

A muscle jumped in his cheek. "My conscience is clear."

"Oh yeah? I guess you must be proud of everything you've done, then. I mean, being the one to capture me would have been enough for most enforcers. But," I added with savage sarcasm, "it takes a *special* guy to tie me up and watch my mind get pulled to pieces."

Something fierce leaped to life in his face, and was gone again just as fast. When he spoke, he sounded

71

coldly resolute. "I told you before. I will do whatever I must."

"I know." I held his gaze. "Only that doesn't mean you like all the things you've had to do."

His expression was unreadable. The fact that he didn't reply, though, was enough to tell me that I was right. *I think I won that round.* Not that I expected him to have a sudden change of heart – he was too deeply committed to his beliefs for that – but the knowledge that he was suffering even a tiny bit over this was enough to cheer me up.

Basking in my victory, I took another swig of Wentworth's syrupy concoction. The soothing sensation of the medicine was spreading throughout my system, and I felt light, almost giddy. I guzzled the rest of it down, making sure to get every last drop. Connor waited until I'd let the empty flask fall to the bed, then handed me the rectangular package. "Eat. This is breakfast."

His voice had returned to something approaching his usual smooth tone, except it was a bit ragged around the edges, instilling me with a desire to provoke him further. I ripped off the wrapping and found a cream-coloured block inside, and made a show of examining it from every angle before shaking my head. "Oh dear.

I'm afraid you've gone and mixed up the food supplies with the building supplies."

"It's a protein bar, and it's perfectly edible."

"How do you know? Bet this wasn't what you had for breakfast."

"It was, actually."

"Really? Were you being punished for something?"

"I realize it might not seem very appetizing, but it contains all the nutrients you require."

I started to toss the bar from hand to hand. "What if I don't want it? It's going to be much harder to get me to eat this than it was to make me take the medicine." I threw it back and forth one last time, before waving it at him threateningly. "Plus, I'm armed now. This thing's so hard that if I hit you with it, I could probably kill you."

Connor didn't respond.

"What, no smile?" I asked flippantly. "Not even to acknowledge my plucky resilience, my gutsy defiance in the face of overwhelming odds?"

He retained his statue-like composure for a second longer. Then his lips twitched, and he *did* smile, a sudden flash of brilliance that sparkled across his eyes like light over water. "Ashala, please eat the protein bar."

With effort, I tore my gaze away from his face.

Breathe, Ash. Just breathe. It wasn't fair that a being of such imperfection could look so perfect. Why couldn't I see the flaws in his character running through his features, like hairline cracks through marble? Feeling awkward in a space that seemed too small for the both of us, I searched around for something to say. "Um … what's that noise outside?" Even as I spoke, I realized the wailing sound had stopped some time ago. But Connor understood what I meant.

"It was a test."

"A test of what?"

He glanced at the bar. I sighed and took a bite. It was completely tasteless, but food was energy, even when it came in unappealing block form.

"Wait, let me guess. It was the oh-no-the-detainees-are-escaping alarm? Or the better-run-because-Miriam-Grey-needs-a-new-test-subject alarm? Or," I finished witheringly, "is it the alarm that goes off if ever a government employee has an independent thought?"

"It's the fire alarm."

There was a disarming hint of laughter in his voice, and it was making me uncomfortable. I wanted him to be angry or annoyed, to create some kind of distance between us. "What, doesn't it work properly? I bet the

Inspectorate will have something to say about that on their big visit on Friday!"

"The alarm works fine. We're simply running a systems check to ensure everything is functioning as it should."

"Sounds like Neville's worried they're going to find something wrong. Like a memory-reading machine, for example."

As I'd expected, he had nothing to say to that. I knew he'd never admit out loud that Neville had been keeping secrets. I took another mouthful of the bland bar and retreated into silence, thinking about the Inspectorate and wondering if I could find a way to tell them about the machine.

The creation of the Inspectorate had been the first major victory the reform movement had achieved. Pro-Illegal groups like Friends of Detainees, together with concerned Citizens throughout Gull City and its associated towns, had put so much pressure on the government over detainee treatment that they'd appointed an independent Citizen's committee to inspect detention centres. Problem was, although both the current Inspectorate members were known to be sympathetic to Illegals, they were required to announce their visits well in advance. This particular inspection had been scheduled for weeks, which meant Neville would have already worked out how to hide what he didn't want seen.

But I know something he doesn't. I knew that two days from now, on the same day the Inspectorate would be here, an Illegal with a ridiculous alias would launch an attack. Unfortunately, the Serpent wasn't attacking the centre itself. He was aiming for something in the mountainous terrain which bordered it on two sides. The Tribe had known for a while that something was happening in the Steeps, because enforcers kept going out there, even though there was nothing for them to patrol except rocks. The Serpent had refused to share information with us, though, so I had no idea what he was attacking. But if the Serpent was going to use his reality-bending ability – however that worked – or if there was any kind of explosion, people might be able to see the attack from the centre. It would be a good distraction, if I could find a way to take advantage of it.

Connor's voice broke into my busy thoughts. "Ashala? You need to finish the bar."

My lack of enthusiasm must have shown on my

face, because he added, "Once you've eaten it, we can go outside for exercise."

"*Exercise?*"

"You are to receive half an hour of exercise every day."

"I didn't get half an hour yesterday."

"Yesterday you were a patient in the hospital. Today you are a prisoner in the cells."

Rules. The government loved their rules. Although I couldn't complain this time since they were working in my favour. I'd barely been outside since I came here, and it would be useful to get an idea of the layout of the centre. I polished off the bar and rose, only to find myself standing not more than two paces away from Connor. I almost sat down again, wanting to escape the unwelcome proximity – or rather, wanting to escape the fact that it *wasn't* as unwelcome as it should be. Except before I could do anything he turned and strode out the door.

I followed, making sure to keep some distance between us as we began to walk down yet another white corridor. My thoughts drifted back to Friday. I seemed to have a lot of small pieces of information, which altogether might add up to a big opportunity.

The Inspectorate, the Serpent, the fire alarm. Something was stirring in my mind. Something that was almost a plan.

And I didn't know why, but I had a weird feeling that I'd thought of all this before.

DAY TWO

THE PARK

This is very odd.

I was sitting on a bench, looking out over, of all things, a *park*. Stretching out in front of me was a grassy oval with spindly young trees, gleaming composite benches and a whole lot of shiny play equipment at the far end. If it wasn't for the high wire fence around it, and the rest of the centre beyond that, I could have been in any park, anywhere. It was all so strange that I felt slightly dizzy.

There were saurs screeching in the distance, loud enough that some of them must still be in the part of the grasslands that was nearest to the front of the centre. The lizards had apparently decided the large numbers of staff moving into this place constituted a potential threat to their territory, and they'd been stalking about for weeks now. The direction of their screeches let me know roughly which way the main gates were, but other than that, I had no better idea of the layout of the centre than before. My sense of direction was usually pretty good, but every time I thought I'd glimpsed a pattern to how the structures were set out, it slipped away, as if the knowledge wouldn't stick in my head. All I could say for certain was that there were lots of buildings, far more than seemed necessary for a detention centre. It was making me suspicious that Neville had plans for this place I hadn't begun to fathom.

There was a sudden flurry of movement from outside the fence, and I sat up, surveying one of the rows of house-like buildings that bordered the park. Doors were opening, and four beige-robed administrators were coming out, followed by a bunch of children in white clothes and collars. *The detainees!* I shot to my feet. Connor, who was standing guard a few paces away, gave me a warning glance. I sat back down again, almost twitching with the effort of keeping still, as the administrators guided their tiny charges through a gate at the other end of the park. Sixteen children in total, and none of them seemed older than ten. There'd be a lot more to come, too, if the Inspectorate found everything in this place was functioning as it was supposed to.

The administrators sat down on a couple of benches, smiling and chatting to each other. They didn't appear to be paying much attention to the detainees, which I supposed was no surprise, since the whole park was one giant cage. It was nice to see the kids running around, and to hear them giggling and yelling. Then I realized that one of them was watching me. A thin, spiky-haired boy, who was perched on the top of a climbing frame like a big lizard in a tree. My heart flipped over. *Jaz?* Except of course it wasn't him, just a kid who vaguely resembled my lost Firestarter. This boy had a longer, leaner body, his hair was inky black instead of brown and something about the stillness of his stance and the tilt of his head reminded me of the saurs. *He has to be a Scaly.* For some reason, animal-speakers often started to resemble the animals they communicated with. The boy raised his arm to chest height, moving his hand along in a quick serpentine motion.

My mouth fell open. *That looked almost like … a snake!* Could it have something to do with the Serpent? Maybe the boy knew about what was going to happen on Friday? I didn't see how, though. Perhaps all he was trying to do was tell me his ability by making some sort of reptile sign.

He seemed to be waiting for a response to his signal. I checked to make sure Connor wasn't looking, and hastily made the same snake sign back. It was all I could think of to do to let him know he had a friend in me, and it seemed to satisfy him. He nodded, and tipped his head towards the other detainees. Puzzled, I followed the direction of his stare. *What is he trying to show me now?* It was just a bunch of children playing silly games – three girls, running around with their arms flapping like wings, a boy jumping up and down in one spot, another boy and a girl speeding across the playground. I almost gasped out loud when it dawned on me what they were doing. *They're telling me their abilities.* Three Chirpers. One Rumbler. And two Runners.

Concentrating, I studied each detainee until I'd figured it all out. *Three Chirpers, one Rumbler, two Runners, four Growlers, three Leafers, one Waterbaby and one Pounder.* Plus the Scaly boy. I turned away, hoping they'd realize I'd got the message. I was so impressed by them that it was hard to keep the smile off my face. They might be detainees on the outside, but on the inside every one of them was thinking like a free person. These kids were Tribe in their hearts. And if there was any kind of confusion on Friday, we might be able to help each other.

An entire scenario began to form in my mind. If we could make it to the main gates, the only thing between us and the grasslands was a long stretch of gravelly earth. Unfortunately, the saurs had a very keen sense of borders, so unless someone was stupid enough to provoke them, they wouldn't help us by crossing onto the gravel. *But if we could make it to the grass...* The big lizards knew my scent, and I should be able to get them to understand that the children weren't a danger. Anyone who tried to come after us, though, wasn't going to be so treated so nicely.

I was trying to think of a way to communicate all of that to the Scaly boy when, from somewhere to my right, someone called, "Justin!"

I jumped. A lanky, pale-haired enforcer was approaching from the outside of the park, waving at Connor. He didn't look more than a year older than

I was, which meant he'd probably only graduated from enforcer training a few months ago. His thin, earnest face was set in an expression of extreme seriousness, and when he stopped on the other side of the fence, he was standing so straight and still that I was surprised he didn't strain something. Clearing his throat, he asked, "Can I have a word, Justin?"

"Stay here," Connor told me, before striding over to the other enforcer. The two of them began discussing something in voices too low for me to overhear, and I shifted my attention back to the boy, only to find that he wasn't on the climbing frame any more. Worried, I searched for him, and found him mingling with the other children. The kids suddenly scattered, making a tremendous noise as they chased each other around the park, and the boy began to meander in my direction. *The idiot!* Connor was standing with his back to me, but he was half-facing the children. Even if the administrators were distracted by what the other children were doing, he'd notice the kid for sure. I shook my head furiously, gesturing to Connor. The boy shrugged, plainly unimpressed, and kept coming. He was getting closer and closer, and I was growing steadily more frantic. Then he stumbled abruptly to a halt, his eyes wide, and ran back into the noisy crowd of children.

From behind me someone whispered, "Ash!"

Twisting around, I found a petite, hazel-eyed girl staring at me through the wire of the fence. She had short blonde hair, freckled skin, and was wearing a collar and detainee uniform. It couldn't be. Except it was.

"Briony?"

"Hey, Ash."

I glanced at Connor. He was deep in conversation, and still turned towards the kids. Moving as surreptitiously as I could, I crossed the short space to the fence. I pressed my brown hands to Briony's pale ones through the cold wire, and scanned her face. She seemed OK, but knowing her, she had no idea how much trouble she was in.

"What happened, Bry? How did they catch you?"

Words rushed out of her in a typical Briony-like fashion. "When you didn't come back, Ember sent Daniel to Cambergull, and everyone there was talking about how you'd been caught, and probably killed! *I* said we should go to the centre and try to find out whether you were OK, only *Ember* said it was far too dangerous. So I pretended like I agreed with her, because there's no arguing with Ember, and snuck away to find you on my own."

"You shouldn't have done it, Bry!"

"I was worried about you, and besides, I didn't expect to get caught. Then some enforcers found me, and they were carrying those streaker weapons. And I didn't know if I could outrun a blast from one of those, since I'm nowhere near as fast as Daniel. I thought I'd better give myself up, and here I am."

She sounded almost cheerful. If I could've got through the fence, I would have shaken her. "Have they hurt you?"

"Oh no." She frowned. "Except they took my stuff."

That was the last thing she should be worried about, but I knew that however trivial it might seem to me, it wasn't to her. Briony *clung* to her things, especially the hiking boots she wore everywhere, and the little knife she always carried. They were the last gifts her parents had given her, before they sent her away.

"At least you're OK, Bry."

"I was frightened at first, but these places aren't as bad as everyone says, are they? I mean, there's a park and everything! And I met the Chief Administrator, who was so nice to me."

"You met Neville Rose?"

She nodded. "He said I might get an Exemption! Even though I'm a Runner, and Runners don't usually get them. But since my ability's not very strong, it might be OK."

She was fizzing with excitement. I wanted to shout at her, "You can't possibly be that stupid," but I knew that she could. This was Briony, a girl who lived in a make-believe world where the Citizenship Accords would be repealed any day now, and she would be able to go home to her mum and dad. "Bry," I said carefully, "there's no way they'll ever give a Runner an Exemption. He's going to string you along, try to get information out of you."

She shook her head. "He doesn't want anything from me. He wants something from you."

"Something from me? *What?*"

"I don't know. He said it isn't anything bad – and you'll give it to him, won't you? To help me?" She bit her lip. "You don't blame me for Connor, do you? I thought he was an administrator, and he was a good guy when I knew him as a kid. I'd never have introduced him to you otherwise."

I squeezed her fingers. "Connor fooled all of us. It's OK."

She brightened instantly, as I knew she would. Briony hated people being mad at her. She had to have everyone's approval. It was why she clashed with Ember, who'd always been impatient with her flightiness. In fact, I was willing to bet she'd come here for no better reason than because Ember told her she shouldn't.

"Bry, you can't trust Neville Rose."

"I know that. I'm not stupid."

No, she wasn't, not entirely. Her wilful blindness to reality could lead her to do some very silly things, but Bry could be crafty in her own way. As if to prove it, she continued, "What I thought was, we can *pretend* to be going along with him, to get what we want. We can trick him, you and me together."

She smiled at me, and I felt sick. This was what Bry did whenever she wanted something – she smiled her extraordinary smile, the one that was like sunlight, all brightness and warmth, and waited for people to respond to it.

I tried to make her understand the threat looming over her. "Listen to me. Neville's not as harmless as he seems—"

A shout cut across our conversation. "Get away from there!"

Spinning around, I found Connor approaching.

He stalked up to the fence and addressed Briony coldly. "Step *back*." She scurried backwards, looking lost and uncertain.

I spoke quickly. "It was my fault, everything was my fault."

The other enforcer hurried to Briony's side, scowling. "You were supposed to wait at your quarters, Briony. If you cannot be trusted to follow the rules, the privileges the Chief Administrator has given you will be revoked."

It was a mild rebuke, under the circumstances, but it was delivered in a harsh tone of voice, and Briony wilted. I watched as she started to smile at him, and then stopped herself. *At least she has that much sense.* Only it hurt to see her faith in that smile falter.

Connor subjected the other enforcer to an icy stare. "I think you had best escort her to where she is supposed to be, Evan."

The lanky enforcer took Briony's arm. I didn't like the intensity in his dark eyes, or the way he seemed so focused on her. I'd bet guarding Briony was the first important job they'd given him, and he was obviously keen to succeed at it. I clutched at the fence as he led her away. Bry was never going to survive in here. And Connor, who had used her to get to me, didn't care. *In the end, we're all just Illegals to him.* He would stand by while they did horrible things to Briony, the girl he'd known as a child, in the same emotionless way he'd stood by when they'd done horrible things to me. Except I was a fighter. She wasn't, and Connor knew it.

Briony and the enforcer dwindled into the distance. She kept glancing back at me, like I was going to be able to help her, until she vanished behind one of the white buildings. Connor spoke my name, once, and again. I stayed where I was. Finally, he reached out to touch my shoulder, and that was more than I could stand. I lashed out, my fist driving towards his jaw. He moved at lightning speed, catching my hand in his, and for a second we stood locked together, our faces centimetres apart.

"*Stop,*" he hissed. "If nothing else, think of your audience."

I glared up at him, choking on rage. But he was right about having an audience. The children were watching, their small faces pale and worried. They were much closer than they'd been before, and so were the administrators, who were standing between them and us. I took a deep breath, and another. I didn't want to get anyone else in trouble on my account today, especially not a kid. Staring bitterly at Connor's perfect features, I whispered, "I hate you."

His mouth twisted. "I know."

He let me go, and walked over to the administrators, waving at the kids and speaking sharply. The Scaly boy was standing ahead of the rest, like he'd been the first one to run towards me. Connor came back, pausing to say something to him. I tensed, but the kid was all right. The moment Connor moved past him, he gave me a toothy grin, and I managed a small smile in return, warmed by his defiance.

It wasn't until we were leaving, when I was waiting for Connor to open the gate in the fence, that my tired mind put everything together. *This wasn't exercise.* It was another part of the interrogation. It was no accident that Briony's guard had lost track of her, or that Connor had lost track of me. Neville had wanted to show me that he had captured a Tribe member. He'd known I would understand the danger she didn't. I could even guess at which of Briony's memories the machine would find first. It would be the one that hurt her the most, the memory of the day her mum and dad sent her away.

Briony never talked about it, only about how much they must miss her, how glad they'd be to have her back. With Bry, though, you had to listen to what she didn't say as much as what she did. From things she'd let slip, I knew that her mum and dad had adored her until she was thirteen. Then they'd discovered she had an ability, and overnight they'd gone from being proud to being ashamed. They'd helped her to get out of Gull City after making her promise she would never try to contact them again. Briony had found her way to a group of Illegals hiding in some caves along the coast, and then, when that didn't work out, to us. I didn't think those other Illegals had meant to be cruel, but they'd tried to make her understand that she could never go home. They hadn't seen what I had – that Briony needed to believe in her happy ending, or she couldn't go on. If the machine shattered that faith, it would shatter her.

Connor swung the gate open, and I walked numbly through it. I'd thought yesterday had been bad, that I'd been robbed of my freedom and forced to make hard choices, but I knew now that I'd had no idea how bad it could get. *This* was real powerlessness. This terrible situation where one of my own was in trouble, and I couldn't help them.

I had no idea what to do.

DAY TWO

THE OFFICE

I stared at the clock on the wall. Two minutes and thirty seconds since Connor had escorted me into this cheerful room and, in all that time, Chief Administrator Neville Rose hadn't said a thing.

Neville's office was a bright, happy place, filled with books, files, photographs and a pile of awards for "meritorious service". There was an empty chair beside mine that was clearly meant for Briony, but for now it was only myself, Neville and Connor, who was standing guard in the corner behind me.

The Chief Administrator stirred, and for a second I thought he was going to say something. He didn't, though, just kept gazing sadly out the window. *Is this some kind of contest, to see who speaks first?* I had to admit, it was getting increasingly hard to resist the temptation to fill the silence. Trying to distract myself, I studied the enormous map of the world that took up all of one wall. It was colourful and pretty: in the centre of the ocean, which covered most of the earth's surface, sat the single landmass that had emerged after the shifting of the tectonic plates during the Reckoning. I focused on Gull City, my eyes following the road that led out of it and through to the Gull City towns – Eldergull, Aspergull, Halligull, Stonygull and Cambergull. Then the grasslands, and the Firstwood, and beyond that Spinifex City, and its towns – Junifex, Sivafex, Kallfex…

"I had people working all night, Ashala."

Neville had finally decided to speak. I ignored him, pretending to be fascinated by the map as he continued, "It took a while to track down the boy you knew as Jaz. His name was Jade Nelson and, as I'm sure you can imagine, his parents were devastated to hear that their son is dead. It's a dreadful time for that family. Their eight-year-old daughter drowned a month ago."

I jumped in surprise. Jaz had a *sister*? He hadn't told

me that! But then, my live-in-the-moment Firestarter had hardly been the type to dwell on the people he'd left behind.

Neville sighed. "His parents never stopped searching for him, Ashala. Never gave up hope that they might see him again one day."

He was deliberately targeting a vulnerable spot, and I wasn't going to let him know how much it hurt. "If his parents wanted him to stay at home then they shouldn't have booked an appointment with an assessor."

"They loved him, and they were doing what was best for him. Whatever you thought of detention before, you've seen how detainees are treated, now. The houses. The park."

"And," I shot back, "let's not forget the machine."

He gave me a stern look. "That machine is only necessary for Illegals who have broken the Citizenship Accords, or those who are hiding things from the government. It would never be used on ordinary detainees."

Yeah, it would. Neville would put almost anybody on that machine if he suspected they had useful information, and Miriam Grey would do it for fun. But I knew he'd never own up to that. "You can build as many houses and parks as you like. It doesn't make this place any less of a prison."

"Do you expect me to believe that Illegals are better off in living in the Firstwood? I know what your life there is like, Ashala. I've spoken to your friend Briony."

My fingers dug into the arm of the chair before I forced myself to relax, aware that he was watching for a reaction. Neville went on. "Briony's told me how difficult it is for you in that enormous forest. The way you struggle to find food for everyone, and how desperately cold it gets in the winter."

I turned my head away, letting my hair fall over my face to hide my expression. With any luck, Neville would think I was contemplating my pitiful forest existence. And the truth was, it hadn't been easy, especially at first when there'd been so few of us, although Ember's encyclopedic knowledge had helped a lot. She'd been the one who showed us what plants could be eaten and how to prepare them, taught us to grind seeds to make flour for our bread, and found herbs to use for medicine before we had a Mender. But even in the early days, when there hadn't been Leafers to make the food garden grow, and when the stock of supplies brought in by new members or purloined from the towns had been small, it had *never* been as bad as the stories Bry had been telling.

Neville had gone silent, and I realized he was waiting for me to respond. "It is a hard life," I lied, and then added pointedly, "but it's a free one."

"Are you so sure all of your Tribe wants that kind of freedom?" He took off his glasses, cleaning them on his robe. "I know now why you call yourself Ashala Wolf. You believe that each member of your group has some sort of connection with an animal. You with wolves, and Briony with – treecats, wasn't it?"

Briony, what have you done? It was so like her, to have done such a good job of lying about how grim life was in the Firstwood, only to let something truthful slip out when she wasn't paying attention. Unsure of how much she'd revealed, I kept my mouth shut as Neville said, "Your followers might believe that they each have a bond with an animal. You and I know better, though. You invented it, didn't you? To make them all think that they're special?"

I did not! But it was better to let him think I had, so I didn't answer. Besides, I couldn't have explained the animal bonding, even if I'd wanted to. It didn't have anything to do with our abilities, it just seemed to be something that happened in the Firstwood. And Neville would never understand what it was like to run with wolves the way I could. Or call crows from the sky like Ember, or have the night vision of a treecat like Briony.

Neville put his glasses back on, gazing at me over the top of them. "You might have convinced your Tribe that they're better off in the Firstwood, Ashala. You might have even convinced yourself. But consider this: if you do have such a special connection with animals, why couldn't you prevent the saurs from taking Jaz? Because you do realize that, if he'd been in detention, he'd still be alive."

Those words struck me like a blow to the chest. *Don't let him get to you!* It was hard, though, when the memory of how badly I'd failed Jaz was so raw and aching. *I tried to save him, I did...* For a mad, stupid second, I wanted to say that out loud, as if it mattered. Like I could somehow plead my case to the world and be absolved of guilt. Only I knew there was no forgiveness, not for Jaz. Or for Cassie.

Neville nodded over my head at Connor, and I heard the door open as he left. *He's gone to fetch Briony.* She was in terrible jeopardy, the same as the others had been, the ones I hadn't been able to save. Everything seemed to tilt and go grey around the edges. Then I felt a faint sense of steadiness and strength, almost as if someone had laid a reassuring hand on my shoulder. I grabbed hold of that feeling, clutching on to it until my vision cleared.

Connor came back in, along with Briony and her guard. She sat herself down in the chair next to mine, and Neville said, "I think that you gentlemen can wait outside."

Yeah, we wouldn't want enforcers ruining the cosy atmosphere. Connor left with his usual quick grace, but the other enforcer lingered, casting an intense stare at Briony before making his way out. I wondered if he really thought that Bry and I were going to overpower Neville if they weren't here to stop us. I mean, I certainly had a few ideas – a couple of those meritorious service trophies might be heavy enough to make a good weapon – but I was hardly going to try anything with the two of them right outside, not to mention all the other enforcers who were patrolling the centre.

Once they were gone, Neville spoke. "I called Briony's father this morning, Ashala. Her parents were overjoyed to hear that she's been found at last."

Bry reached out to put her hand on my arm, pinching my skin gently, and I knew she was trying to tell me to play along. "If I had an Exemption, I could be with them, Ash."

On cue, Neville chimed in, "The government doesn't usually give Exemptions to Runners, but I think they might consider it if I make a good case. And in the future I might have rather more influence than I do now. I've put my name forward as a candidate in the Gull City Prime election, you know."

No, I hadn't known, and the prospect of him becoming the Prime was positively terrifying. Naturally, Bry didn't see the implications. She and Neville seemed to be trying to out-smile each other. I looked away from them both, trying to calculate how much of a disaster it would be if he actually won the election.

Like every other city in the world, the day-to-day governing of Gull City and its towns was managed by an Assembly of thirteen elected representatives. But it wasn't the Assembly who was responsible for the big rules that set out what had to be done, or *not* done, in order to maintain the Balance. It was the Council of Primes who made the Accords. It took a majority vote of the Council to enact a new Accord, or to alter an old one, so Neville couldn't act on his own. Given enough time, though, he could probably persuade the Primes of some of the other cities to vote with him. *Which means he could make the Citizenship Accords a lot worse than they already are.* And stupid Bry was still smiling at him.

Her smile suddenly faded, and for a second, I thought she'd understood how much trouble we were in. Until I realized she was reacting to Neville, who wasn't smiling either. "The problem I have," he told her, "is that I work for the government, and the government is concerned about the Tribe. Very concerned. So I couldn't let a Tribe member go, not unless there was some … co-operation."

He hadn't so much as glanced in my direction, but we both knew who he was talking to. "Exactly what do you want?" I asked.

He answered, in an earnest tone, "I want you to tell the Tribe to leave the Firstwood."

"What?"

"I promise you," he hurried on, "they won't be punished. I'm prepared to treat them like ordinary detainees, despite the fact that they've broken the Citizenship Accords."

I couldn't believe it. He was serious. I stared at him in bewilderment. My first thought was that Chief Administrator Neville Rose had gone completely insane. My second was he wanted to win the Gull City Prime election. With increasing numbers of Citizens asking the Question, heads of detention centres weren't as popular as they used to be. Getting even a few Tribe members to come into detention would help to put an end to the unpleasant rumours about him. In fact, just having Ashala Wolf, the leader of the Tribe, ask them to come in might be enough to convince people that Neville was the kindly guardian he seemed. I could be getting him a pile of votes. Worse still, once rumours spread that the leader of the Tribe said detention was OK, there was an outside chance that an Illegal somewhere might turn themselves in because of it, some kid who wouldn't realize that I'd never say such a thing voluntarily.

Briony's voice interrupted my worried speculations. "You'll help me, won't you, Ash?" She leaned over to give me a quick hug, taking the chance to whisper in my ear, "We both know none of the Tribe will ever leave the Firstwood, so it doesn't matter what you ask them to do."

She settled back into her chair, and I knew she'd never understand why it *did* matter. Or that regardless of what I agreed to, Neville was never going to give her an Exemption. He would invent one delay after another, and all the while she'd be in danger, a piece of leverage to be used against me. She'd be oblivious to what was happening, too, and somehow, that made it worse. She was so vulnerable, my flighty Briony, with her happy endings and her blonde hair and her smile.

My thoughts seemed to stutter to an abrupt halt. Something was bothering me, and I wasn't sure what. It was almost like I could feel a hand tugging at the corners of my memory, as if a piece of my mind was trying to remind me about something important that I'd seen. No, something I *hadn't* seen.

"You didn't smile," I said.

"What?" Bry asked.

"Before. At the park, when the guard was taking you away, and you looked back at me. You didn't smile." *Even though you were asking me for help, and you always smile when you do that.*

"Well ... I..." She cast a nervous glance at Neville, and drew closer to murmur, "I was frightened, Ash."

Were you, Bry? A lot of things were rapidly piling

105

up in my mind, tiny things that didn't seem like anything until you put them all together. Enforcers on an unscheduled supply run into Cambergull. How Briony had been the only one to come to the centre. The way she said she'd been captured by enforcers with streakers, when those things weren't standard issue yet. *I don't think I've seen a single enforcer carrying one since I came here.* Most of all, the lack of a smile.

Focusing all my attention on her pretty face, I said, "I know what you've done." The guilt that flashed across her features was gone so fast that I would have missed it, if I hadn't been looking for it. But I *was* looking for it.

I pushed her away. "Traitor!"

She immediately started babbling. "I'm sorry, Ash. I didn't mean for it to be like this. I'm sorry you got hurt, and about Jaz and everything, but honestly, he should never have eaten that rabbit..."

What was she blathering about? "What does this have to do with – wait, *you're* the one who told the government about the Pact?"

"I didn't think anything would happen, you have to believe me. I wanted to go home. They said I could go home!"

"You were home, Bry!" I was so overwhelmed with rage, I was almost sputtering with it. Briony had betrayed us all, selling the Tribe out to the government, and for nothing more than an illusion. In a single, angry moment, I shouted out the truth she couldn't bear to acknowledge: "And it was a better home than you'd ever had with your parents, because they don't love you. They think you're some unnatural thing, and they'll *never* love you."

The colour drained out of her face, and for a second she just sat there, pale and trembling. Then her eyes went flat and scarily mindless and she leaped for me, knocking the two of us to the ground. Bry was screaming, over and over, "They do love me. They do! They do!" We rolled across the floor, banging into furniture and toppling books as Neville jumped to his feet, calling for the enforcers. She was shrieking and clawing and kicking, really trying to hurt me, and I was so enraged that I was fighting right back. She tried to scratch at my eyes, and I slapped her hand away, striking the edge of her jaw, which was painful in a satisfying kind of way. She howled, throwing a vicious punch at my side, and another. Something sharp dug into me, and Connor and Evan charged in, dragging the two of us apart.

Briony clung to Evan, clutching at her face as if she'd sustained some severe injury, which I knew she hadn't. For some reason, Connor kept trying to get me to sit down in the chair. He was shouting something, only it took me a second to understand what it was. "Ashala! You're hurt!"

What? I looked down, puzzled to find my white shirt marred by a spreading red stain. *I'm bleeding? How?* But then I realized.

They hadn't taken away all her possessions after all. Briony had still been carrying her little knife.

DAY TWO

THE WOUND

I slid to the floor, the world shattering into fragmented images. Evan, hustling Briony out of the room. Neville, screeching for someone to fetch Wentworth. And Connor, hands pressed to the wound in my side to stop the bleeding. He'd done this before, I thought vaguely, when I'd received that other injury. Had it really only been two days ago? Then everything faded into darkness.

When I regained consciousness, blurry figures wearing red robes were swarming everywhere. Someone spoke urgently. "Doctor, the blade was poisoned!"

Wentworth shouted, "Somebody get that collar off her!"

Confused, I thought, *My neck isn't hurt.* Then I realized she must want to Mend me, and the rhondarite would stop her ability from working on my wounded body.

The stone band was pulled away, and I tried to fall asleep and Sleepwalk. But my ability wouldn't work. Instead, I drifted, sometimes rising to the surface of consciousness and sometimes falling beneath it, as if I was being carried along on the tides. It would have been peaceful, except that the connections my mind had made in Neville's office spread out around me like a net floating on water, trapping me amongst painful truths.

I'd thought I'd been unlucky when I was captured in Cambergull. Now it seemed a bit *too* unlucky that a troop of enforcers – including the one who knew exactly what I looked like – had happened to be there at the same time as me. *Briony told them where I was going to be.* And her story about how Ember hadn't sent anyone to the centre after they'd heard what happened. That should have struck me as wrong instantly, and would have, if I hadn't been so caught up in being terrified for Bry. No matter how futile or dangerous Em had thought it was, she definitely would have

110

sent someone. Daniel, probably, since he was the fastest of the Runners. Although Briony herself was much quicker than she'd ever let on. She had to be, or she couldn't have got in and out of the Firstwood fast enough to maintain contact with the government without arousing suspicion. *Why didn't I see it?* Why hadn't I noticed something was wrong, before she'd told them about the Pact, before Jaz had died?

Grief washed over me, weighing me down, and I began to sink. I fell gently away from consciousness and life, drifting through nothingness, until my feet touched what felt like dirt. The blackness winked out, leaving me standing among trees – big tuarts, and smaller peppermints, and in between and around, all the other plant life of the forest. The Firstwood? *Sort of.* Everything was brighter than it should be, the colours so vivid it almost hurt to look at them. Plus, I was glowing with a faint blue light. Was this the Balance?

When Citizens died, their spirits were supposed to go to the greater Balance, the world soul. I thought Illegals did too, even though the government said our fate was uncertain, since we were outside the natural order. Only if this was the Balance, then I was ... dead. I supposed I should have been upset about that, but all

111

I felt was an overwhelming sense of relief. *If I'm dead, I'm free.* No more worries, no more responsibilities and no one else to save. The government couldn't hurt me, and I couldn't hurt anyone else, couldn't *fail* anyone else, ever again.

I surveyed my surroundings. Souls were meant to either exist in the Balance as energy or be born back into a body, and it didn't seem like I'd become energy. So I should be on my way to being reborn. I brightened, thinking it'd be great to come back as a wolf, or maybe something that could fly, like a hawk. Anything other than a Citizen. Except it wasn't clear how I was meant to get to my new life. There didn't seem to be any pathway to follow, or anyone to guide me either. "Hello?" I called. "Is anybody out there?"

A twig snapped behind me, and I spun around to find myself facing a tall, olive-skinned girl. She tipped her head to one side, gazing at me out of eyes that were a peculiar shade of light green. "Hi, Ash."

I gasped. "Georgie? You aren't … you're not… Georgie, are you dead?"

She shook her head, sending her long black curls flying around her shoulders. "I think I'm dreaming."

"You can't be."

112

"Why not?"

"Because this is the greater Balance. You can't get here by dreaming."

"But," she replied, in a bewildered tone, "I *am* here."

"I know! Are you sure you're not dead?"

She laughed. "I'm alive, promise. I came because you need me."

"I do?" An idea popped into my head. "Hey, are you my guide? Are you just appearing as Georgie, like the part of my subconscious that appears as Ember?"

"I don't know. Am I?"

"Well, *I* don't know!"

She shrugged. "I guess neither of us knows. Anyway, what's important is, we have to go."

"To the next life?"

"No, Ash! To see the Serpent."

I gaped at her in dismay. "The Serpent? Is *he* dead? Did the government catch him?"

For a second she looked very confused. Then her face cleared, and she said, in a slow, careful tone, "No, Ash. Not *that* Serpent. The, um, other one."

"What other one?"

"You'll see. Come on."

She tore off through the trees, and I ran after her,

following along behind as she emerged from the undergrowth to pelt along one of the forest tracks. The geography of this Firstwood seemed to be pretty much the same as the one I knew, almost as if it reflected my forest. *Or maybe this is the real Firstwood, and ours is the reflection.* That was a freaky thought.

It made me happy, though, to see the familiar pathways travelled by the Tribe, and I marked each branch of the trail in my mind as we passed it. If I turned there, I'd eventually reach the clearing that was our summer camp. There, I'd find my way to where the waratahs grew, the big red flowers from which we harvested a thick, sweet honey. There, I'd go to the cave system that was our shelter in winter. The caves were also where Ember had her laboratory, mixing up her various herbal concoctions and inventing stuff. I almost took the path to find her, before remembering that I didn't *want* to see Em in this place, since I still wasn't sure if you could be here without being dead.

Georgie ran on until there were no more pathways branching off the trail, and I knew where we must be going. I sped up, outpacing her slightly, and reached the sandy shore of the lake before she did. Leaning over,

I rested my hands on my legs, catching my breath and looking out over the water. This was *my* lake. I was the only one who swam here, because everyone else thought there was something spooky about the dark water. I had to admit, there was a kind of broodiness about it, but I'd always loved the way the lake was so unfathomably deep and mysterious. It was especially impressive now, the blue water shining with dazzling light where the sun hit it, and coloured with purple shadows where it was shaded by the overhanging trees. There was no Serpent, though. In fact, there didn't seem to be anyone here except for us.

"Are you sure this is the right place, Georgie?"

She nodded, and came to stand beside me. "Yes. Because when I meet you in the Balance, this is where we come."

I rolled my eyes at her. "You do know that makes no sense, right?" To my horror, I saw that she was starting to disappear, fading away around the edges. "Georgie, what's happening to you?"

"This is when I wake up, Ash."

I put my hand on her arm, as if I could keep her with me by hanging on. "Georgie, if you're really sleeping, I need you to remember something. Tell Ember that

Bry's a traitor. Do you understand? If she ever contacts you, she can't be trusted."

"It's all right. We already know."

"You do? How can you know?" She didn't answer, and she was disappearing quickly now. "Georgie! Don't be dead."

"You either, Ash."

She smiled at me, and vanished.

I barely had time to register that she was gone before I heard a popping noise, and another. Bubbles were rising from the centre of the lake, slowly at first, and then faster and faster. I took a curious step closer to the water. Suddenly, a huge, sinuous shape broke the surface, sending ripples rolling outwards to splash against the shore.

An *actual* serpent? *Run, Ash!* Only my legs wouldn't obey the commands of my terrified brain. I stood trembling as the massive snake slid upwards, its pale blue scales shimmering with rainbows in the light. The creature bent towards me, swivelling its head until it was upside down, and a deep, male voice rolled across my mind. **Hello.**

There was something about the way he was watching me from his upturned silver eyes that was strangely comic, and I suppressed a hysterical urge to laugh as I replied, "Hello yourself."

You are very small.

"You … you're kind of big."

I am, aren't I? He turned his head the right way up. **You do not tend to your pain.**

"Um, I'm not in pain."

Yes, you are.

"No, I'm—" I stopped abruptly, aware of a deep, throbbing ache in my chest.

You give up too easily. Because you will not forgive.

My chest was burning now, and I was starting to feel hot all over, kind of feverish. "Who am I supposed to forgive?"

Yourself.

"I *can't*."

Why not?

"B-because," I stuttered, "Jaz and C-Cassie are dead."

Death is a great transformation. But it is not an end.

The shivers racking my body were getting so bad that I could barely stand, and I was in no condition to argue the meaning of life – or death – with a giant snake. "I think I'm sick."

It is your pain.

"Can you help me?"

Yes.

"So help me!"

His long tongue flicked out, coiling around my body. Alarmed, I tried to fight free of his grasp. "What are you doing? Let go!" The Serpent lifted me up and flung back his head, sending me soaring through the air. I hit the lake with a tremendous splash, still yelling, and swallowed a mouthful of water as I plunged downwards. I tried to struggle up to the air and found myself suspended in the depths, unable to move as the water I'd gulped down flowed through me like an electric wave. My entire body continued to shake, only now it was from the inside out, as if every tiny cell within me was rattling against the ones next to it. Then something broke free inside my chest, streaming out to vanish into the lake, and I shot to the surface, gasping for air.

Flailing and treading water, I searched for the Serpent, and found him coiled high above me. I started swimming, keeping a wary eye on him as I made my way to the shore.

"What did you do that for?" I demanded as I squelched out.

I was helping.

"You were *not.*"

I made you better.

"No, you didn't." Except the second I spoke, I realized that the pain was gone, and my body wasn't shaking any more. More than that, I felt lighter, as if a weight I hadn't even known I was carrying had been lifted. "What is that, some kind of magic water?"

It's not the water. It's what's in it.

"And what's that?"

Me.

I suppose I should have expected that answer. "You're like a Mender?"

There was a liquid, tinkling sound in my head. Laughter?

In a way. He preened in the sunlight. **You will see them clearly now.**

"See who clearly?"

The transformed ones.

I remembered his earlier words – *Death is a great transformation.* "Do you mean Cassie and Jaz?" I peered around eagerly. "Are they here?"

Yes. And no.

"Which is it?"

Which is what?

"Yes, or no?"

I cannot tell you what you do not wish to know, granddaughter.

"Of course I wish to know!" Then my brain caught up with what he'd said. "Hang on, what do you mean, granddaughter?"

He didn't make the laughing sound again, but I got the distinct feeling he was enjoying my reaction. **I am your many times grandfather, one of the creators of your people.**

"That's … that's impossible." It was ridiculous to be telling a giant snake that anything he did was impossible. "You made Illegals?"

Not Illegals. Your people in the world that was, before the great chaos you call the Reckoning.

Before the Reckoning? There weren't any Illegals back then. Except there were different peoples, different races. Ember had told me about it, once – how things like my skin not being the same colour as hers, or the way Pen's eyes were almond shaped, used to mean something. After the end of the old world, when there were so few humans left, everyone stopped worrying about things like that.

"Are you saying that in the old world, my, um, people were made by giant snakes?"

My kind took many forms, granddaughter. He sighed deeply, and that sigh seemed to flow out of him and through the Firstwood, stirring the leaves in the trees. When the great chaos began, I was sleeping deep in underground water. My resting place broke apart and I was cast out into the end of everything. I journeyed for a long time, gathering all the scraps of life that I could find. Rising up higher, he added softly, I brought them here. Then I sang, reminding life of its shapes, strength and its many transformations. Until life remembered its nature, and grew.

I choked. "*You* made things start to grow again after the Reckoning?"

I made things grow here. There may be other creators elsewhere. I am one of the old spirits of the earth, granddaughter. I do not know how many of us survived the great chaos. He dipped downwards, coming so close that I could see tiny drops of water on his shimmering scales. But, yes, this one place is mine. **The trees were the first to return. Then I sang the lizards into being, to guard what I had created. And everything else followed.**

This couldn't be true. Somehow, though, I knew it was. "Do you live here, in my world, I mean?"

I live in all worlds, and in the spaces between them.

"I swim in this lake all the time. Why haven't I seen you before?"

I've been sleeping.

"Sleeping?"

I required much rest.

"It's been more than three hundred years since the Reckoning."

It was not an easy task to make life grow. I began to stir from my slumber when you came to the Firstwood, and I woke completely when you began to speak of me.

Speak of him? Then it dawned on me what he meant. *The Serpent.* "I'm afraid I wasn't exactly talking about you."

He made the laughing noise again. **Weren't you?**

"No, there's this Illegal, you see, and he…" I let my

voice trail off, realizing the uselessness of trying to explain.

The snake's eyes swirled. **You have forgotten my story. But then, you have forgotten many things, haven't you?**

"I haven't forgotten anything!" Only that didn't sound right. "I mean, I don't *think* I've forgotten anything."

It does not matter. A wave of emotion seemed to flow out from him and wash over me, a feeling of affection mixed with a sort of proprietorial pride. **What matters is that you can call upon me, if you ever need my help. You might be the last to carry the bloodline of those who I created, in the world that was.**

"Can you help me become a wolf?"

You are not going on, granddaughter. You are going back.

"What do you mean, back?"

The Serpent didn't answer, but light flashed, so bright it seemed to burn my eyes. For a few seconds, all I could see was a blue glow. When my vision cleared, there was no Serpent, no lake and no Firstwood. Instead, I was lying on a bed in a white-walled room.

Sunlight streamed in through a large window, and the air was filled with a clinical scent. *The hospital.*

I was still alive.

I blinked, hoping my surroundings would change. They didn't. *It isn't fair! How can I be alive?* And what had that experience with Georgie and the Grandfather Serpent been, if not the Balance? Surely, it couldn't have been a dream. It had felt so real.

Connor was standing at the end of the bed, arms folded across his chest. He moved to stand beside me, and I hastily levered myself into a sitting position. I was wearing the collar and a crisp white shirt. I felt underneath it where Briony had stabbed me, and found the faint ridges of a scar. Wentworth must have worked her magic, again.

Sighing, I looked up at Connor. "You know, for a dangerous Illegal surrounded by enforcers, I'm having a very difficult time getting myself killed."

And Connor said quietly, "Ashala. Briony is dead."

DAY THREE

THE HOSPITAL

"Dead?" I gasped. "She can't be dead. I just saw her."

Connor shook his head. "You've been unconscious for some time."

I pointed to the window. "But it's still afternoon."

"Yes. Thursday afternoon."

It was the next day. "It didn't feel like that long."

He pressed his lips together into a thin line. "It did to me."

"What happened to Bry?"

"She was killed while attempting to escape."

I tried to make sense of that, and couldn't. "Why would she want to escape? She was working for you."

"Yes," he acknowledged tiredly, "but the Chief Administrator was only prepared to give her an Exemption if she could persuade you to ask the Tribe to surrender. Until then, she was being treated like any other Illegal."

"Where'd she get the knife then?"

"She had a … relationship with her guard. He allowed her to keep the knife."

"A *relationship*? With some enforcer she'd known for a couple of days?"

"She'd known him far longer than that. Since she they were children."

I snorted. "Exactly how many future enforcers could Bry have grown up with…" But my voice trailed off as I made the obvious connection.

When Briony had introduced Connor to me, she'd claimed she'd been friends with him when she was young, and that she'd recently run into him again on a trip into Stonygull. I'd realized yesterday that she'd probably always known he wasn't an administrator. Now it seemed she'd been lying about other things too.

"It wasn't you she knew as a kid, was it?" I asked. "It was Evan. He was the one who was her friend."

Connor nodded, and I mentally re-evaluated every

assumption I'd made about Bry's enforcer guard. Small moments replayed themselves in my head, like the way he'd been so focused on her at the park, and the glance he'd given her before he'd left her in Neville's office. I'd thought he'd been concerned about doing his job. Now, it seemed as if he might have actually been concerned about Briony. "So, Evan was the one she ran into in Stonygull?"

"It would be more correct to say she sought him out in Stonygull."

"And he reported to the government that she was willing to inform on us. Only," I added bitterly, "they didn't send him to the Firstwood when it came to it. They sent you."

"Yes."

"Because they trusted you. Because you'll do whatever is *necessary*."

Connor didn't respond to that, just gazed at me with something like his usual cool reserve. But he wasn't quite as statue-like as normal. There were faint shadows under his eyes, like smudges on marble. I got the sense that he was feeling almost as exhausted and edgy as I was, and I was glad of it. Because it was right that Bry's death should cause Connor and the

127

government some pain. Especially since something else must have happened, in the time I'd been unconscious, for her to have run.

"Exactly what did you do to her?" I demanded.

Connor raised an eyebrow in surprise. "What?"

"You must have done *something*. Bry believed she'd get an Exemption. She wouldn't have tried to break out without a reason."

"She thought she'd killed you, Ashala! There was some kind of plant toxin on the knife. Not even Wentworth was certain that she would be able to save your life. If you'd died…"

He didn't finish the sentence, but he didn't need to. *Bry wouldn't have had anything to bargain with.* Plus, she'd have been the only Illegal from the Tribe left for Neville to interrogate. "She must have been terrified."

Connor shrugged, as if he didn't particularly care if Bry had been scared or not. I did, though. Maybe I shouldn't, but I couldn't help it. Even after everything she'd done, she was still one of my own, and I knew she hadn't truly meant to kill me. She'd simply lost control when I'd shoved the truth about her parents in her face. I was pretty sure the poison hadn't been meant for me, either, or for anyone particularly. It had been Bry's way of protecting herself. Somewhere in that dreamy brain of hers, she'd realized how dangerous it was to come here.

"I still don't see how she ended up dead. You're telling me that an entire detention centre of enforcers couldn't keep hold of one Illegal?"

He answered irritably, "Evan tried to smuggle her out by disguising her as an administrator. The two of them were almost through the main gate when someone raised the alarm."

"Then what? You lot stabbed her?" Except I knew immediately they couldn't have caught her with a sword, not if Bry hadn't been wearing a collar. "You shot her, didn't you?"

"*I* didn't do anything. I was here, waiting to see if you'd live or not. But she used her ability, and, yes, they shot her."

"I thought streakers weren't standard equipment yet."

"They're not. But they've recently been issued to the guards on the gates and the walls."

I sat in silence for a few minutes, imagining all those armed enforcers on the lookout for escape attempts or an attack from the Tribe. Had Briony understood how many deadly weapons would have been aimed in her direction? She must've been desperate to try and out-Run them. I felt a sudden rush of warmth towards Evan, glad that she hadn't been alone at the end.

"What happened to her guard?"

"He's here, in the hospital."

"They shot him too? What for, to punish the guy?"

"No one did anything to him," he replied evenly. "He went a little crazy when Briony died and had to be sedated. He's here under guard until Wentworth clears him to be moved to the cells."

"Sounds like he loved her."

"Apparently so."

There was a note of surprise in his voice, and it stung. More than stung – it cut, opening up a wound I didn't want to acknowledge was there. "Guess that's not something you could understand, a Citizen loving an Illegal."

Connor drew in a long breath. "No, it isn't. Any more than I understand why you're so concerned about someone who tried to kill you."

"She was still Tribe! She was just another Illegal to you, though, wasn't she? Someone to manipulate and *murder*."

"*I* had nothing to do with her death. And she was well aware of what she was doing when she came here—"

"She was terrified, and vulnerable, and you took advantage of her."

He ran a hand through his hair in an utterly uncharacteristic gesture, and growled, "She was vain and thoughtless and selfish, and she made her own fate, Ashala!"

I lunged at him, forgetting that I was sitting on a bed half-covered with a blanket, and ended up hopelessly tangled. Connor caught me as I fell, dragging me to my feet and holding me against his chest. His heart was pounding wildly, and I could feel the warmth of his breath on my skin. For a weird moment, everything seemed upside down and confusing. Then I shoved him away, snarling, "Get your hands off me!"

Connor took three quick steps back, and we stared at each other across the room. He actually looked upset. But even as I watched, his usual composure began to reassert itself, the emotion vanishing from his features. I glared into his distant blue eyes, hating him for everything he'd done, for everything he was and, most of all, for the glitch in my head that made me

131

react to him as if he was some kind of guardian angel. *No, be honest, Ash – not a glitch in your head. A glitch in your heart, you stupid, stupid girl.*

We stood there for what felt like ages, and I was starting to feel vaguely ridiculous when the door swung open. Neville came in, with a red-robed Wentworth following close behind him. Her pretty, caramel-brown face was anxious, and I shifted uneasily as her dark eyes flicked over me. "I'm glad to see you're recovering, Ashala." Only she didn't sound very glad. Turning to Neville, she added, "She is making excellent progress, but I do think she needs more rest. I'd prefer not to discharge her yet."

"I'm afraid," Neville responded, "that I must speak with her, Rae. She has information about an attack."

With a monumental effort, I choked back a gasp of dismay. Then I opened my mouth to deny everything. Before I could get a word out, though, Neville said, "Don't even try to talk your way out of it, Ashala. You spoke in your sleep."

Talked in my sleep? How would he even know that? *Connor.* Connor, who hadn't been outside when Bry and Evan were trying to escape because he'd been waiting by my bed to see if I lived or died. He'd left out the part where he'd been spying on me. I scowled at him as Neville spoke to Wentworth. "She mentioned details which indicate a genuine threat. Lives could be at stake."

What details? Wait … I'd been having that odd dream thing with Georgie and the Serpent. *Whatever I said, it wasn't the Illegal rebel I was talking about, it was the other Serpent!* But I knew they'd never believe that.

"If you like, Ashala," Neville told me, "you could talk to me here. Whatever it is that you've got caught up in, I'm sure you wouldn't want people to be hurt."

His voice was gently hopeful, and Wentworth responded to it, smiling encouragingly in my direction. Neville was standing slightly in front of her, though, so she couldn't see what I did – the hint of something that wasn't grandfatherly kindness in his features. He was angry. No matter what I said or did now, Neville was never going to stop until he'd extracted every scrap of knowledge from my mind. Doctor Wentworth couldn't save me. No one could. It was the most awful feeling to stand close to someone who was trying to help, and know that I was completely alone. *I carry my friends with me*, I reminded myself, calling up images of Ember and Georgie and the rest of the Tribe. *I carry*

133

my friends with me. The memory of their faces gave me enough strength to hold Neville's gaze as I slowly shook my head.

Wentworth slumped in disappointment, and Neville sighed. "Then I'm afraid I am going to have to ask you some questions, Ashala. You agree it's necessary, Rae?"

"Yes… I mean, if there's going to be an attack…"

She sounded uncertain, and Neville asked in an amused tone, "What do you think I'm going to do, torture her?" He laughed, and Wentworth did too, somewhat sheepishly.

"Of course not! I'm sorry – it's been a long day." She shot a quick glance at me, but I just stared flatly back, knowing she'd achieve nothing by continuing to come to my defence. And there was no point in putting her at risk for nothing, not when the other detainees in this place needed a Mender as good as Wentworth. My lack of response must have finally convinced her because, looking relieved, she said to Neville, "You'll bring her back if she shows signs of a relapse?"

He smiled his best grandpa smile. "Naturally."

I made myself take deep, even breaths as the Chief Administrator ushered my only ally out of the room, watching as he closed the door behind her and swung back to me. His usual air of benevolent kindness had vanished with Wentworth, and I didn't much like what was left behind. "You know," he said, "it really would be best if you confessed what you knew. Justin has reported that you mentioned the Serpent, and Cambergull."

It took every ounce of strength I had to keep my face blank. Cambergull? How could I possibly have let that slip? It hadn't even been in the dream.

Neville waited for a few moments, then asked, "Exactly what were you doing in Cambergull the day you were captured?"

Gathering my courage, I achieved a casual shrug. "I went to check out the new Bureau of Citizenship office."

His brows drew together, and his mouth hardened. I knew he'd heard that lie before. Bry would have repeated it to him, because it was exactly what I'd told her and the rest of the Tribe, except for Ember.

Only Neville didn't believe it, not any more.

DAY THREE

THE TRAP

"Bring her to the machine." Neville strode out, leaving us to follow.

Connor and I began walking, eventually emerging from the cool corridors of the hospital into the warm afternoon air. I tipped my face to the sun, savouring the few precious minutes of being outside. Connor was watching me, but I ignored him. There simply wasn't any point in wasting my energy on arguing with him, or even speaking to him, not when I had to conserve all my strength for what was to come. The wind picked up, swirling through the centre, and I caught a distinct hint of eucalyptus in the breeze. My towering tuarts.

I inhaled, drawing the cleansing scent into my lungs as I called out to the trees in my head. *If I could make it back to you, I would.* But that wasn't going to happen, because Neville would have me hooked up to that machine until I was broken or dead. My only real hope was that the stress of the ordeal would kill me before I gave him the information he was searching for. They'd probably tell Wentworth I died while trying to escape. I smiled, thinking that it wouldn't even be a lie.

The world seemed to be receding around me as we entered the building that held the machine, or maybe it was me that was receding from the world, withdrawing into myself. I clung to that feeling of detachment, thankful for the sense of distance that made it seem like it was some other girl who was walking into the windowless room, drinking the vial of stay-awake liquid and being strapped into the dreadful chair. Grey fussed over the box with Neville at her side, while Connor removed my collar, fitting the final restraint around my neck, and the hoop around my head. He retreated to stand beside the door, and I found myself bizarrely transfixed by his uniform, wondering why it had gone all fuzzy and sparkly around the edges. Then I realized that the entire room was filled with faintly blurring shapes and odd swirls of light.

I focused on the tiny flecks of colour that now seemed to dance across the composite wall, following them to the ceiling. I smiled in delight at the twinkling field of reds and blues and greens and yellows and pinks. It suddenly struck me as very important that every single one of those miniature lights had once been something else, before they'd been put into the recyclers to make composite. Maybe they'd come from awful things, like the remains of old world factories or weapons. Now they were part of something useful, something you could build stuff from. It seemed a shame, though, that they'd been made into a detention centre. *When Illegals finally get rid of the Citizenship Accords,* I promised the lights silently, *you can be a house.* No, this place was too big for a house. Perhaps a school? A library?

Neville approached to loom over the chair, distracting me from the starry ceiling. "Is there anything you'd like to tell me before we begin, Ashala?"

"Yes," I replied solemnly. "Nothing ever truly ends, only transforms."

He made an exasperated noise. "There's no need to put yourself through this ordeal. Why don't you help yourself and tell me what you know about the Serpent's attack?"

"He's not attacking anything. He's sleeping in the water."

"What water? Where?"

"In the Balance. And everywhere else too." My gaze drifted to the lights again, finding comfort in the sight of all those tiny, twirling spirits. Maybe I'd float up to be with them if the machine killed me. Except I wasn't very keen on being part of a detention centre. I called out to them hopefully, "I'd like to be a wolf!"

Neville peered into my eyes and shot a frowning glance at Grey. "What exactly did you give her?"

"She lost consciousness after the last time she was on the machine, even with the drug. I thought it advisable to administer a higher dose."

"I need her coherent!"

"I don't see why it matters," Grey protested. "It's my machine that will get you your answers."

"Your machine can be something of a blunt instrument, Miriam."

"I keep telling you, I've improved it. It's much better than it used to be."

"It is still far from perfect, and she *will* resist it.

She'll be of no further use to me if her brain ends up completely scrambled."

He came closer, patting my hand where it lay confined in the padded restraint. "Ashala, I need you to concentrate. Talk to me about the Serpent. What do you know about his plans?"

"Nothing." I sighed. "The Serpent said I'd forgotten his story."

He didn't seem happy with that answer, and I felt bad for disappointing him, especially when he'd asked so nicely. Then an idea occurred to me. "Maybe I can tell you your story instead."

"I'm not interested in my story, Ashala."

That was a silly thing to say, but maybe he didn't realize how important it was to understand your own story. I hadn't either, until Ember told me.

"Ember says everyone has a tale they tell themselves about who they are. And, if your tale is true, then you see yourself clearly, like looking into still water. But if it's not, then it's more like the water's all rippled, so you can't see yourself at all."

"Ember's one of your Tribe, isn't she? Does she know the Serpent?"

"Ember knows *stories*. You see, I think your story is

the Balance. You tell yourself that everything you do to Illegals is OK, because it's all for the sake of the Balance."

But those words tasted bad in my mouth, all bendy and askew, and I knew I'd somehow messed up the story. Neville was speaking again, asking about Cambergull this time, but I wasn't listening. Instead, I tried to work out where I'd gone wrong. Neville had started to blur around the edges too, but I felt like I saw him better this way. Colours seemed to move through his body, showing me the patterns of thought and feeling that lived beneath his skin until, finally, I understood.

I felt cold, the fog lifting from my mind as Neville came back into focus. He looked expectant, but he wasn't getting any more answers from me. I knew his tale now, and it was a terrible one. The reason Chief Administrator Neville Rose imprisoned and tortured Illegals was simply because he *liked* doing it, and he'd never thought his actions were for the good of the Balance. That was just something he said to other people, part of an elaborate trick he played on the world. He enjoyed causing pain as much as Grey, only he was much worse than her. She was simply mad, a dog gone rabid. Neville held both her leash and his own, and when he let go of the restraint, it was because he'd made a deliberate choice to do so.

Licking my dry lips, I whispered, "You're a very bad man, Neville Rose."

He scanned my face. Then he smiled. It wasn't his grandfatherly smile. It was the knowing smirk of a monster who understood exactly how monstrous he was, and simply didn't care. "I don't think you're going to help me, Ashala. What a shame."

He nodded to Grey, who began pressing buttons on the black box. Unable to stand staring at him for a second longer, my eyes roamed around and fixed on Connor. He was so still and expressionless he truly could have been a statue, and yet the sight of him was instantly reassuring. I wished I could tell myself that my reaction to him was another strange effect of Grey's drug, but I knew it wasn't. For days now, I'd been avoiding a part of my own story, trying to hide from feelings I didn't want to have. Only here, in this room that I wasn't very likely to leave alive, it seemed pointless not to acknowledge the truth. *I love Justin Connor.* He didn't deserve it, but somehow that didn't change how I felt.

Grey stopped pushing buttons, and Connor's gaze locked with mine as I tensed myself for what was to come. The very last thing I was aware of before the blinding flash was his flawless features, crumbling into an expression of utter desolation, and I thought, *This is how the angels looked when they watched the world end.*

The white light faded, leaving me standing once again on the grasslands, disorientated and alone. Everything seemed the same as before – yellowy grasses, rocky hills, distant tuarts. And the far-off thumping that heralded the approach of the dog-beast. I turned to run for the trees, but a giant boulder came thrusting out of the ground, grass and dirt flying everywhere as it rumbled to a stop in front of me, blocking my path. The same thing happened in every direction I tried, except when I faced the sound of the dog's pounding steps.

Ember appeared in front of me. "I'm afraid they've upped the settings, Ash."

"So what do I do?"

"Get hold of the dog's collar." she answered promptly. "I've been thinking and I'm pretty sure it represents the command pathways of the machine. If we have it, we can give him new orders."

"How am I supposed to get it?"

"You grab the thing!" I looked at her doubtfully,

and she added, "You know how when you Sleepwalk you can do impossible stuff because you know you're dreaming?"

"Yeah…"

"This is a bit the same. We're in *your* mind, Ash. If you believe you can do something, then you can."

"Em, I'm not sure—"

But I never got to finish the sentence, because the beast came loping over the horizon. He swerved towards us, letting out a bloodcurdling howl, and Ember vanished.

I yelled, "Wait, Em, I still need your help!" She didn't reappear, and the hound was barrelling forwards at an impossible speed. Focusing on that shiny collar, I ran for the beast, keeping a single thought in my mind as I tore through the tall grass: *I can do this, I can do this, I can do this, I can do this.* Energy burned like fire in my veins, and I sprinted faster and faster until my pace matched that of the hound.

The two of us leaped for each other, but I'd been quicker off the ground, hurtling upwards as he dived for the space where I'd been. I twisted to land on his back, and he snarled, bucking and flinging back his head. Dodging his snapping teeth, I clung on with my legs, feeling frantically around the edge of the metal collar until my fingers encountered a latch. I'd just managed to unclasp the thing when the dog bucked again, sending me sailing through the air with the collar clutched in my hand.

I hit the ground hard, the shock of the impact reverberating through my entire body and knocking the wind out of my lungs. After a moment, I managed to roll painfully to my side and sit up, only to freeze in place when I saw that the massive black beast was standing a few paces away. Except he didn't seem to be interested in attacking me. His entire attention was directed at the collar lying in the grass. I seized hold of it, horrified to find the thing was lined with a series of long, nasty-looking spikes that were wet with blood. The lights were still blinking, and I could see now that there were tiny buttons beneath each of them. *Is that how I'm supposed to give him new commands? By pushing buttons like Grey?* The dog trotted over, bending his head and waiting for me to put the ugly thing back on him. I gazed at the bleeding gouges in his neck, my mind racing. *None of this is real, remember? He's only a black box.* Except it was real, and he wasn't only a black box.

"You're a prisoner too, aren't you, boy? Like me, but with a different collar." He whined, tipping his head to one side.

I staggered over to the nearest rocky hill and threw the collar on the ground, searching around for a sharp rock. When I found one, I crouched beside the metal band, bringing the rock down on it with an almighty smash. The lights went out, but that didn't seem like enough, so I kept going, hitting it over and over until I'd reduced the entire thing to mangled pieces.

Feeling immensely satisfied, I threw the rock away, panting from exertion. The dog ran over, wagging his big tail. He didn't look menacing any more. In fact, he seemed kind of goofy. I grabbed at his nose. "Never again, do you hear me? You're your own dog now." He gave me a big slobbery lick. "Woof!" he barked, bouncing like an overgrown puppy. "Woof, woof, woof!"

"You do realize," said a dry voice behind me, "that you've given the machine power over itself."

I scrambled up guiltily. The dog caught sight of a butterfly, and took off after it, bounding across the grasslands. "He's a good dog, Em!"

"He might *not* have been a good dog, Ash, and there's nothing to prevent him from attacking you –

or rather, your mind – if he wants."

"Why didn't you try to stop me, then?"

"I'm you, remember? How successful have you ever been at stopping yourself from rescuing something?"

"I don't think I've ever *tried* to."

She rolled her eyes. "That's kind of my point. Besides," she added, waving at the hound, "this is what you do best. It's just like the Tribe. People come to the Firstwood all hurt and scared and angry at the world, but the only thing you see is the good in them, the greatest version of themselves that they could be. And somehow, most of them grow and change until they start becoming that person."

"It's not *me* that does that," I protested. "It's freedom."

"It's so not, Ash."

I opened my mouth to argue. But it was ridiculous to have a debate with myself, so instead I watched the dog, who'd given up on the butterfly and was rolling on his back with his metal paws in the air.

"Do you think they know that they've lost control of him yet?"

"They will soon if we don't give him a memory."

I grinned. "Let's give him a totally useless one, like my fifth birthday party."

"Or we could give him the one they want."

"Very funny."

"I'm not joking, Ash."

I turned, puzzled, to find she was holding something above her head, a long stick that curved in the shape of … a *snake*? Panicked, I lunged for it, but found my movements were sluggish and weak. Ember stepped back, easily evading my slow grab. "Sorry, Ash, but I can't let you interfere now." Then she threw the stick into the air, sending it flying towards the dog.

I couldn't even move my head fast enough to see the dog leap for it. But I heard the cracking snap of it breaking, and I knew the secret I would have died to protect was about to be spread out across a screen for my enemies to see. Ember disappeared, and my mind wailed in horror: *This was all some kind of terrible trap!*

Then the grasslands faded away, and I was dragged into the memory of what I'd been doing in Cambergull four days ago.

DAY THREE

THE SERPENT

I toyed with the river stone hanging around my neck, thinking that I didn't much like warehouses. The air was musty, and the windows set high in the wall let in so little light that if I hadn't known it was early morning, I might have thought night was approaching. Sighing, I shifted into a more comfortable spot. I was sitting on top of a big container, and I'd carefully positioned myself so that I had a view of the door but was still half-concealed behind yet more containers. Cambergull was a farming community, and generally these warehouses held either wool or foodstuffs like grain and vegetables. Not this time, though. Everything in here was for Detention Centre 3. I'd been excited about that until I'd discovered the only thing the containers had in them were boring office supplies. Running a detention centre involved more paperwork than I'd ever imagined.

The door to the warehouse slid open, and I tensed as a tall man slipped inside. He was wearing a long coat, a hat and a scarf wrapped around the lower half of his face. *Guess this is the guy.* "Over here," I called.

The Serpent strolled forwards until he was standing a few paces away. I couldn't tell much about him, other than he was broad shouldered, green eyed and – apparently – somewhat paranoid.

"So you're Ashala Wolf," he said in a gravelly voice.

"And you're the Serpent. Nice scarf."

"It is best if as few people as possible know what I look like. I am something of a wanted man, you know."

"The government's not exactly keen on me either, but I'm not going around all wrapped up."

"You live in a forest, Ashala. I must move through the towns and the cities."

"And just what," I demanded, "are you *doing* in the towns and cities?"

"I am building a network, an alliance of Citizens, Exempts and Illegals alike, who wish to see the Citizenship Accords repealed."

That doesn't really tell me anything. "I've heard the rumours about you. You're supposed to have some kind of reality-bending ability."

"I do, but I am not going to tell you about it. I'm here because I thought I should inform you that there is going to be an attack on Chief Administrator Neville Rose's ... project ... in the Steeps."

I straightened. "What *is* Rose doing in the Steeps?"

"That is not information I intend to share."

"Why not?"

"Because you are an amateur."

"I'm a *what*?"

"I admire your spirit," the Serpent told me, "but you have no idea what you're doing, other than encouraging children to 'escape' to a particularly dangerous part of the world. All things considered, I think it would be best if you stayed out of my way."

"Why did you even bother coming to speak to me, then?"

"Because what I am planning is going to stir up a great deal of trouble. I thought it fair to tell you that you might wish to withdraw further into the Firstwood for a while."

I glared at him. "What you're really saying is, the government might think the Tribe had something to do with your attack, being as we're living so near to the centre. They'll retaliate against us."

"Yes," he conceded. "That is a possibility, although I doubt it'll come to that. I'll ensure it becomes known that I am responsible. Besides, after Friday, the government and Neville Rose are going to have far bigger concerns than your group of runaways."

He sounded so dismissive that my fists instinctively bunched, and I wanted nothing more than to leap off the container, and pull that stupid scarf off his face. I might have tried it, too, except it was a bad idea to start a fight with another Illegal when you didn't know exactly what their ability was.

The Serpent said, with an air of finality, "It has been ... interesting to meet you, Ashala Wolf. Now take my advice, and get your group into the woods."

He walked swiftly to the door, and was gone before I could say another word. I sat there for a good five minutes after he left, fuming. Finally, I thought, *I might not know who he is, but I can certainly find out what he's targeting.* I didn't care how dangerous Ember said it was, I was going into the Steeps myself to find out what the high-and-mighty Serpent thought was worth attacking.

Pushing myself off the container, I left the warehouse, rubbing absently at my nose as I considered the best way to approach the Steeps. My mind was busy with plans as I hurried past other warehouses, and started down the road that would take me out of Cambergull. Only I hadn't taken more than a few steps when someone yelled out my name, and I found myself staring straight into a pair of all-too-familiar blue eyes.

I was caught.

DAY THREE
THE PLAN

I returned to the world in the windowless room. There was no way for me to tell how much time had passed, but I had a sinking feeling it hadn't been very long. Everyone was standing exactly where they'd been before – Connor, statue-like by the door; Neville, horribly triumphant at the end of the chair; and Grey behind the black box, saying gleefully, "I told you my machine would get you the answers."

"Excellent work, Miriam. I must apologize for doubting you." Neville moved to stand over me, shaking his head in mock-disappointment. "I really did think you'd put up more of a fight, Ashala. It seems you're not as strong as I thought."

I wanted to slip into unconsciousness, to escape – however briefly – both Neville and the knowledge of how I'd betrayed the Serpent. But I remained awake and aware. Swallowing, I forced out some words. "The Serpent won't come now. He must have heard I've been captured."

"I'm afraid," he told me smugly, "that no one outside this centre knows if you survived the wound you took in Cambergull. The Serpent may gamble on you having died before you were questioned. Besides, even if he doesn't come, it does me no harm to be prepared. But if he does ..." Neville's smile widened, his teeth gleaming in the light, "then we have him."

"Neville? Are we going to continue?" Grey asked eagerly.

The Chief Administrator shook his head. "No, Miriam. I have preparations to make, and I think she's had enough for today. Anyway," he added, gazing down at me, "this is going to become much easier from here on in, isn't it, Ashala? Because you understand now at exactly what point you'll break. So the next time, you'll break a little before that point. And then a little earlier still. Until finally you'll tell us what you know without the need for any persuasion at all." He leaned in close. "You're *mine*, Ashala Wolf."

I spat in his face.

Neville reared back, his eyes flashing with fury. For a second I thought he was going to strike me. *Go on, Neville. Hit me. Hurt me. Kill me.* But he regained control of himself, taking out his handkerchief to mop at his cheek. "I'm afraid you're going to regret that." His voice was sorrowful, but it came out of a monster's face, one alight with anticipation at the many ways he could make me suffer. I shuddered, and he smiled slyly as he turned away, pausing to issue some low-voiced instructions to Connor before leaving the room.

Connor came to free me from the chair, and it dawned on me that I didn't feel anywhere near as bad as I had after my last time on the machine. But Connor didn't know that. *The second he releases my hands, I'm going to grab his sword and make a hole in my chest too big for Wentworth to Mend.* I waited impatiently as he removed the hoop from my head, unclipped the restraint from my neck and put the rhondarite collar back on me. When he began untying my wrists, I tensed, ready to lunge, but found myself strangely held in place. It felt almost as if the air itself was pushing against my body, preventing me from moving. *What is this, another weird reaction to being given too much of that stay-awake drug?* I was still trying to fight against the pressure when Connor finished with the restraints and lifted me from the chair, picking me up as if I weighed nothing.

I couldn't move at all now, not even to open my mouth to speak, and I started to get scared. But as we entered the hallway the pressure eased enough for me to gasp, "I need to see Wentworth – something's wrong with me!"

"If you're experiencing paralysis," he answered calmly, "it's a temporary side effect of being exposed to the machine at a high level. It should pass soon."

I exhaled in relief. Then I thought, *Wait, that doesn't seem right.* If I was paralysed, I should feel numb, not as though some invisible force was moulding itself to my flesh. In fact, if I didn't know better, I'd think someone was using an ability on me. A surge of sudden hope sent my pulse racing. Could there be a free Illegal around here somewhere, someone who could use their ability from a distance? Were they trying to let me know that they were around?

My mind was still whirling in speculation when we

arrived at my small cell. Connor laid me gently down on the bed, and moved to shut the door. The light coming in through the tiny window told me the sun was setting. *Good, Neville's going to have to move his enforcers into position at night.* It'd take longer to navigate the Steeps in the dark.

The odd pressure in the air vanished, and I sat up. Connor was propped up against the wall in front of me, looking uncharacteristically relaxed. Some of his hair was falling over his face, and his shoulders were slumped in what could only be described as a slouch. "I'm glad," he said, "that you don't want to kill yourself any more."

I stared at him in amazement. He was right that I'd temporarily given up on killing myself in favour of finding out if there was an uncollared Illegal somewhere in Detention Centre 3. But how had he known what I was thinking?

Connor smiled faintly, and continued, "I was ready to stop you this time. I wasn't, back in Cambergull."

"What are you talking about?"

"This was all your plan, Ashala."

"*What* was my plan?"

"Being captured and interrogated."

"Yeah, right!"

"I know it sounds unlikely. But it's true. You thought it was the only way to free the detainees – and expose Neville – without the government coming after the Tribe."

"You're talking nonsense."

"You just think that because you don't remember." Reaching inside his shirt, he pulled out a black cord with a small stone attached to it.

"That's my river stone!" I gasped.

"I know." He pulled the cord over his head, holding it out to me, and I grabbed for it. As my fingers closed around the stone, Connor said, "The phrase you want is, 'This is the real world.'"

For some reason, it seemed important to repeat those words. "This is the real world? What is that supposed to…" Before I could finish the sentence, the stone started to vibrate, sending a weird buzzing sensation into my fingers. I tried to drop it, but the pressure in the air was back, holding my hand in place. The buzzing increased, travelling up my arm and into my head. In an instant, everything disappeared. Then, astonishingly, I was pulled into yet another memory, a memory of something I'd inexplicably forgotten. Until now.

* * *

Ember had cleared a big patch of dirt with her foot. Then she'd picked up a stick, and sketched a rough picture of three circles sitting inside each other.

I rolled my eyes. "Em, this is exactly how you explained this to me when we first decided to bring other Illegals to the Firstwood."

"I know, but what I'm trying to tell you now is how you'll see the world once you've lost your memories. Can you think about it for a second, please?"

I stared obediently down at Ember's system of dividing information. The third ring, the smallest, represented the people in the Tribe who knew the least about our secrets. These were the newcomers, the youngsters and a few others who Ember didn't consider to be entirely reliable. Then there was the middle ring of long-term Tribe members, and finally the first ring, the largest one. That last circle was made up of Georgie, Ember and me. And now Connor and Daniel too, I guessed.

Ember tapped the biggest ring with her stick. "You'll lose this knowledge, Ash. So you won't remember all of what I can do, or any of what Georgie can do. And you won't know about the saurs."

"Or," I put in, "about Jaz, or Connor."

She nodded and moved the stick to the second ring. "This knowledge goes too. You'll forget some of the Tribe are still in contact with their relatives, and that those relatives help us out with information and supplies. All you'll be left with," she concluded, tapping the third circle, "is this."

"Which means," I said grimly, "that I'll know what Briony knows. Em, if I haven't said it, I'm sorry for saying you were paranoid to want to keep secrets. How did you know, so long ago, that there'd be someone like Bry—"

"I didn't. I just thought it was unwise to be telling anyone who happened to come along everything about ourselves. Anyway, it wasn't all about security. Hiding my ability was more because people aren't very comfortable around me if they know I can change memories. As for Georgie..." She shrugged, not bothering to say what didn't need to be put into words. We'd both agreed Georgie's ability was best kept hidden. She was too fragile to have people pestering her for answers that she couldn't give them.

Ember tapped the stick on the ground again. "What I'm trying to explain is that it's not about

164

losing small pieces of information. This stuff shapes your entire understanding of reality. I don't think you realize how badly not knowing these things could affect you."

"I know it'll be awful, but it's the best way to fix everything. Besides, it'll only be for four days."

"A lot can happen in four days." She was silent for a moment, then added tentatively, "We could send you in closer to the Inspectorate visit..."

"We're cutting it close as it is. Anyway, you said my 'subconscious' needed time to work with the machine."

"It might not be necessary. It's more of a precaution."

I shook my head at her, knowing she was trying to find a way to make things easier for me. "It's a precaution we need to take. We can't afford for anything to go wrong."

"I know that. But from everything Connor's told us about the machine, it sounds like it works like my ability, although it can't do what I can. It only *finds* memories, so I don't think it'll be able to tell a real memory from one I've manufactured."

"Yeah, but like you've said before, if my mind – or

the bit of you that'll be in my mind – has a chance to experience the machine before we give it the Serpent memory, then we'll definitely trick it. Everything depends on Neville believing the Serpent is about to attack the Steeps. Otherwise, this is all for nothing."

I rubbed at Ember's circles with my foot, messing up the lines and thinking about how strange the world would become once my memories were gone. "You know, Em, I *still* don't understand how you're going to do this."

She brightened. "I've been thinking of a new way to explain it to you." Taking a breath, she announced, "It's like the rock pool!"

I eyed her dubiously. "The rock pool?"

"You know how there's those rocks underneath the water, first the big one, then the five smaller ones sitting on top of it?"

"Yeah. I remember what the rock pool looks like." Probably better than she did, because I loved that pool. I'd spent hours lying on an overhanging tree branch, looking down at the reds and greens and blacks of the marble rocks.

"Imagine," Ember said, "that the pool is your mind. The surface of the water that reflects the sky, is like the surface of your mind, processing everything that's happening right now."

"O–K."

"The way memory works is, we make sense of the things that are happening now by putting them into context, which is provided by things that happened before. So the underneath part of your mind, the bit under the surface of the water, is your past experiences. Those past experiences give you a structure that you slot your present experiences into. Like the way the presence of the rocks affects the currents of the water. Are you with me so far?"

I didn't know if it was the rock pool thing, or the fact that she'd already explained all of this to me about five times before, but she was making sense. I nodded, and she continued, "And the way the structure gets formed, is that some memories are more important than others. They're key events that shape our characters and determine how we interpret everything. Which means if I submerge some of your key past memories into your subconscious – so the surface of your mind doesn't have access to them any more – the context into which you fit your more recent experiences changes. Imagine that the rocks are key events; I'm sinking them way down into the water, beneath the sand at the bottom of the pool."

"Oh, I get it. The water would change too, wouldn't it? Because the rocks aren't there any more, the water would move differently."

"Yes! Except I'm not sinking all the rocks, because I'm not submerging all your memories. So imagine there are lots of big rocks, and those are the ones that I sink – the key events. If the big rocks aren't there, then all the smaller rocks that sit on top of them..."

"Will sink to the bottom of the pool."

"That's right. They'll be disconnected and out of order. Only the mind hates chaos, so the current of the water will take those rocks – those memories – and arrange them into a pattern that it knows. Without the key memories, it'll use something else that it's familiar with. Something that it won't even know isn't true."

A smile broke over my face as it all came together. "I'll adopt the version of the world that the third circle knows. Like the water rushing into the space left by the big rock, and sweeping the little rocks around into a new position."

She looked pleased, although I wasn't sure if it was with me for understanding or herself for explaining so well. "That's exactly it, and you understand why the mind won't try to heal itself, right? Why it won't try to bring the big rocks back up?"

"Because you'll stop it?"

"No, not entirely. The real reason you won't bring those memories out of your subconscious is because you don't want to. This would never work otherwise. I'd have to take the memories out altogether instead of hiding them, and it would probably send you insane. But the memories I'm sinking are centred around people you love, and protecting what you love is your strongest instinct. You'll keep those memories safe until Connor gives you the river stone, and you say the code phrase to activate it."

"And the stone will have *this* memory in it?"

She shrugged. "This, or some other memory of us discussing the plan. That way, both your subconscious and your conscious mind will know it's OK to remember. They'll work together to bring the memories back into your mind. You'll have a part of me with you to help too."

"Yeah. Em, I get how you can invent memories,

and even change memories and submerge memories. Sort of. But I *don't* get how you're putting yourself in my head."

"It's not me exactly. I'm going to copy one of my memories, a core memory which contains the essence of who I am, and put it in your subconscious. In lots of ways, we are our memories, Ash."

I stared at her and said, not very intelligently, "Um."

She took a deep breath. "Think about it this way. After you shared memories with Connor, you could sometimes feel what he felt, couldn't you? Especially when he was experiencing strong emotion?"

"How did you know that?"

"Your mind experienced the memories that are the essence of who he is. It created a link between you. Like an echo of him, in you. Which I warned you about, by the way."

"Yeah, but it worked out fine."

Now it was Ember's turn to say, "Um." *I wish those two would get along.*

After a few moments of awkward silence, I asked, "So I'll feel what you feel too?"

She shook her head. "No. It's my ability, so it

170

works differently for me. It's more like, you'll have a fragment of me in your subconscious, which can help you. As if I've put a new rock beneath the surface with the other rocks."

"I won't even know this memory is there, right?"

"It'll be in your subconscious, so you won't know it's there. But it means I'll be able to help you and guide you through."

It was reassuring to think that I'd have a part of Ember with me, but I didn't tell her so. I didn't want her to know how scared I was about this whole thing, because she'd never let me do it if she did. So I stood there quietly, listening to the birds and looking out through the trees.

The memory began to gradually dissolve, melting and blurring until it had slipped away from me completely.

I expected to find myself in the cell again, once the memory was gone. Only I didn't. Instead, I was drifting in darkness, and I wasn't remembering any more. I knew that I was somewhere within my own mind. Someone came floating out of the blackness towards me. *Ember again?*

"You're the Ember in my head," I said as she drew near. "The one I saw when I was on the machine. Only you're not really part of my subconscious, are you? You're the fragment of Ember that she sent with me."

She grinned. "That's right, Ash."

"The capture, the interrogation, the Serpent – we planned it all?"

"Yes."

"Right … well … that's…" *Insane.* "Did it work?"

"So far."

"Why don't I remember?"

"Because it's not a good idea for your memories to come rushing back all at once, and out of order." She held out her hand, opening her fist to reveal four river stones. Each one was different – one flat and diamond shaped, one twisty and red, one curved like a claw and one a beautiful shade of blue.

"These stones," Ember explained, "represent the secrets that you couldn't risk being taken by the machine. The key events, centred around people that you love. Are you ready for them?"

I reached out, and she put the rocks into my hand. "You have to remember in order," she told me sternly, pressing my fingers against each of them so I could feel the different shapes. "This is the first, this the second, this the third and this the fourth. You got that?"

Flat diamond, twisty red, claw, blue round. "Got it."

"Then remember!"

She vanished, and lights started popping out of the darkness, brilliantly bright, as connections cascaded through my mind. The rocks flew out of my hand to spin through space, growing bigger and bigger until they were three times my size. Electricity sparked, becoming crackling currents that swept me up and sent me swirling around with the tumbling stones. I was almost overwhelmed, blinded and dazzled by the lights. But then I remembered the sequence, and launched myself forwards, grabbing hold of the diamond-shaped rock. Heat seemed to flow from the stone into my body, and I leaped from stone to stone. *Flat diamond, twisty red, claw, blue round.*

Four sets of memories came blazing through my brain, transforming everything I thought I knew about the world.

THE SECRETS
GEORGIE

FOUR YEARS AGO

Something tickled my nose. I rolled over without opening my eyes, trying to find a more comfortable spot for my head to rest against the lumpy pack of supplies. The tickling didn't stop. *Go away, insect,* I thought sleepily. Stupid fly ... ant ... wait, spider! My eyes flew open, and I batted at my face until a green bug shot through the air and went *splat* against a rock. Not a spider. *Sorry, bug.*

I stood and brushed myself down, in case there *were* any spiders. Then I realized I was alone. *Where's*

Georgie? WHERE IS SHE? After a scary moment, I spotted her sitting on top of the hill we'd been too tired to hike over last night. She was facing away from me, looking at something I couldn't see from here, and totally unaware of me fighting off imaginary spiders. Yawning, I walked over and climbed up to join her. Georgie didn't turn around, even though she must have heard me coming. *Great, she's out of it again.* But when I reached the top and saw what she was staring at, I went all silent and frozen too.

Stretched out in front of us were waves of long yellowy grasses, broken up by patches of colourful wildflowers and rocky hills which rose upwards like turtles surfacing from the ocean. And beyond the grasslands were the trees, a sprawling forest of tuarts so tall they seemed huge even from here. The Firstwood. We were *here*. I glanced at Georgie, pleased to find she wasn't wearing that frighteningly blank expression, the one where she seemed like her mind had gone on holiday and left her body behind. Instead, she looked – actually, I didn't think I'd ever seen anyone look like she did right then. Except, maybe, in the picture that hung in our school library, the one that showed Hoffman on the day the flood

176

waters had started to roll back from the land, and he'd realized humanity would survive the Reckoning after all.

Georgie shifted, her face growing worried, and I thought something might be wrong. Then she asked quietly, "Ash, is this the real world?"

I grinned in relief at hearing her say something so normal – well, normal for her. "Yes, Georgie. This is the real world." I said it with total confidence, like I was absolutely certain, and I was. But Georgie wasn't, and never would be, and I understood why. It wasn't easy for her to keep track of the world-that-was, not when she spent so much time peering into worlds-that-could-be.

Reassured, Georgie went back to staring out over the grasslands. *She's OK. She's herself.* I'd gone along with her crazy scheme of creating a life for us in the Firstwood, and it was working. She was connecting again, in her own Georgie way, and she seemed happy, not sunk in gloom the way she'd been in the city.

Now that we were finally here, though, I couldn't help thinking about the other person who should be with us. *It does no good, Ash. You know it does no good*. I couldn't stop the entire sequence of events from playing out in my mind as, for the thousandth time, I tried to work out where I'd made my mistake.

This whole terrible thing had begun when Georgie had told me she'd "seen" something bad happen to Cassie. As usual, she hadn't been able to give me any details. "Looking at the future," Georgie had once told me, "is like watching clouds." Which sounded like nonsense before she explained. "You know how clouds make shapes, and sometimes you're not sure what those shapes are? So first you think it's a dog, and then you look away, and when you look back you think it's a bird instead." Plus, the way Georgie told it, she had no control over what clouds she saw, or for how long. And the "weather" of the future changed all the time, sending possibility upon possibility flitting randomly through her head.

What Georgie had known about Cassie was that something bad was coming, and it involved the government. I'd thought my Firestarter sister was going to be detained, and I'd made a plan for the three of us to run away together. Only, somehow, my parents had figured out that Cassie had an ability. They'd called an assessor and, exactly like Georgie had said, something bad happened to Cassie. I just hadn't been quick enough to get Cassie out, or smart enough to realize the assessor was coming. I hadn't been *enough*.

My chest tightened until I could only take short, shallow breaths. Spots started to appear in front of me, and everything tilted the way it had right after I'd found out Cassie was dead. The doctor in Gull City had said I was suffering from panic attacks. As if I needed to be told. I mean, obviously I was panicked. I didn't understand why everybody *wasn't* panicked. Didn't people realize how quickly everything could fall apart? *You look away for an instant, you spend the day at a friend's house, and when you come home your sister is gone...*

"Ash!" Georgie tugged my arm, sounding terrified. "Ash! Ash!"

With effort, I forced my thoughts away from Cassie and concentrated on the world around me – the solid bulk of the hill, the hard stones beneath my hand, the wind on my skin. Finally, everything started to right itself again, and I could breathe more easily. "I'm all right, Georgie."

She tightened her grip on my wrist, her pale eyes fixed on me in a super-focused way that was a little scary. "You're thinking about Cassie. You told me *I* wasn't allowed to keep thinking about her, and now you're doing it."

"I'm not. I mean ... I'm..." I shook my head helplessly, unable to prevent the words I'd been holding inside from spilling out. "I was so mean to her, Georgie. You remember how she used to follow me around everywhere, and I pushed her away."

"Because you didn't know she had an ability. You thought you'd have to leave her behind one day, when you ran from the government. Once you found out she was a Firestarter, you were the best sister anyone could want."

"I've only known that for a year. I wasted all that time, and now she's gone, and it's all my fault."

"It was not your fault! Your mum and dad were the ones who called the assessor. And what about the enforcers? And, the government? You always say everything's the government's fault."

I had to laugh at that, a short, painful laugh that turned into a cough at the end. "I guess I do."

She continued to stare anxiously at me. "I *need* you, Ash. "

"I know, Georgie. It's OK..."

"Because I'm like a kite."

"Um, a kite?"

"I go flying around from future to future, and it'd be so easy to drift away and fly for ever. Except I have you, and you're the person who holds the string, the one who pulls me back to the ground." Biting her lip, she said in a small voice, "If you're lost, Ash, then so am I."

I put my hand on hers. "Georgie, it was *definitely* the government's fault."

She laughed, and so did I, and the tension was broken. We went back to sitting in silence, but a more comfortable one this time. Then Georgie said brightly, "Look, a saur!"

There was a menacingly large black shape approaching from the distance. I clutched at Georgie. "If we're not on its territory, I think it'll leave us alone. So what we have to do is go back down to our packs real fast and real quiet. You got that?"

She nodded. I twisted around, slithering backwards. Georgie shifted as if she was about to follow.

Then, suddenly, she stood up and ran down the *wrong side* of the hill. I leaped to my feet, slipped and skidded. By the time I'd clawed my way back, Georgie was out on the grasslands, and the saur was moving in her direction at an unbelievable pace. I belted after her, shouting, "Georgie! You're going the wrong way!"

But she started skipping towards the monster, and I put on a new burst of speed. I had to reach her before the saur did! Grabbing hold of her arm, I tried to drag her backwards. She planted her feet on the ground and grinned at me, looking like a naughty kid who was playing a trick on her mum. *What does she think she's doing? Has she totally flipped out?*

The saur was getting so close now that I could hear the ripping as its claws tore through the grass. Georgie *still* wouldn't move. I flung myself in front of her as the saur charged towards us, waving my arms wildly. "You want to eat somebody? Eat me!"

The huge reptile skittered to a halt. It stood there, staring down at me, while I gaped back at it, my knees shaking and my heart slamming against my chest. From this close, I could see it wasn't all black. There were thin orange stripes running along its scaly body, and it was *huge*, so big that the top of my head was level with the top of its front legs. The beast flicked out a long blue tongue, and if Georgie hadn't been behind me, I would've fled. But I knew I had to keep between her and the saur, so I stayed where I was, watching in terrified silence as it licked at the air above my head. *What is it doing?* Then I remembered – lizards smell with their tongues. And it seemed to be ... puzzled.

Maybe it didn't know what we were? It'd been years since anyone had been foolish enough to wander into the grasslands and be eaten by saurs, so this particular saur might not have seen a human before. That could buy us enough time to escape. Or at least, enough time for one of us to escape. Without looking away from the beast, I whispered over my shoulder, "Georgie, I want you to go. Don't run, because I'm pretty sure it'll chase after you if you do. Just walk back to the hill and off the grasslands."

There was a moment of silence, during which I hoped Georgie was following my advice. Only when she spoke, I could tell she hadn't moved. "The speckled egg will hatch in the next no moon."

What on earth was she going on about? "Georgie, you have to leave!"

But she'd already caught the lizard's attention. Its golden eyes focused on her as she continued talking. "You can tell the mother that her last child will hatch with stars."

A strange, raspy voice demanded, **How do you know about the egg?**

My jaw dropped. The saur was *speaking*? But it hadn't even opened its mouth. The voice came again, and I realized I was hearing it *inside* of my head.

How do you know?

Georgie stepped forwards to stand beside me. "Because I know. It's a future."

The lizard's eyes flared in something that might have been anger, and I put in hastily, "She has an ability, like a special power, that lets her see things that are going to happen before they do. So your, um, speckled egg will be OK."

There was a tense silence, during which he – she? – gave Georgie and me a thoughtful stare. He, I decided. I had no way to tell, but I thought the saur was a male. He didn't seem to know what to make of us, and I certainly didn't know what to make of him. Or of

Georgie, who'd obviously been seeing things she hadn't told me about. I cast a sideways glance at her, to find she was giving the saur a cheerful wave.

"I'm Georgie, and this is Ash. What's your name?"

He stretched out his neck, seeming to preen a little, and rolled one golden eye towards us. **I am Wanders-too-Far.**

Putting as much enthusiasm as I could into my voice, I exclaimed, "Wow, that's a very impressive name. Very adventurous."

The saur didn't reply, but I got the feeling he was pleased. Encouraged, I said, "Well, we just came to tell you about that egg. So we'd like to go now, if that's OK with you."

You are humans.

Georgie nodded. "That's right."

We have songs about humans. They harm their young.

The way he said that, it sounded like the worst thing in the world. I opened my mouth to deny it, but it was such a blatant lie that the words stuck in my throat. After all, Georgie and I wouldn't have been here if humans didn't harm their young. Luckily, Georgie wasn't as lost for words as I was.

"Not me, and not Ash! Ash doesn't hurt people. Ash looks after everyone."

Wanders-too-Far seemed to be considering that, and I put in, "Also, among humans, *we're* young. We're ... babies, really. We're running away from the adults, the big humans, who are trying to hurt us. So," I finished firmly, "if you eat us, you'll be no better than they are."

Wanders made a hissing sound. A *laugh*? **You are not my young, human. Why should I protect you?**

"Because ... because ... we're useful! Like Georgie – she told you about the egg, and she could tell you about other things too. And I can do anything in my dreams."

He gazed at us without blinking, and I got the feeling he was thinking hard. For what seemed like a long time, everything was quiet except for the sound of our breathing – Georgie's normal, and mine too fast – and the murmur of the grass in the breeze.

Finally, Wanders spoke again. **Humans should not know of us.**

It took me a second to figure out exactly what he meant. "You – the saurs are hiding, aren't you? That you can talk, I mean?"

Our songs say humans fear difference, and when they are afraid, they will find a way to destroy what they fear. Unless they do not know it is there.

I had to admit, that was a good plan. "But we won't tell anyone, not ever, I promise."

Georgie chimed in. "We don't even have anybody to tell. All we want to do is live in the forest."

You wish to live with the trees? He gave his hissing laugh again. **Your kind call this forest the Firstwood. Do you know why?**

I'm getting a history quiz from a saur? "Because this is the first place trees began to grow again after the Reckoning. It's the first place that anything began to grow."

These trees grew from seeds that survived the great chaos. They carry within them the memories of their ancestors, the lost forests of the old world. They do not forget what humans have done.

He doesn't think the trees will want us here. "Look, if you don't want to let both of us go, just leave Georgie alone, OK? She's already proved she can help you."

"No, Ash!"

Ignoring her, I rushed on, "People in the city, other humans, think she's crazy. She could tell everybody saurs can speak and no one would believe her. She's not a danger to you, I promise."

"No!" Georgie shoved her way in front of me. "If you're going to eat her, you have to eat me too."

"I'm trying to help you, Georgie!"

"I don't want that kind of help."

The two of us glared at each other, while Wanders watched us both. **You do not seem like the humans the songs speak of, and Keeps-the-Memories will be pleased to know her egg will hatch.**

I asked, "Are you going to let us go?"

No, young one. You wish to live with trees, so it is they who must determine your fate.

He dipped his head towards me, coming closer until I could make out his individual scales and the thin line of black around the gold of his eyes. He was ... alien. Beautiful. Terrifying.

You will make your plea to the forest. Perhaps the trees will let you stay. But be warned, whatever bargain you make with them, the saurs will ensure you keep it. And if the forest decides

you must go, then we will finish you.

Wanders drew back, and I looked towards the trees. Those old trees that remembered how humans had caused the end of the world. They seemed to stare right back at me.

I wasn't sure they liked what they saw.

THE SECRETS

EMBER

FOUR YEARS AGO

So now it was only me, and the Firstwood.

Georgie was waiting a few paces back, and Wanders was lolling in the grasses to my right, along with two new saurs who had joined him in the three days it had taken to cross the grasslands. I got the feeling Wanders was secretly cheering for us, but those other two looked hungry. If there was going to be any eating, they'd be the ones who would be doing it, and I didn't think they'd be a bit sorry either.

Rocking back on my heels, I stared up at the

tuarts that towered over all the other plant life of the forest. They were so tall I could barely make out the tops, and so wide that Georgie and I would've had to join hands with about ten other people to circle the trunks. But more than that, they were seriously spooky. Standing near these trees was like being outside right before a bad storm breaks, when the air goes heavy and electric, and you know you need to get indoors fast. I reached out to touch the grey bark of the nearest tuart. My fingers tingled, and grew slightly numb. *As if I need another sign that this is no normal forest.* Wanting to be sure I had the Firstwood's attention, I pressed my whole hand to the tree, and started talking.

"Um, hello, Firstwood. My name is Ashala. My friend Georgie and I would like to live here. I know you remember the bad humans in the old world, the ones that caused the Reckoning, but Georgie and I are nothing like them; I promise you we're not. If you let us stay, we won't eat any of the animals, or cut down any trees, or do anything else you don't like." I paused, taking a breath. The air around me seemed to have grown even heavier, more expectant, and I hurried on. "I don't know if there's any way we can help you, but if there is, we'll do it. We've got abilities – Georgie can see the future, and I can do stuff in my dreams. We could be useful people to have around, and we'll do *anything* to stay. Just let me know what you want."

For what felt like for ever, nothing happened. Then a fiery bolt shot up my arm and exploded into my head. I yelled, trying to pull away, but my hand was stuck to the rough bark of the tree like it'd been glued there. Images poured into my mind, nightmarish pictures of things I'd never seen before. Strange vehicles with metal jaws, weird saws with teeth that roared, and humans, always more humans, cutting and hacking and slashing and killing. I slumped to my knees, shouting in my mind, *It wasn't me! It wasn't me who did that!* But the pictures kept on coming, filling my body with pain and my mind with the shocked confusion of dying forests. I realized the trees wanted to know why.

I knew what that was like. Two months ago, I'd wanted to know why too.

Staggering to my feet, I sent the Firstwood a picture of my own. Me, walking in circles over the burned earth that was all that remained of my house.

I'd been as bewildered as the trees, totally unable to grasp how my mum and dad could have thought it was a good idea to call in the assessor. Even though I'd always known my parents were good Citizens, I couldn't quite believe they'd done it. For days, I'd wandered through a world that made no sense to me, feeling as if I'd gone suddenly stupid or crazy. Until I'd asked myself what I would've done if I were them, and it had dawned on me that I wasn't the one who was mad, or dumb, or wrong.

I rested my face against the tree, and whispered, "There is no reason. Do you hear me? There's no reason good enough to hurt my sister, or to kill a forest. I *know* that. I'm not like my mum and dad, or the government, or the humans who caused the Reckoning. I won't hurt you or anyone else because I think you don't count as much as me. And if anyone ever comes for you with machines or saws or axes or anything, they'll have to get through me first."

The Firstwood went silent. There were no more horrible pictures, and no normal forest noises either. No birdsong, no wind in the leaves, no scurrying animals. The only thing I could hear was myself, sniffling pathetically. I couldn't even remember when

I'd started crying, and now I didn't seem able to stop. I let my tears dribble onto the bark, and a new image came into my head, one of bare, broken earth. That picture seemed to blur into the scorched ground where Cassie had died, and all I could see or feel was an aching nothingness. For a long moment, the Firstwood and I were sad together. Then something started growing in the emptiness. Tiny green sprouts shot up out of the earth. The sprouts became saplings and the saplings mighty trees, and around them, other things grew too. Small streams of water swelled into rivers and filled hollows in the earth to make pools. Peppermints, flowers and shrubs sprung up beneath the shelter of the tuarts. Birds nested, wolves denned and saurs hatched from their eggs. And beneath and within and between it all was a shining shape that was somehow the beginning and the end of everything.

The glowing thing flowed around me, and my whole body hummed with life. I found myself shouting out, giving words to the joy and defiance of the Firstwood. "I live! We live! We survive!"

I was flung back into total awareness, as if someone had shaken me awake from a deep sleep. No pictures any more. Just me, huddled against the base of the tree with Georgie crouched at my side. "Ash? Ash? Are you OK?"

"Yeah, I think so." I stood up, feeling strange, kind of warm and comfortable and ... safe. "Actually, I'm terrific, Georgie!" I lurched out onto the grasslands, looking for the saurs. *No humans for dinner today...* But they were far away, skittering into the distance with their awkward, super-fast run. "Hey, the saurs left?"

"Yep. The wind talked to them."

"It did? What did it say?"

Georgie shrugged. "How I am supposed to know? The wind didn't speak to me."

"Then how did you know it spoke to the saurs?"

"Because it blew, and they lifted their heads and listened."

Guess that makes sense.

"And," she added cheerfully, "Wanders said that it's up to us to decide what to do with the other one."

"What is that supposed to mean?"

"I don't know. I thought you would."

"Why would *I* know?"

"Because you know lots of things, Ash."

"I don't know this, Georgie. Didn't you ask him any questions?"

She shook her head, and I sighed.

I had no way of finding out what Wanders had been talking about, but hopefully it'd become clear, since I didn't want to get on his bad side. I spun in a circle until I was facing the trees again. Those tall, clever, *beautiful* trees. "Come on, Georgie!"

Grabbing hold of her hand, I ran into the Firstwood, pulling her with me up to the top of a rise before I let go and stopped, trying to take in the whole of the forest that was now our home. The scattered, towering tuarts, and beneath them the twisting peppermint trees, and further down still a whole lot of plants I'd never seen before. My attention jumped from one odd piece of nature to the next: a flower with a yellow stalk which flared upwards into curved green tips; a stumpy black trunk with long grasses spraying out the top; and a shrub hung with brown pods filled with black seeds that peered out like creepy little eyes. Everything was strange, and yet I felt I fit in here in a way that I never had among the familiar streets of Gull City. It was as if I'd come shooting up from the earth with the tuarts and the rest of the woods had grown around me, leaving an Ashala-shaped space that only I could fill.

I live. We live. We survive.

I belong.

I glanced over at Georgie, who was twirling around and humming. "Georgie? Why didn't you tell me about the egg and the saurs?"

"You didn't believe me."

"Yes, I would have—" Then I stopped, realizing what she'd said. Not "you wouldn't have believed me", but "you *didn't* believe me". So she'd seen a future where she told me the saurs could talk, and it hadn't gone well. "Um, sorry."

She stopped twirling and wandered over. "You said lizards can't talk with their minds. You said I must've misunderstood the shape of what I saw."

I knew it would do no good to tell her that I'd never actually said anything like that. "I'm sorry. You were right."

"I was, wasn't I?" Then her eyes widened. "Hey, do you hear that?"

I did, now that she'd pointed it out. "Is that somebody singing? There's not supposed to be anyone here but us."

I began to move towards the distant melody, with Georgie trailing after me. The two of us picked our way through the undergrowth, following the sound of the song until we came out onto the banks of a wide river. There was a red-haired girl sitting in a tree that overhung the water. She must have seen us, but she kept on singing in a high, clear voice. Georgie waved, and called out, "Hello! HELLO!"

The girl still didn't react, and I put my hand on Georgie's arm, stopping her mid-wave. "She knows we're here. I think she's ignoring us."

"Who is she?"

"I don't know. Maybe she's the other one Wanders was talking about?" I gazed thoughtfully at the girl. I didn't know how she'd even got past the saurs in the first place, but somehow she had, and it seemed like the lizards thought she was now our problem. *She's a long way above the ground too.* I listened to the words of her song. Something about winter, and being alone. OK, so she was sitting in a high place, singing a depressing song. This probably wasn't good.

"Georgie," I said, "I'm going to climb that tree and try to speak to her. You stay here, OK?"

She nodded, and I strode over to the base of the

tree. It was a tuart, but a young one, so there were branches low enough to reach from the ground. The girl finished her song as I began to climb, so the only thing I could hear as I went up was the wind, growing stronger as I got higher. The tree started to sway, and I held on tighter, levering myself onwards until I swung onto the same branch as the girl. She was still quite a distance away from me, but there was no way I was going to edge out to her. Heights didn't bother me, but the movement of the tree in the breeze, combined with the sharp rocks sticking out of the water below, was enough to make me cautious.

Holding on to the trunk, I said, "Hi. I'm Ashala, and that's Georgie down on the ground."

She kept on staring at the swirling water. "This is the largest river in the forest," she said distantly.

"Um, OK."

"It runs for a long, long way. I don't even know where it ends. But I've been thinking about how far it might go. How it could run past the tuarts, and out of the Firstwood, into ordinary forests, and then down to the sea. If I fell in, it would carry me away."

"If you fell in," I informed her in a helpful tone, "you'd probably bash your head on one of those rocks. Then your body would get stuck in the reeds, and fish would eat your face."

She whipped her head around to frown at me out of mismatched eyes. "Who *are* you?"

"I told you, I'm Ashala. Who are you?"

"Ember. What are you even doing here?"

"Right now, I'm talking to you."

"I *meant* in the forest. How did you get past the saurs?"

I shrugged, not wanting to share any information about the lizards. "Guess I was lucky. How did you get past them?"

She pulled at the sleeve of her top. "Haven't you noticed that I'm wearing yellow? I came here from Spinifex City, in the other direction."

I thought about that. Spinifex City sat in desert-like country that bordered the western side of the vast Firstwood, and if what I'd learned in school was right, it was true that there were no saurs on that side. But there *were* insanely territorial big cats who killed anything wolf-sized or larger, and hung the body in a tree as a warning to other trespassers. "Then how did you get past the sabers?"

"By going underground. Through the tunnels."

"Through the *what*?"

"There are tunnels that run beneath the Firstwood. Or at least, beneath part of the Firstwood."

A scary picture flashed into my head, of troops of enforcers bursting up from secret passages. "Does anyone else know about the tunnels?"

Ember shook her head. "Just my father and me, and he ... he won't tell. Besides, they're all collapsed now. I barely made it through." She looked me up and down. "You're obviously an Illegal, but you don't need to worry. No one's coming to detain you."

"Or you," I retorted sharply. "You're obviously an Illegal too."

She held up her hand, displaying a tattoo of three spiky blades of Spinifex grass contained within a circle. "Yes, I am, but I have a Citizen tattoo."

Impressed, I said, "You fooled an assessor? What's your ability?"

She rolled her eyes like she wished I'd stop pestering her with questions. But I was pretty sure, at this point, that she was glad to have someone to talk to, so I wasn't surprised when she decided to answer. "I manipulate memories."

"You what?"

"I can take memories from people. And I can share them, change them and even invent ones that never happened. Only," she added angrily, "I can't forget. Not anyone I meet, not anything I see or read or hear. I remember everything in perfect detail."

"That doesn't sound so bad."

"Then," she snapped, "I expect you've never lived through anything you don't want to remember."

I thought of Cassie, and didn't reply.

Ember went quiet too. I watched her curiously, trying to figure her out. I'd thought at first she was a bit strange, but now it seemed more like she was angry, or upset. Really upset, in the kind of way that made you do crazy things, like climb very tall trees.

"Why are you in the Firstwood?" I asked. "With that tattoo, you could've stayed in Spinifex City. Or gone anywhere else in the world."

She didn't move or look at me, but she whispered, "My father's dead."

"Was it the government?"

"No. He was sick. There was something wrong in his head. The Menders couldn't help him, and I couldn't help him, and he died, not very long ago."

So you came here. I could see now why she'd gone

down into those unstable tunnels, not caring if she ever came out again. Expecting not to come out, probably, and being kind of glad of it, because then she wouldn't have to feel that endless ache of grief any more. I knew what that was like. "My sister's dead too. The government killed her during an assessment." *I understand how you feel.*

She shifted closer to me. "I'm sorry about your sister."

"I'm sorry about your dad."

"He and I were going to change things for Illegals. He was helping to start a movement, getting Citizens to ask a question about whether people with abilities are part of the Balance."

My doubts must have shown on my face, because she added defensively, "I know it doesn't sound like much, but Alexander Hoffman said that *all* revolutions begin with a question. It's got people thinking about if there's a good enough reason to even have Citizenship Accords. We had lots of other ideas too."

"Yeah? Like what?"

She hunched her shoulders. "It doesn't matter now. I can't do it on my own."

"You're not alone. You've got us."

"I don't even know you!"

"Hey, I climbed this tree for you. Plus, I don't know if you've noticed, but Georgie's made you a picture." Looking puzzled, she peered downwards to where Georgie had been busily putting a bunch of stones together, making a sprawling pattern on the sand. "I think," I said cautiously, "that it's supposed to be a flower. Or maybe a puppy."

Ember giggled, a pretty, musical sound that floated over the forest. Her face was transformed by that laughter – she looked happy, and hopeful. Georgie squinted up at us, grinning, and I waved at her. Then I cast a calculating glance at Ember. "I've had about enough of this tree. I'm going back to Georgie."

For a second I was worried that she wasn't going to follow me. But she started to inch towards the trunk, and the two of us began the long descent to the ground. "So," I said as we made our way down, "what exactly were the other ways that you and your dad were going to make things better for Illegals? Besides the question thing, I mean."

"We were going to change how people thought."

I paused, looking up at her. "Wouldn't it be better,

I don't know, to storm a detention centre? Take on some enforcers?"

Her eyes blazed with a sudden, ferocious intensity, and when she spoke, she sounded as certain as I did when I told Georgie the world was real. "You can't transform a society for the better with violence, Ashala. Only with ideas."

THE SECRETS

JAZ

SIX MONTHS AGO

I don't know how long I lay on the grass, sobbing into Jaz's last footprints. Eventually, Ember and Daniel came and found me. Ember stroked my hair, making soothing noises, while Daniel lifted me off the ground in his strong brown arms, and carried me back to camp. I thought, *I want to die.* For four days, I didn't move or speak. Then, on the fifth day, the wolves came.

It started with a single howl, a long, eerie wail right before dawn. Then another, at a different pitch.

And another, different again, until the whole forest echoed with their cries. It sounded like there were hundreds of them out there, even though it was only a twelve-wolf pack. I tried to ignore them like I'd ignored everyone else, but they went on, and on.

Finally, I stood up, stumbling out of the caves where the Tribe was camped. It was icy cold outside, and I wrapped my arms around myself, peering into the grey dawn light until I spotted one of them. I knew which one it would be. The same wolf who had been sitting at my feet when I'd woken up on that very first morning in the Firstwood. He'd hardly been more than a pup, back then. Now he was big and lean, his orangey-brown coat shining with health and his pale yellow eyes watching me above a toothy canine grin. He yipped once, and ran off, clearly expecting me to follow like any wolf in his pack would. And I did, wanting to do something, anything, other than think of Jaz.

I ran lightly, swerving to avoid trees, racing over rocks and through shallow streams with the rest of the pack, never hesitating and never losing my footing. I ran until there was no Jaz, no saurs and no Tribe. Just me, the wolves and the sights and smells of the forest, rushing past me and around me until I was almost dizzy with it. When I couldn't run any longer, I stumbled to a halt and threw back my head to howl my grief to the forest.

The wolves slowed to a trot, and then a walk. Pack Leader circled back to where I was standing. I would've liked to keep going, but I had a stitch in my side, and my legs were shaking with exhaustion. He nosed at my knee like he was trying to tell me something, and he was. I couldn't explain how I understood him, any more than I could explain why everyone in the Tribe developed a bond with one of the forest animals. None of us could communicate with our animals as well as Georgie could with those creepy spiders, but I understood Pack Leader. He thought I would be OK now. The terrible thing was, I did too, and I didn't *want* to be OK. I didn't want to be able to go on, not without Jaz, not after I'd failed to save him like I'd failed to save Cassie. And I hated knowing that I could.

I started to pace back and forth, to walk off the stitch and gather my strength for the long, weary trudge back to camp. The wolves faded into the forest, and my heightened senses retreated with them until I could see and hear and smell no better than any other human. I kept pacing long after the pain in my side was gone, wanting to delay going back into the caves. I didn't want to face the others and see their disappointment. Or, worse still, their approval, since most of them believed I'd done the right thing. *They'd be furious if they knew it was me that was meant to die.*

"Ash!" A cheerful voice interrupted my thoughts. "Here you are."

I spun round to find Georgie approaching through the trees, all rosy and warm in her grey woollen coat, and carrying my own coat over her arm.

Eyeing her grumpily, I asked, "How'd you know where to find me?"

"You needed me, and when you need me, I come."

"I *didn't* need you, and that doesn't even make any sense."

She handed me my coat. "You're cold. Put this on."

As I shrugged myself into it, she said, "We have to go the grasslands now. To see Jaz."

My hand crept up my throat, and I stared at her in horror. "His – his body? But he would have burned."

She shook her head. "No, Ash! Jaz, as in, the *actual*

210

Jaz. He's alive. The saurs came to tell us." She reached for my hand. "Come on! They're all waiting."

She started walking, and I stumbled along behind her. I felt confused, overwhelmed, wanting for it to be true that Jaz wasn't dead but not daring to believe it. We wound our way out of the trees, through the tall grasses and around the red rocky hills, until I saw them. First, an enormous, yellow-striped saur that I didn't know, lounging against a hillside. Then Ember, sitting near another saur who was instantly recognizable. After being born so late, Hatches-with-Stars had never grown to her full size, or into her proper colour. Her scales were pale blue instead of black, her one stripe was a red line down the side of her neck and she wasn't much taller than I was. But what grabbed my attention was the boy standing a few paces in front of them all. Only it wasn't Jaz. His hair and eyes were black, and he was too thin and *way* too still. *It's not him. It's not.* I was sure of it. Right up until he grinned triumphantly, and said, "I told you they'd be won over by my endearing personality."

I tore forwards, flinging my arms around him. "Jaz!"

211

He hugged me back, his wiry frame seeming to have gained new strength. "Hey, Ash."

"You're alive!" He started to wriggle in protest at being held too tight, and I let him go, touching his changed face in disbelief. Even his smile was different. It was a bit snarly, and somehow seemed to have a lot more teeth in it. "Is it really you? It doesn't look like you."

"Of course it's me." Then he added accusingly, "You never told me the saurs speak with their minds."

"It was a secret. Hey, how do you know that, anyway?"

"Because they told me." He puffed out his chest. "I'm one of them now."

I studied him, noting the darkening of his hair and eyes, which reflected the saurs' own black scales, and the reptilian elegance to his movements. "You're a *saur*?"

"Yep!" He jerked his head towards the lizards. "You see that big one? His name is Tramples-my-Enemies. He was the one that came to get me and took me to the others. They said, since I'm an eater of flesh, and *they* are eaters of flesh, I belong with them. Then they had a ceremony that went on for a whole night and day. Did you know they sing?"

"Yeah. I mean, I've never heard them, but I know they do."

"It's amazing! The songs have stuff in them I've never heard about before, stuff from the old world. Only, I'm not supposed to talk about the ceremony. It's a saur thing, you know? But it joined me to their pack." He fixed his black gaze upon me, his brow creased in concentration, and words formed in my head. **I can speak like this now, Ash.**

I gasped. "Jaz!"

"Cool, isn't it? I can't do it over long distances yet, like the others. I'll learn, though."

"You ... you're not coming back?"

"Sorry, Ash. I can't. I'm not Tribe any more. You can't tell anyone else I'm alive, either."

"Why not?" As soon as the words were out of my mouth, I realized why. "The Tribe would start asking questions about the saurs if they saw how you'd changed."

"Yeah, and the saurs don't want anyone to know they can talk, except for you and Georgie and Ember, of course. Also, there's the Pact." He gazed at me with an un-Jaz-like severity. "We saurs want the Pact to be kept, so it's better if people think something terrible happens if you break it. And something bad *could* happen, Ash. Not everyone can become saur like me." Then the seriousness vanished from his face. "Guess what? I have a new name too! I'm Blazes-with-Fire!"

Tramples-my-Enemies lifted his head, directing a stern look at Jaz. "OK." Jaz sighed. "So I'm not Blazes-with-Fire *yet*. I will be one day, though, when I've earned it. Saurs can get new names if they change so much that their old one doesn't fit any more."

"Really? Then how come Hatches-with-Stars is still Hatches-with-Stars, and Wanders-too-Far is still Wanders-too-Far?"

"Hatches will always be Hatches. She's special. And Wanders-too-Far *does* wander too far! Last week he went all the way to the other side of the Firstwood, until he was almost in saber territory. Tramples-my-Enemies and Gnaws-the-Bones had to bring him back."

"What do they call you then?"

Jaz shuffled his feet, and mumbled something. I bit back a smile. "Can't-be-Still? *That's* your saur name?"

"It's my name for now. Only I'm practising being

very still. Then they'll see the name is wrong, and they'll have to give me a new one."

I looked away so he wouldn't realize I was struggling not to laugh. *Sounds like the saurs have Jaz all figured out.*

Hatches rose to her feet, shifting from one clawed foot to another. She seemed kind of anxious. "Jaz? Is she all right?"

He waved his hand dismissively. "She's fine. She's just worried I'll go back to camp with you, even though I've told her I won't. Hatches is my best friend among the saurs."

"Oh yeah?" I strode over to the small saur, gazing up into amber eyes that weren't that far above my own. "I want you to take care of him, OK?"

From behind me, Jaz let out an outraged cry. "Ash! I can take care of myself. I'm saur!"

I ignored him, and so did Hatches. She pranced closer, and pictures started to form in my mind, giving me a view of the world from the perspective of the smallest of the saurs. Trying to join in games with the other saurs, and always being pushed away. Having her meat killed for her, even though the other younglings were hunting for themselves. Swimming in the shallows of the seven pools while the others leaped from the rocks into the deeps. Then came images of the new saur who was even smaller than she was. Jaz flinging himself into a saur game, being immediately tossed out and diving right back in again. Jaz trying to eat raw meat, throwing up and starting a cooking fire that set the grasses alight and had to be stomped out with tough saur feet. Jaz chattering endlessly – would Hatches help him sharpen very small rocks so he could glue them to his fingernails to make claws? Could Hatches listen to him practise his hissing to see if he had it right? Did Hatches think, if he was extra good, that Tramples-my-Enemies might let him ride on his back? Hatches-with-Stars, the saur who had never quite fit in, wasn't alone any more. And she more than loved Jaz. She adored him, with a devotion so intense it bordered on worship.

The images faded, and Hatches tilted her pale head at me.

"It's OK. I get it. I know that he ... that he..." My throat closed over, and I stopped, took a breath and forced out the words. "I know that he belongs to you now."

She made a high-pitched trilling noise, and despite

everything, I had to smile at the sheer joy in the sound. Jaz came up beside me. "Ash. Are you crying?"

"Only a little."

"But aren't you happy for me?"

"I'm very happy for you, Jaz. I'm going to miss you, that's all."

"Oh!" His face cleared. "That's OK. I'll still come and visit. I dunno when, though, because I have *heaps* to learn about being a saur. It would've been so much better if they'd raised me from an egg."

I didn't even know what to say to that, so I hugged him again, and whispered, "I love you, Jaz."

"Love you too, Ash!"

"You know, if you ever need me, for anything..."

"Yeah, yeah, I know." He pulled away impatiently. "I have to go now. Keeps-the-Memories is going to teach me a song. I'll try to mindspeak you over a distance. It'll be good practice!"

Tramples-my-Enemies rolled to his feet, while Jaz swung himself onto Hatches's back with quick, inhuman grace. He fastened his arms around her neck, and grinned at me, one last time. Then, in an instant, he was gone, carried away by Hatches, with Tramples running along behind. Ember and Georgie both came and stood beside me, putting their arms around my shoulders in silent support. I watched as the saurs disappeared into the distance, the landscape blurring in front of me. *He's not my Jaz any more.* But I couldn't be sad, not when he'd looked so carefree, perched on Hatches's back.

Wiping at my eyes, I turned to face Georgie and Ember. There was something I had to say to Em, something I'd been thinking about a lot over the past three days. I'd gone over and over that final journey with Jaz in my mind, until I'd understood what Ember had done, what she *must* have done. "Did you *really* think I wouldn't figure it out, Em?"

She went pale. Georgie looked from her to me, and asked, "Figure what out?"

I glared at Ember. "I had a plan, Georgie. I was going to dose Jaz with the sleepy herb, and give myself to the saurs in his place. Except he worked out what I was doing and switched my water flask with his. Only," I snarled, "Jaz wouldn't have recognized that herb if he'd tripped over it, and he definitely wouldn't have known how much to put in the water to send me to sleep. Unless he had help from someone who *did* know."

218

I expected Em to deny it, or to start babbling an apology. She didn't. "I did what I thought was right."

"What was *right*? You sent him to his death!"

"Jaz made a mistake, Ash, and he chose to take responsibility for it, and you should've let him. Being a leader doesn't mean always taking the blame for other people's mess. Besides, Jaz begged me to help him. He knows you're important—"

"I'm *not* more important than Jaz!"

"Yes, you are!" she snapped. "I don't know why you can't understand it, but you *matter*, Ash. You transform things in a way that no one else can, and I know you're going to change everything for Illegals. If everyone has to die to protect you, so be it."

I stared at her in shock. Ember had always said we'd one day make the world better for Illegals, but I'd never realized how big a role she'd been expecting me to play. Or how far she'd go to keep me safe. "Ember ... you can't..." I couldn't seem to put what I was thinking and feeling into words. Then Georgie's voice broke the silence, sounding angrier than I'd ever heard her. "You got it wrong, Ember."

Em and I looked at her in surprise as she continued. "It's the other way round – if *Ash* has to die to protect everyone she cares about, then so be it. You have to let her love. Because it's the only thing more powerful than hate."

OK, this isn't very helpful. "Georgie—"

"Don't look at me like that, Ash! I know you think I'm not making sense, but I am. It's just that you don't know. You don't understand, because I never told you what you almost did."

"What are you talking about?"

Georgie bit her lip, seeming unsure of herself. "I don't know if this is when I tell you. I haven't *seen* when I tell you."

"Georgie! Tell me *what*?"

"You hated once, Ash. Back in Gull City, you hated the government for what they did to Cassie."

"Yeah. I know."

"No, you *don't* know. Because what you don't remember is, how you were going to kill people. A lot of people."

Ember and I both spoke at once. *"What?"*

Georgie focused her pale-green gaze on my face, and explained, "After Cassie died, when you were staying at my house, there was this day. We were upstairs in my room talking about Cassie, and you suddenly ... changed. Your eyes went all white, and you were Sleepwalking. You told me there were bad people out there in the city, and you were going to go punish them. I think you meant everyone who worked for the government. You said you wanted to kill them all."

Ember made a choked noise, and I gaped at Georgie. She kept on talking. "You were really going to do it, Ash. So I sat on the window ledge in my room, and I said if you left, I was going to throw myself out of it. I said it over and over, until your eyes went back to normal and you were yourself again."

"Georgie, I don't ... I don't remember any of that!" Except I *did* remember something. A vague recollection of a long-ago dream, when I'd wanted to go somewhere, only there'd been this shining, fragile thing, and I knew it would break if I moved. *Had that been it?* "What you're saying isn't even possible. I mean, I can't use my ability when I'm awake."

"You *might* be able to," Ember said thoughtfully. "If you were in some sort of dissociative state."

"Some sort of what?"

"When someone is very distressed, they can go into something called a dissociative state. Sort of like being asleep, but when you're awake. That might have happened to you."

Dissociative state? Sleepwalking while awake? The whole world was spinning around me. "I'm *not* a killer."

"Of course you're not." Georgie said. "Only, Ash, you feel things deeply. All the way to your bones, and you were *so* angry after Cassie died. You had so much..."

I finished the sentence for her. "Hate." I had. I could remember the taste of it, a constant acid on my tongue. The one thing I'd thought about had been getting back at the government. Until Georgie had gone all sad, and stopped talking or eating much. Then I'd had to worry about her instead.

"Georgie," I said wonderingly, "the way you were after Cassie died, when you went all sad, you did that on purpose, didn't you? To get me to leave the city?"

"Yes. I knew you had to go, Ash. To get away from the hate."

I couldn't believe it. All this time I'd thought I rescued Georgie, when she'd been the one who rescued me. I was still trying to wrap my mind around this new version of my past when Georgie said to

222

Ember, "You have to let Ash *be* Ash. Caring about people, helping people, that's what brings her back to herself. It's the reason she didn't attack anyone that day. She wanted to help me more than she wanted to hurt them."

Ember looked stricken. "I ... I didn't understand. I was ... I think I was wrong about Jaz. I *know* I was wrong. I'm sorry, Ash! I'm so sorry."

I couldn't deal with Ember right now, so I just nodded and walked away, wandering over the grass to the edge of the flattened area where the saurs had been. I breathed in the cold air, inhaling the faint scent of rain and absorbing everything that had happened. After a while I heard footsteps, and glanced back to find that Georgie was coming towards me. Ember was headed in the other direction. "She's leaving?"

"She knows you're still mad at her."

"I have a right to be mad." Although my anger was fading now. "I don't know why she's so convinced I'm going to change the world!"

"Because you can make dreams come true."

"That's just my ability."

"Yes," she agreed, "but I wonder sometimes, is it

223

our abilities that make us who we are? Or do we have the abilities we do *because* of who we are?"

"I don't even know what that means."

"You bargained with saurs, Ash, and made a home in the Firstwood, and started the Tribe. You *have* changed the world, and you didn't use your ability for any of it. So maybe Sleepwalking is an extension of who you are inside."

"I didn't do any of those things by myself, and I wouldn't have even come here without you." Thinking about how badly I'd misunderstood her, I added, "Thanks for everything you did, four years ago."

"It's OK. Only, you do know that it wasn't really the government you wanted to punish that day, right?"

"I know." I'd pushed all my rage, all my hate, onto the government, but there'd always been something else underneath. "I wasn't a good sister, Georgie."

"You loved her, and she loved you. And if you could have saved her, you would have. Ash, *please*. You have to forgive yourself, for Cassie."

I was quiet for a long time before I confessed the truth to my oldest friend. "Georgie. I don't think I can."

* * *

Jaz says get salt.

It had been four days since Hatches had sent the mysterious message into my mind, and I still didn't understand what it meant. *Of course,* I thought, as I walked back from the lake with my hair still dripping wet from my swim, *Jaz probably doesn't want salt at all.* Messages between humans and saurs sometimes got garbled, especially over long distances. I wished I could answer Hatches back, but the lizards couldn't hear us in their heads the way we could hear them. Jaz was the only one who could have an entirely mind-spoken conversation with either human or saur, and despite months of effort, he usually had to be pretty much within sight of someone to do it.

What was really worrying me, though, wasn't the message itself, but the distressed feeling that had come with it. *You saw Jaz a couple of weeks ago,* I reminded myself, *and he was fine.* True, he'd been a bit upset, but that was because I'd given him an update on the information our new enforcer friend Connor had been giving us. Jaz hadn't been pleased about the traitor in the Tribe.

225

There was the sudden sound of running feet, and Ember came bursting onto the path ahead of me, her cheeks red with exertion. "Ash! Come quick! Daniel's back, and he's hurt."

I plunged into the trees, heading for the large clearing that was our warm-weather camp, until Ember called, "The caves!" Switching direction, I angled upwards to the trail so I could run without having to tear through the undergrowth. The Tribe had moved out of the caves about a week ago, more than willing to exchange the cold nights and mornings of early spring for open sky above our heads and the lemony scent of the tuarts in bloom. Daniel had left for Gull City before that and must have assumed we were still there.

I'd sent Daniel to check out a series of weird rumours about a terror campaign in Gull City, some kind of attack that people had at first thought was the work of the Tribe, but now seemed to be linked to the Serpent. Which was strange, since firstly, the Tribe wasn't responsible for any kind of terror campaign, and secondly, Ember had basically invented the Serpent.

My feet hit the trail, and I picked up speed, pounding along until I pelted through the northeastern entrance to the cave system. Inside, I found Daniel stretched out on the sandy floor, with Georgie on one side of him and Pen on the other. He didn't have any wound that I could see, but he was drenched in sweat and his lean body was shaking. Georgie was smoothing his hair, while Pen had one small hand pressed to his chest. The Mender's dark, slightly slanted eyes were wide open, staring at nothing, and her normally smiling mouth was pressed into a thin line. *It's bad, then.* I went still, knowing better than to distract Pen when she was Mending. After a while, Ember came in behind me, and whispered, "Georgie found him. I told the others that there'd been a rockfall, and some of Georgie's spiders were hurt."

"Good story," I whispered back. It was too – no one would come up here to check out what was going on if they thought there were a bunch of anxious spiders crawling around. We relied on Georgie to keep the critters away from the side of the caves that everyone lived in.

"No one else saw Daniel," Ember told me. "The others still believe he's out scouting for a new camp site."

I nodded, thinking that a few months ago, our

biggest problem really had been finding a camp site deeper into the Firstwood and further away from the site of the new detention centre. And I wouldn't have cared what the others knew. But that was before I'd met Justin Connor and learned about the Tribe member who was betraying us. Luckily, we didn't have to worry about our resident traitor right now, because we knew exactly where she was, and it wasn't in the forest. Briony was off meeting with her government contact. I wished that I could do something about her, only I couldn't, not yet.

Pen finally stirred, and took her hand away from Daniel's chest. He'd stopped shaking, but his eyes were still closed. She stood up, and walked over to Ember and me. "He's done too much Running and exhausted himself. He needs to sleep now. You can try talking to him, but not for too long."

"Thanks, Pen. Don't say anything about this to the others, OK?"

"Yeah," Ember chimed in. "Remember, as far as they know, you were doing a favour for Georgie, helping out her spiders. This is very important."

"Don't worry," Pen answered earnestly. "You can count on me."

She left, and Ember and I walked over to Daniel, kneeling down beside him. Georgie didn't take any notice of us. She wasn't paying attention to anyone but Daniel, and I could see why. *He still looks bad.*

"Daniel," I asked, "can you hear me? Can you tell me what happened?"

His eyelids fluttered open, revealing green eyes murky with fatigue. "It's Jaz. The government has him."

My chest felt like it was being crushed in a vice, the air choked out of my lungs. I was dimly aware of Ember asking Daniel urgent questions, and Daniel responding, but I couldn't hear anything over the roaring in my ears. Ember reached across and squeezed my arm. "Ash, I'll do this. Go wait outside."

I stumbled out, down the trail and into the forest. Pressing my back against a tuart, I slid to the ground, curling against the comforting presence of the tree. To my horror, I realized I was whimpering. *Get a hold of yourself, Ashala! You're no good to him like this.* I'd just barely managed to get my panic under control when Ember arrived.

"It'll be OK, Ash," she said, sitting at my side. "We'll get him out."

"What happened?"

"He was picked up by a patrol in Gull City." I opened my mouth to ask what Jaz was even doing in the city, but she held up a hand to stop me. "It's complicated, so you have to let me tell it in order."

I subsided into silence as Ember began, "When Daniel arrived in the city, the streets were crawling with enforcers searching for an Illegal waging what the government was calling psychological warfare. Except the so-called warfare was nothing but clouds."

"Clouds?"

"Yep. A Skychanger was changing clouds into reptile shapes that looked like saurs. That's why people thought the Tribe might be involved. Daniel dodged the patrols and made it to our storage unit, which is where Jaz came to see him. He wanted Daniel's help to rescue his sister. His *Skychanger* sister."

"His..." I put my hand to my head. "I didn't even know he had a sister! But, wait, Daniel thought Jaz was dead, and the saurs..."

"I know, I know. Apparently it took Jaz quite a while to convince Daniel that he truly was Jaz." Ember sighed. "It's a mess, and Jaz'll have to answer to the saurs for telling the secret, I suppose. But, Ash, Jaz was indirectly responsible for the entire psychological warfare situation. He discovered that the saurs who can talk to each other over the longest distances were from the same hatching, as in, siblings. So he tried to mindspeak to his sister, and it worked, sort of. Jaz managed to pick up on what Phillipa was feeling – which is pretty good, considering how far away Gull City is – but he didn't realize what effect the contact would have on her. She started having recurring saur dreams, and since she's all of seven years old, and a Skychanger..."

I groaned, seeing how everything had started to go wrong. "She can't control her ability."

"Nope. It's leaking out of her. Probably had been for a while, but I suppose nobody reacted to clouds that looked like dogs or cats or whatever else she made them into. But big scary lizards?" Ember shook her head. "When the hunt for the Skychanger started, Phillipa panicked. Jaz felt her fear, and decided to go to Gull City to see what was wrong."

"He should've asked me for help."

"He didn't even ask the saurs, Ash."

"Because they wouldn't have let him go. Of all the stupid, reckless—" I stopped, and drew in a shaky

231

breath, knowing it was pointless to be mad at Jaz now. "OK, tell me what happened next."

Ember studied my face, clearly wanting to make sure I was all right, then continued, "Once Jaz reached the city and saw how many enforcers were around, he did something sensible and hid out. Fortunately, being closer to Phillipa meant he could mindspeak with her better. He couldn't get her to stop making the shapes at first – you know how much practice it takes to control an ability – but he did get her to make the shapes less like saurs and more like snakes."

"That's why everyone started thinking it was the Serpent!" I felt a surge of pride. "That was smart."

"Yeah. Only Jaz was stuck. He wanted to take Phillipa out of the city, except he couldn't rescue her on his own. He decided to wait, figuring that the patrols would eventually stop, or you'd send someone you trusted to investigate when you heard about the 'terror campaign'."

"So Daniel and Jaz tried to rescue Phillipa, and Jaz got caught?"

"Not exactly. Daniel wouldn't help him."

"*What?* Why not?"

"Because it was still dangerous to be out on the streets. Daniel had trouble making it to Dockside without being stopped, and Jaz's family live in the Hub. Daniel wanted to Run back here and get me. With my genuine tattoo, I could've passed any Citizenship inspection. He thought he'd convinced Jaz it was a good idea..."

"Don't tell me," I said. "Jaz tried to get his sister himself."

"He crept out while Daniel was asleep. When he woke up, he went after him, but by then it was too late. Jaz had been picked up by a patrol."

"Of course he was picked up!" I snapped. "He looks like a Scaly now! It's a miracle he wasn't detained before. When did this happen?"

"Three days ago. Daniel almost killed himself Running back here, Ash. He feels really bad."

He should have known what Jaz was planning! But I could hardly blame anyone for believing Jaz was going to do one thing when he was going to do another, not when I'd fallen for that once myself. "Jaz will be locked up by now."

"Yes, but think. He was detained in the city. They'll never match his new face with his old photo, and he's clever enough to give a false name. They'll assume he's an orphan."

"And," I said with rising hope, "orphans get sent to Detention Centre 3. Which is where Connor is."

"Exactly! The government is probably going to put Jaz in the one place where we have a friend on the inside. The next time we see Connor, we can get him to make sure Jaz is on the list of detainees to be transferred there."

The icy feeling of dread that had seized me since I'd heard Jaz had been taken eased a little. "We can save him!"

"That's what I've been trying to tell you. Only – there's something else."

More bad news? I wasn't sure I could stand it. "What is it?"

"Jaz's sister. Her name is Phillipa. But she calls herself Pepper."

She said that last word as if it was very important. "What does that ... the message! 'Jaz says get salt.' Jaz says get Pepper?"

"I think so, yes. He must have made contact with Hatches after he was caught."

It would have taken a superhuman effort on Jaz's

part to reach Hatches all the way from the city, and it made me feel like whimpering again to think of him being so desperate. "Of course we'll go get her. You and me, Em. We'll need a plan."

"I'm already thinking about it, Ash."

It was ridiculous, but the prospect of a dangerous rescue mission was improving my mood. Levering myself to my feet, I stared out through the trees in the direction of faraway Gull City. Wherever Jaz was, I knew he couldn't hear me. But I sent my thoughts out anyway, along with the wish that they'd somehow reach him.

We'll get Pepper, Jaz. Then we're coming for you.

FIVE WEEKS AGO

I shivered, pulling my coat more tightly around myself as I peered out the doorway of storage unit number 338. From where I was standing I could smell the sea, and see dozens of units facing each other across a wide aisle, their smooth composite surfaces glowing eerily in the moonlight. The unit I was in belonged to an upstanding eighty-two-year-old citizen named Elizabeth Douglas. Or, as we knew her, Daniel's grandma Bessie.

It was weird to be back in Gull City, and the weirdest thing of all was I'd forgotten there were things I loved about it – the winding streets, the quotes from Hoffman etched into walls and over doorways, and the tang of salt in the air. I liked too the way you could read the history of the city in its architecture. The oldest parts were cobbled together out of bits and pieces of the old world, while the newer sections were filled with gleaming composite structures, produced once people had got the recyclers working. But none of that was enough to make up for the constant creeping terror that I would be detained. I didn't know how Em had been able to stand it in the week that she'd been here. Her genuine tattoo let her ride the Rail without fearing the close scrutiny of a spot Citizenship inspection, so she'd made it to the city much quicker than I had. I'd only arrived this morning. But every moment in this place had been a scary one, even with a fake tattoo on my wrist and the security of knowing that Briony believed Ember and I had gone deep into the Firstwood to check out a new camp site.

Ember had gone to fetch Pepper a while ago, and I

wondered uneasily if something had happened. Maybe the kid had got last-minute jitters and changed her mind? But from what Em had told me, Pepper had been a willing ally ever since Ember had made that stupid snake wriggle at her. Jaz had told his sister that if he didn't come for her, whoever showed up in his place would identify themselves with the sign of the Serpent. I'd laughed when Daniel had explained that, thinking only Jaz could invent a secret wave for an imaginary Illegal. Then I'd realized Jaz had been trying to protect the Tribe, making sure Pepper couldn't link anything to us if she was found out and questioned before we could reach her. And I'd felt like crying instead.

There was a noise in the distance, and I huddled into the unit, straining my eyes to see into the night. A grey-coated figure emerged from the darkness, leading a dark-haired child, and I ran out to meet the two of them. "Any trouble, Em? Did anyone see you?"

She shook her head. "We were fine. This is Pepper." I smiled down at Jaz's sister, and Ember pressed Pepper's hand into mine. "Let's go, huh? You take her, and I'll go get our stuff."

I could hear the strain in her voice, and I knew she

wanted to get out of here as much as I did. I began walking, pulling Pepper with me as I looked for a gap running down the side of one of the units. This place was organized so that the main passageway was criss-crossed by a narrow corridor every fifty units and a much bigger one every hundred, but it was the smaller space I wanted. While it was better not to be shut in when I Sleepwalked – mostly because I could, and would, smash my way out – I wasn't comfortable falling asleep out in the open either. Not here in the city, with no friendly tuarts to stand guard.

I found a gap and ducked into it. Pepper was quiet, but she didn't seem worried, which was making *me* worry that she didn't understand what was going on. We'd decided not to break the news about Jaz being captured yet, but Ember should have explained everything else. Except I knew what Ember's explanations could be like. *Too many big words, and not enough full stops.* Halfway down the narrow space, I let go of Pepper's hand, and said, "Pepper, you do know we have to leave your mum and dad behind? But," I added quickly, "it's going to be much safer for you where we're going."

There wasn't much light between the units, but

even so, I could make out Pepper's ferocious scowl. "I'm *glad* to leave them behind. I remember when they made Jaz go away."

"You do?"

"I woke up when he was climbing out the window. He said one day he'd come and get me, and he did! Well, he had important things to do, but he sent Ember."

Right. I strongly suspected that before the mind-speaking had brought Pepper to his attention, Jaz had forgotten all about coming back, because he'd never so much as mentioned a sister. But I wasn't going to tell her that. "Jaz wanted to make sure you were safe."

She drew herself up proudly. "I climbed out the window and down the tree even quieter than he did when he ran away. *And* I helped Ember throw my suitcase into the ocean."

"That's great! You understand that people will think you drowned? Your parents won't notice you're gone until morning, and when they find your things in the sea..."

My voice trailed off. I couldn't see Pepper's exact expression, but I swear I could feel her looking at me

239

like I was an idiot. "Of course they'll think I drowned. Didn't Ember tell you about my note?"

"Your note?"

"I wrote, 'Dear Mum and Dad, I'm running away to sea like Captain Albatross.' It was an excellent note. Ember said so."

"It sounds like a terrific note. Who's Captain Albatross?"

Her mouth dropped open. "Don't you read?"

I was saved from having to respond to that by Ember coming around the corner of the unit, carrying a pack slung over her shoulder. She passed me the flask I'd brought from the Firstwood. Taking hold of it, I hesitated, glancing down at Pepper. She seemed pretty tough, but if anything was going to scare her, it would be what was coming next. "Pepper, do you know how we're going to get to the forest? I'm going to ... to..." There didn't seem to be a good way to say, *I'll be Walking through the world with my eyes all white, and I won't really see you or anything else since I'll be dreaming, but I should be able to get us out the city by doing something impossible.*

I looked at Ember, who shrugged. "There's no good

way to explain Sleepwalking, Ash. Pepper knows it'll be very strange, but she'll be perfectly safe. Don't you, Pepper?"

She nodded vigorously. "Ember will take care of me."

With an effort, I bit back the words, *I'll take care of you too!* It was good that the kid liked Ember, especially since Em would need to reassure her if things got scary. *I just wish she liked me as well.* Comforting myself that I'd have time later to win her over, I opened the flask and took a deep drink of the sleep-inducing concoction inside. Then I handed it back to Ember and stretched out on the cold ground, closing my eyes and letting the tension drain out of my body. Which wasn't that easy, because this was still new to me. It was only in the last year that I'd been able to control my ability at all, thanks to some techniques that Ember had devised. After much experimentation, she'd discovered two key things about Sleepwalking. Firstly, in order for my ability to activate, I needed to realize I was dreaming. Secondly, it was possible for me to send a set of simple instructions to myself between when I was almost asleep and when I was actually asleep.

I let my mind drift, allowing thoughts to pass by

without holding on to them, and I started to lose awareness of my surroundings. There was no Ember, no Pepper, no storage units and no city. Only me, floating in nothingness. I imagined a piece of paper in my hand, and concentrated on what I had to do. *Take Pepper and Ember. Make sure no one sees you. Get to the Firstwood.* I would've liked to give myself more detailed instructions, but we'd discovered that three basic ideas was the absolute limit of what I could manage to keep in my head in a dream. Pouring all my will into those thoughts, I repeated them over and over, until the words appeared on the paper. I let the note go, watching it float away. Relief washed over me. There was nothing more to think about, and I could let myself slip into unconsciousness now. I started counting backwards. *Ten, nine, eight...* With every number I seemed to grow heavier, sinking downwards into the dark. *Four, three, two, one* – and I was asleep.

I was sailing in a boat across the ocean, enjoying the feeling of the wind on my face and the sight of the albatrosses swooping through the air. Suddenly, a small, brown-skinned girl appeared in front of me. Her big eyes shone out from beneath her tangled dark curls, and I could see every tiny detail of her face – the long eyelashes, slightly crooked eyebrows and a scar on her cheek from where she'd fallen down the front steps when she was two. She was the most beautiful thing I had ever seen, and it broke my heart. Because this was Cassie, and Cassie was dead. *I'm dreaming. None of this is real.* The second I realized that, Cassie vanished. A piece of paper materialized in her place, and I glared at it, hating the lifeless thing for not being my sister. Then I grabbed the note, reading what was written there, and knew what I had to do.

The boat and the water and the birds winked out. In their place, buildings sprang up everywhere, one after the other, until I was surrounded by hundreds of menacing structures that stared down with blank window eyes and howled at me out of long door mouths. I started to search, ignoring the eerie wailing of the doors as I tried to find my friends who were trapped somewhere in this horrible place. *There they are!* Leaping forwards, I threw my arms around the enormous black crow and the furry brown kitten, hugging them against me. *They're OK. We're all right.*

Only we weren't, not really. The three of us were in terrible danger, and we had to run. But we needed to be careful, because the buildings were watching. They thought they saw everything, but they didn't know how special we were, and if they found out, they'd swallow us whole.

I tried to make a protective bubble around us, a magic bubble that would turn whatever was inside it invisible. But I couldn't get it to form. I concentrated harder, fighting to rise above my fear. *This is MY dream, and I can do ANYTHING I want!* With terrifying slowness, the bubble shimmered into existence. The crow and the kitten and I floated within it, bobbing in our perfect sphere. From the outside, we were now a passing gleam in the night, a faint glistening in the air. I looked up at the buildings that could no longer see me, grinning my defiance. Then I bent my knees, and jumped.

The bubble moved with me, bouncing off the ground and soaring into the sky. From up here, I could see a wide white pathway snaking among the buildings and winding into the distance. *That will lead us home!* Our bubble started to fall back to the earth, and I leaned forwards, aiming it for the path. We rebounded off the surface, rising up into the night, and I laughed in delight as we left the buildings behind. On and on we went, each bounce taking us further away from danger, until I was dizzy with exhilaration and power. I was a saviour, a victor, a hero, and nothing and no one could stop me.

Then the crow attacked.

She raked her claws across my neck, sending me stumbling sideways and breaking my concentration. The bubble was on the descent, and it wobbled in the air and sank to the ground, rolling back and forth along the path as I struggled with the crow. *Has she gone crazy?* I tried to fend her off without hurting her, but she came at me again and again, screeching and pecking and flapping, until finally, I grabbed hold of one of her wings. The crow swept the other one around, slamming it against my face – and everything changed.

There was no bubble, no flying, no magic. Instead, I stood on the ground, gazing into the wide eyes of a pale-skinned girl, and holding her right arm in my left hand. She had the other arm raised as if she was going to strike me, and from the way my cheek was stinging, it felt like she already had. I let her go, backing away and looking around in confusion. I could see a child standing some distance away, but no crow and no kitten. *Where am I? Where are my friends?* Comprehension crashed over my bewildered mind, and I staggered, resting my hands on my legs. Ember ran over, pulling my hair back from my face in case I threw up, which I sometimes did after I'd Walked. "It's OK, Ash. You're OK."

I coughed and hacked as I tried to get control of my heaving stomach and shaking body. I wanted to collapse in a heap, but I felt I'd shatter into pieces if I did, as if being on my feet was all that was holding me together. So I kept breathing, slowly and evenly, staring down at the earth. *No, not the earth – a road.* We weren't even in the Firstwood. "Where?" I managed to ask.

"I think we're close to Cambergull."

"Not far enough!"

"Don't be silly, Ash. We didn't need to get all the way home, just out of the city and away from any search for Pepper."

"Sorry. So sorry..." Tears dripped down my chin. I'd had one thing to do, and I felt horribly guilty that I hadn't been able to do it. I sobbed harder, overcome by my failure and ineptitude.

"What you're feeling," Ember said calmly, "is a reaction to the Sleepwalking. You know that. And you probably wouldn't be in such a state afterwards if you'd use a different symbol to tell yourself you're dreaming."

"My only chance ... to see her. Can't remember ... all the details of her face that way ... when I'm awake."

She sighed. "Oh, Ash."

I don't know how long I stayed like that, hunched over and crying and shaking. Eventually, though, I began to feel better, enough for my battered brain to realize why Ember had started a fight with me. "I wouldn't wake up, Em?"

"No, and you were starting to tremble and weren't breathing properly. I knew you were exhausted."

"You were right." Sleepwalking burned through my energy, and once it was all gone, I woke up, no matter where I was. Which could be fatal. Like, for instance, if I was bouncing around in a giant invisible bubble... I shuddered at the horrifying image of Ember, Pepper and me falling from the sky to slam into the ground. Ember had tried various mixes of what she called smelling salts, but while they brought me out of normal sleep, nothing could rouse me from Sleepwalking. That was why I never deliberately used my ability without Ember, who knew how to tell if I was reaching my limits, and could try to keep me in a safe place long enough for my exhaustion to kick in and snap me out of it.

My stomach had stopped roiling, and I straightened up. We were on the highway that linked the Gull City towns together. To the right of the road were the tracks for the Rail, but beyond that, and on the other side too, were forests. There were no mighty tuarts in these woods, but it was still comforting to see trees looming over me in the moonlight. "We better get moving."

"We could wait longer."

"No. Let's go. I can walk." Just not very fast, or very well. But after an effort like this, my ability wasn't going to work for a few weeks, and we had to get to the safety of the Firstwood as soon as we could. I searched for Pepper, and spied her small form waiting at the edge of the tree line. *I've probably scared the kid off me for ever.* Dragging myself towards her, I said in the friendliest, most reassuring voice I could muster, "Hey, Pepper. Are you OK?"

For an awful moment she was silent. Then she bounced on her feet, and exclaimed excitedly, "We flew! We actually flew! That was the most awesomest thing to ever happen to me ever. Can we do it again? *Please.*"

I gaped at her. Pepper moved closer, putting her hand in mine. "I'm sorry I wasn't nicer to you before, Ashala. I was just scared about running away and everything." She sounded remorseful, like she was the saddest, sorriest little girl in the world. I would've believed she was, too, if I hadn't heard that exact tone so many times before from Jaz. She looked up at me, tears sparkling on her lashes. "You're not mad, are you?"

Behind me, Ember muffled a giggle. I ignored her. "No, Pepper, I'm not mad."

"Can we go flying again sometime?"

"Of course!"

She flung her arms around my waist, and I hugged her right back. There was a warm, contented feeling around my heart, and it wasn't one bit diminished by the fact that I knew I was being shamelessly manipulated. Staring into Pepper's upturned face,

I smiled ruefully. "You're a *lot* like your brother, Pepper."

Jaz's sister grinned a wide, familiar grin. "I know!"

THE SECRETS

CONNOR

FOUR MONTHS AGO

I should never have hit him with the stick.

What I *should* have done was follow him and find out what an enforcer was doing in the forest. But it had been such a shock! There I'd been, gathering wood for the fire, and suddenly there was this enforcer, and all I could think was that he might have been the one who killed the rabbit Jaz ate. The next thing I knew, the piece of firewood I had in my hand was connecting with the back of his head, and the enforcer went down. Which was right about when my brain started working again, and began informing me of all the potential consequences of assaulting someone from the government. Visions of troops of enforcers descending on the Firstwood had danced through my mind, and for a few panicky seconds I'd stood there over his body, thinking, *What have I done?* Then a worse possibility had occurred to me: *Have I killed him?* I hadn't, though. Just knocked him out, which was bad enough. So I'd dragged him into the bushes and run for Ember. I needed her to help me decide what to do.

And the first thing she'd said was, "You shouldn't have hit him with a stick."

Since I *had* hit him, though, Ember thought we might as well find out what he was doing here. So the two of us had carried him through the Firstwood, with me taking his arms, and Ember his legs, and Ember's crows flying ahead to warn us if someone was coming. I didn't want the rest of the Tribe involved in this; it was bad enough that we were. We'd gone to the "secure" side of the cave system, the part that was infested with Georgie's little friends. No one ever came here without Georgie's permission. They knew that they'd get bitten if they did, and that meant being temporarily paralysed or permanently dead, depending on the size of the spider.

I looked out over the trees without really seeing them. I was in one of the high caverns that opened on to the forest, and ordinarily I loved the view. Today, it made me feel sick to think how I might have put it all in danger – the tuarts, the saurs, the Tribe, everything – by giving the government a reason to attack us. *I wish Georgie would hurry up!* I'd left Ember with the still-unconscious enforcer because Georgie had said she needed to show me something important, except then she'd had to go make sure the spiders understood not to bite the prisoner. Finally, I heard footsteps, and Georgie came hurrying in. "He's waking up, Ash. But you have to come with me before you speak to him."

She grabbed hold of my arm, pulling me through a few of the smaller caves and stopping in front of one of her "maps" of the future. It was made up of all the usual ingredients – vine, string, scraps of clothing, seeds and rocks, the odd button or piece of glass that caught the light. All of it was tied together in a complex set of connections that stretched out across most of the cave wall. It meant nothing to me, but I knew every part of that web represented possibilities to Georgie. She reached out, pulling forwards one of the objects tied into it.

I peered at the tiny, carved wooden figure. "Is that a bird?"

"No," she answered. "It's an *angel*."

"OK..."

"He looks like one."

"Who? The enforcer?" I examined the map more closely. The winged figure was all over it – the same carving, tied in again and again. "This is a shape you're seeing in more than one future? That means it's significant, right?"

"Yes, and the shape of the angel – it's the shape of a friend."

"He can't *possibly* be a friend! Unless ... maybe the angel isn't him?"

Georgie just looked at me, and I sighed. "Yeah, OK, I've never seen a real-life person with a face like that either. Are you sure about the friend thing?"

She shrugged. "It's what I see. Except I don't know what I don't see."

Which meant, in all the futures she'd glimpsed, the

angel was a friend. But she didn't know if there were a whole lot of other futures she *hadn't* seen, where the angel was an enemy. Georgie added, sounding frustrated, "And I don't see lots, Ash. Because this map is about the detention centre, and I'm pretty sure rhondarite is messing it up." She pointed at big, blank areas of the web where there were only a few strands of vine and string. "You see, the futures of that place are basically the futures of everyone in it, and a lot of those people will be wearing rhondarite collars, which blocks my ability. So there're these massive gaps..."

"Yeah, I get it." I stared glumly at the angel figure. "I'm not sure I know what to do about this. I'll keep it in mind when I talk to him, though."

"I think," she told me, "that you have to trust your heart, Ash."

"That's not very—" I broke off, leaping backwards as I spotted something grey and furry coming over the top of her shoulder. "You've got one on you!"

She picked up the spider, putting it on the wall. "It's one of the small ones, Ash." Which was to say, it was the size of a fist instead of a dinner plate. I deliberately didn't watch where it went as it scurried away. I knew there'd be heaps of spiders crawling on the ceiling, but as long as I didn't look up, I could pretend they weren't there. "They know not to fall on me, don't they? Or jump? Or come anywhere near me?"

"They're not that interested in you."

Yeah, she always said that. I could feel them all watching me out of their miniature spider eyes, and I knew that they knew I didn't like them. I hunched my shoulders defensively as I headed back to Ember and the enforcer, making my way through the labyrinthine passages until I saw a dim glow in the distance. Even when fully charged, solar lamps weren't super bright, but the ones we had were more than enough to light the cavern where we were holding our prisoner.

Ember was cross-legged on the floor, facing the enforcer, who was sitting with his wrists and ankles bound and his back to the wall. His appearance had been startling enough in the daylight when his eyes were closed. But in the soft lamplight, with his pale skin almost glowing and his eyes shining a bright, impossible blue, I had to try *very* hard not to stare.

Then he smiled, and I gave up trying.

"Ashala Wolf. I am Justin Connor."

I shoved my hands into my pockets, doing my

absolute best to glare at that extraordinary face as he continued, "I'm afraid I must tell you that someone in the Tribe is betraying you."

Ember choked, and I snapped, "They are *not*."

"The government knows about your Pact with the saurs."

My gaze flew to Ember's. She'd always thought there might be more to the rabbit killing than the random stupidity of a few enforcers, and it seemed like she'd been right.

"If what you're saying is true, then who is the traitor?" Ember demanded.

"I don't know yet."

She snorted. "Convenient."

He ignored her, addressing me instead. "I swear to you, I am not your enemy. I am an Illegal too."

"You're an *enforcer*!"

His lips curved into another of those heart-stopping smiles. "Yes, I know."

Ember stood up. "If you're an Illegal, prove it. What's your ability?"

"I can fly." And with that, he rose above the ground – not far, but enough for us to see that he was hovering above the floor. Then he sank back down again, breathing heavily. "Of course," he said, "it's easier to do when my head isn't hurting so much. Do I have you to thank for that, Ashala?"

I didn't answer, feeling so stunned by the revelations of the last few minutes that I was struggling to form thoughts, let alone words.

Ember wasn't as overcome as I was. "So you have an ability. That proves you're an Illegal, but it doesn't prove you're not working for the government. You could be their spy."

He sighed. "You must have seen my tattoo when you tied my wrists. Do you think they'd allow an Illegal to wander free with a Citizenship mark? I am proof that the government is lying when they say no Illegal ever passes a Citizenship test. Also, why would I warn you that you have a traitor among you?"

I lifted my chin. "Maybe we don't. Maybe you're trying to win our trust by deceiving us."

"Is that what you really believe, or is that what you want to believe?"

I wanted to shout, *Yes, it's what I believe!* Only I wasn't sure. Ember wasn't either, I could tell by the way she'd lapsed into thoughtful silence. He glanced from one of us to the other, and added, "I am willing to do whatever it takes to prove myself. I'll undergo any test you like."

Ember smiled, and it wasn't a very nice smile. "You might be sorry you said that." She turned to me. "Let's talk."

We walked out of the cave, standing where we could still see our prisoner, and huddled together for a hushed conversation.

"What do you think, Ash?"

"I don't know! Georgie believes he's a friend. She's *seen* an angel in one of her futures."

"A *what*?"

"You know, like the statues in Gull City."

"Oh. Yes, I see the resemblance."

"She saw betrayal a few months ago too," I admitted.

"You never told me that!"

"I thought... I'm sorry, Em, but I thought it was you, with Jaz."

She looked crushed, and I said quickly, "I'm so sorry, I shouldn't have assumed."

"No, it's all right. Look, I can test this guy. Read his memories."

"Then he'll understand what you're capable of!"

"I could always alter his memories afterwards,

259

take away the ones of what happened here."

"Didn't you once tell me that taking memories when people don't want to give them up can break their minds?" She was so obviously astonished, it was almost comical. "Sometimes I *do* pay attention, Em."

"We have to know why he's here!"

"And if he's not a friend? What then?"

She went quiet, then said, "We could ... dispose of him."

"You mean *kill* him?"

"It wouldn't take much. Just a bite from one of the big spiders—"

"Em! How can you even suggest that? What happened to changing the world without violence?"

"I never meant we shouldn't strike back when we're under attack, and we are! Either from him, or from a traitor. We've *got* to defend ourselves, or the whole Tribe could be lost."

I looked away. The mere idea of having to kill anyone made me feel like throwing up. *If he's a spy and we let him go...* Ember wasn't wrong about the Tribe being in danger. All the lives I was responsible for – not only the Tribe, but the tuarts and even the saurs – seemed to weigh down on me. It was as if I could feel the massive bulk of them all, pressing upon my inadequate shoulders. "We do have to find out if he's telling the truth," I acknowledged. "But we decide *together* what happens after that. Don't go and hide things from me, like with Jaz. OK?"

"I won't, Ash."

We stepped back into the cave. Ember strode over to the enforcer, and announced, "I have an ability that allows me to read other people's memories. Are you still sure you want to be tested?"

He raised an eyebrow. "An impressive power. Yes, I'm sure. Is it possible for you to show my memories to Ashala?"

"To me? Why?"

"Because," he replied, staring right at me, "you are the reason I came here, Ashala Wolf."

I had no idea what to make of *that* statement, and I waited for Ember to tell him she couldn't do it. She didn't, and after a minute, I asked, "Em?"

"It is possible," she admitted. She moved closer to me, saying softly, "In fact, it would make it easier if he wants you to have his memories, since his mind will give them up more easily. But when you experience someone else's memories, Ash, you let things into your head that you can never get out again, maybe awful things. It could make a kind of ... link ... between you and him."

That didn't sound good, and the truth was, I didn't want to know any more about someone we might have to kill. Except it wasn't fair to ask Ember to do things that I wouldn't, especially not when I knew she'd do almost anything to protect me.

I nodded at our prisoner. "All right, Justin Connor. I get your memories."

His eyes lit up, blazing with – triumph? Happiness?

Ember hissed in my ear, "Ash! Are you sure?"

"I'm sure."

She took a step back, studying my face. Whatever she saw there must have convinced her that I wasn't going to change my mind, because she said, "Sit down then, because this is going to take a while, and *don't* interrupt."

I positioned myself on the floor, and she moved to the far corner of the cave, grabbing a flask of water from the pile of basic supplies we'd assembled. I watched as she filled a cup and picked up a stone from the floor, dropping it into the water. Then she came over to kneel beside the enforcer, pressing the cup into his hands before clasping her own hands over his. When she spoke, her voice had a soothing, steady rhythm to it that made me feel like falling asleep. "I need you to concentrate, Justin Connor. Look at the water in the cup. See the surface, how it reflects? Focus on what you want to show Ashala, the memories that demonstrate who you are. Imagine them reflected in the water."

The enforcer hunched over the cup, and the water began to move, sloshing against the sides. Then I realized it wasn't the water; it was him, shaking. His skin grew paler, and his shivering more intense, until I could hear his teeth rattling together. Ember didn't seem worried. She kept talking, repeating the same phrases, while the enforcer looked worse and worse. I started to get scared that something had gone wrong, and was about to defy Ember and interrupt, when he sagged against the wall. It seemed like he wouldn't have been able to endure another second and, despite everything, I was glad it was over. But when Ember spoke again, I realized she wasn't finished yet. "Good. Now I need you to imagine the memories flowing out of the water and into the stone."

I thought he wouldn't – or couldn't – do as she said.

Eventually, though, he leaned forwards. He didn't shake so much this time, but he kept sliding sideways and then jolting back upright, as if he was keeping himself conscious by sheer force of will. All the while, Ember kept talking. "Every one of those memories are passing into the little stone, flowing in one by one until they're all held safely inside the pebble, locked away. No one can reach them now unless they speak a special word that will let the memories out. Imagine the word that unlocks the stone."

On it went, Ember speaking and the enforcer staring at the water, until finally he slumped, gasping, "Done."

Ember took the cup from him and came over, holding it out to me. "You need to take out the stone."

I hesitated, glancing over at the enforcer. *Is he even conscious?*

"Don't worry, he'll recover. The stone, Ash."

I fished out the pebble, feeling awed at what Ember had done. "You can put memories into water and stones?"

"Sort of. My ability works on the mind. The water and the stones aren't that important. They're just devices, things for the mind to focus on."

"Oh. Um, what do I do now?"

Ember put the cup on the floor and sat down beside me. "Hold the pebble, say the keyword – which you'll need to ask him for – and you'll have the memories."

I clasped my hand around the stone and turned my attention back to the enforcer, only to find he was already watching the two of us. He seemed better, or at least, not about to collapse.

"So, enforcer, what do I say?"

"The word you want is 'Ashala'."

"Very funny."

"What makes you think I meant it as a joke?" And, astonishingly, he winked at me.

Is he flirting with me? Uncomfortably aware that I was almost blushing, I focused on the stone, closed my eyes and said, "Ashala." I felt an odd buzzing sensation, one that seemed to travel from the stone all the way up my arm and into my head. Images started to form in my mind, and it was strange. Very strange.

From somewhere, Ember's voice said, "Don't fight it, Ash." So I tried to stop thinking, and gave myself up to Justin Connor's memories...

✦✦✦

When I was seven, I knew my father didn't love me.

But I didn't mind. There was simply no room in his heart for anyone but my mother. Besides, Mum told me often that she loved me, her little Connor, more than anyone. It was our secret, although I thought sometimes, from the way Dad watched me, that he knew it too.

It was Mum who insisted he take me away on the day the assessors came to Eldergull. "Go out with him on the boat," she said. "I'll have no son of mine near an assessor." And because he could never refuse her anything, we had gone. We'd made a good catch, and he was happy. Until we spotted the smoke billowing into the sky.

The quake had been sudden and terrible, leaving almost the entire town in ruins. Dad feared, at first, that Mum was trapped in the rubble like so many others. But when we reached the place where our house had been, we found that she was not. She lay in the street, out in the open air, with the sun on her face. She looked almost peaceful.

Only she was quite dead.

266

❖❖

When I was ten, I was in danger of dying myself.

Dad didn't fish any more. He drank instead. I'd learned to watch his moods, so that I could recognize when I was in danger. On this night, though, I'd been reading a book, and become so lost in the words that I'd failed to notice his steady decline. Until the book was torn from my hands, and he loomed over me with his fist in the air. His face was more twisted with rage than I'd ever seen it, and I thought, This time, he really will kill me.

I had seconds to act, and I did, saying quickly, "Don't you want to get whoever killed Mum?"

He roared, "You did, boy. If it wasn't for you, I would've been there. I would have saved her."

It was a familiar accusation, and I knew better than to respond to it. Instead, I said, "But it wasn't a natural quake."

Dad swayed from side to side. "What do you mean, it wasn't a natural quake?"

It didn't surprise me that he didn't understand what I meant. It always seemed to take other people so much longer to comprehend the simplest things. I sometimes felt like the rest of the world must be moving through water to arrive so painfully slowly at obvious conclusions. Besides, I'd been putting together the pieces of this particular puzzle for a while now, and even I still didn't have the whole of it.

"There's never been a quake like that in Eldergull," I explained, "not before and not since. And Cary's sister, Beth, was a Rumbler. She was being assessed that day."

My father lowered his fist, and I pressed my advantage. "Beth died in the quake, but there were no assessors killed. So whoever made her lose control is still out there somewhere."

Dad stared at me as if he'd never seen me before. Then he staggered to the table, picked up the bottle that was sitting on it and stumbled outside. I listened, with dawning hope, to the sound of alcohol being poured onto the ground. He lurched back in, steadying himself against the door frame, and said, "Son, we have work to do."

When I was twelve, we finally discovered the name of Beth's assessor.

Dad sank into a chair, his thick arms thudding onto the small table where we ate our meals. "Talbot. Prime Talbot. No wonder it was so difficult to find him. That bastard's come a long way in five years." He eyed me speculatively, and said, "There's nothing else for it. You'll have to become an enforcer."

I swallowed. "An enforcer?"

"Talbot's terrified of being assassinated by Illegals. They say he has three body doubles, and the only ones who get close to him are his enforcer guards. And to get into the Prime's guards you have to be the best and brightest. So that's what you'll be. My son, the greatest enforcer that ever was."

I looked at my father. He didn't drink any more. He didn't eat much either, or do anything, except plot revenge. But it was a big improvement on how he'd been, and I hadn't yet given up on the dream of having a proper father someday. So I said, "Yes, Dad."

"Thing is," my father rumbled, "you'll have to learn to control that air-shifting ability of yours. There'll be no room for mistakes, if you're to pass for a Citizen." He rose out of his chair, and barked, "Stand up, boy! Make this table and these chairs float for me."

I jumped to my feet, and summoned my ability.

269

It always amazed me when people talked of air as being still. Couldn't they feel the way it was constantly moving, how it ebbed and flowed in currents, reacting to the movements of everything in it? I called to the air, speaking to it in my mind, letting it know what I needed done. The air answered, rushing up under the furniture until everything rose towards the ceiling.

Dad strolled across to stand by my side. I thought he might lay an approving hand on my shoulder. Instead, he drew back his fist, and struck.

I stumbled, losing my connection with the air. The table and chairs came crashing down. "No, no, no!" my father roared. "You'll have to do better than that. Lift them up again."

I straightened with difficulty. Dad circled around me as the furniture drifted steadily upwards. Then he hit me again.

I was a quick learner. The table and chairs did not fall.

❖

When I was fourteen, I passed my assessment and received a Citizenship tattoo. And I began to split in two.

270

Connor the Illegal, Connor my mother's son, started to recede from the surface of my consciousness, becoming safely cocooned within Justin the Citizen, Justin the enforcer-to-be. My Justin self was a mirror, a perfect reflection of the expectations of others. The Justin me made jokes about Illegals with my enforcer classmates; won a prize for an essay about the imminent threat that abilities posed to the Balance; and passed my father's increasingly extreme tests of control. My peers were satisfied, my instructors were satisfied, my father was satisfied.

Deep inside I occasionally screamed. But that was all right, because nobody ever heard.

❖❖❖

When I was sixteen, I became the youngest Citizen to ever receive an enforcer uniform, and submitted my application to become a bodyguard to the Gull City Prime. I was almost through the lengthy approval process when Prime Talbot had a stroke, and died.

I said to my father, "At least he's dead." But Dad didn't answer.

For the next two weeks, Dad rose from his bed, sat

at the table and didn't move again until the evening, when he went back to bed to sleep. He seemed to grow smaller every day, shrinking further and further into himself. Until, one day, he didn't get up at all.

The doctor said that a blood vessel had burst in his brain. One of those awful, unexpected things that are impossible to predict. There was nothing that could have been done. And Justin-the-enforcer agreed that it was a terrible, unforeseeable tragedy.

But I knew that I had failed my father for the last time.

I celebrated my seventeenth birthday alone, and adrift. My entire life had been defined by one consuming purpose, and without it I was lost. I knew I should find another path, but it just seemed like too big an effort to do anything except continue to exist in the life I'd made. So that was what I did, until the day that Chief Administrator Neville Rose came to see me.

The grey-haired man offered his sympathies on my father's death, and spoke of how proud Dad must have been of such an exemplary son. I endured it in silence. Finally, he said, "I must tell you something. This is very difficult, but I think it's important for you to know. Justin, your mother was killed by an Illegal."

For a mad moment, I almost shouted out that I was an Illegal. But the habit of caution was too deeply ingrained, and my defence system snapped back into place. Connor sank into the shadows, while Justin sat up, white-faced and staring, as Neville explained how a Rumbler had caused the Eldergull quake. Nothing about the assessor. Justin-the-enforcer was appropriately horrified, outraged, thirsty for revenge. But Connor-the-Illegal was curious. Neville Rose was going to a great deal of trouble to obtain the loyalty of someone he believed was a perfect enforcer, and I wanted to know why.

There were more meetings, in which Neville spoke of how he feared the government would lose its way after the death of the great Prime Talbot, especially with the reform movement gaining increasing support. He told me about his own political ambitions, and how he wanted to carry on Talbot's vision for the future. Eventually, he explained that in his new role as the head of Detention Centre 3, he needed enforcers who were willing to bend the rules in the interests of countering the threat from Illegals. What was more, he wanted my help with a special project, something to do with the runaways living in the Firstwood.

I was given a file about the leader of the runaways, and told to study the contents. I did, and my Justin self displayed only those emotions that Neville expected to see – outrage and disgust that anyone would so blatantly defy the Citizenship Accords. Deep inside, though, I reacted differently. I read that file over and over, until I knew by heart the story of a girl who, like me, had lost someone to the government. It seemed almost as if her voice was speaking to me from the crisp white pages. I told myself that it was absurd to think that, and yet I could not escape the growing conviction that she was someone who I had always been destined to know, or even that I somehow knew her already. That was absurd too. But I began to miss her, just the same.

Then it occurred to me that there was more information in the file than there should have been. How could they have such a detailed description of someone who had run away from the city four years before? How could they know how many people were *in the Tribe, or about the Pact with the saurs?*

I thought, She is being betrayed.

The sense of aimlessness that had plagued me since my father's death vanished, burned away by the fire of a new purpose, a single, simple mission.

Save Ashala Wolf.

The memories evaporated, leaving me blinking and disorientated in the dim light of the cave.

Ember was sitting right in front of me. "Ash? Are you OK?"

"I'm fine."

"You're crying."

I lifted my hand to my cheek, surprised and yet not surprised to find it wet with tears. "I'm OK. Promise." Grabbing hold of Ember's arm, I asked, "Can you do that in reverse? Give one of my memories to him?"

"Yes. But, why?"

"Because I'm asking you to. Get the water and the stone and whatever else you need. Please."

"Ash—"

"Don't argue with me, Ember! I need you to do this."

She pressed her lips together, and stalked off to

the corner of the cave, leaving me looking right at Connor.

"I think," I said, "that you can untie yourself now."

Ember froze in amazement as the ropes around his wrists and ankles began to unwind, and I asked, "Have you got that water yet, Em?"

She came over to me and picked up the cup that she'd left on the floor, tipping out the old water before filling it again and dropping in a new stone. "Are you sure about this?"

"Yep." I smiled at her. "This is important. And thank you."

She sniffed, looking mollified, and handed me the cup. We went through the whole thing, like she had with Connor and – wow, it *hurt*! It felt like I was literally shaking apart. When we were done, I slumped forwards, gazing at Connor with new respect. I'd put *one* memory into the stone, and my head was pounding fiercely. How much worse must he have felt when he'd already been hit with a very large piece of firewood? *Swung with a lot of force, too.* At this point, I was starting to feel quite bad about that.

I dragged myself over to him. I couldn't have stood

up if my life depended on it, so I half-crawled across the floor with the cup in my hand, and held it out, watching as he took the stone. Then I tossed the cup away, careless of the water running onto the floor, and pressed his hands closed around the pebble.

"The word you want," I told him, "is 'Connor'."

He laughed, an unexpectedly joyful sound that echoed around the cavern, and said, "Connor."

His face went blank, staring at something I couldn't see, although I knew what it was. He was experiencing the moment when I'd come to the Firstwood, and the things I'd felt when I'd touched the tuart. I started talking – even though I knew he probably couldn't hear me – wanting to explain what it all meant. I liked to believe that I understood the Firstwood's message better, now that I'd had years to think about it. "People, animals, trees – everything grieves, and regrets, and mourns what's passed. Only nothing is ever truly gone for ever. This is the place where life began again, where *I* began again. Whatever we were before, whoever we were before – it doesn't matter. Because we're all made new here. We live. We survive. We belong."

He came back to himself slowly, his eyes focusing

on mine. He looked vulnerable. Wounded. Hopeful. And he whispered, "Ashala."

He didn't say anything more. But I knew what he was asking.

I shifted closer, brushing my lips against his cheek. "You're Tribe now, Connor. Welcome home."

THREE MONTHS AGO

I loved the forest at night. The way the grey tuarts went silver in moonlight, the curving shadows between the trees, and the changed sounds and movements of the Firstwood as the owls, treecats, bats and other night animals woke to hunt. That was why I was out, wandering beneath the stars and heading in no particular direction. Well, that, and because, once again, I couldn't sleep. It had been four weeks! Where *was* he?

Ember kept telling me, patiently and often, "He can take care of himself, Ash." And, when that failed to reassure me, "You know he won't come back until he finds out who the traitor is." She was right, but it didn't stop me worrying. It wasn't that I didn't think he could protect himself. I knew that he could.

But I also knew how much that self-preservation cost him.

There was a noise somewhere behind me, and I turned to see Ember stepping out from the trees. "Honestly, Ash, you *would* be wandering around out here when I need to find you. He's back."

I bounded forwards. "Is he all right?"

"Of course he's all right. He's waiting in the caves."

She started walking, and I followed behind her. Except she was moving too slow, *much* too slow! Hopping from one foot to the other, I asked, "Exactly where is he waiting?"

"In the largest of the caverns that opens onto the woods."

I took off, tearing through the undergrowth until I was pounding through the narrow entrance to Georgie's side of the caves, and down the tunnels to the big cavern. Connor was standing in the opening with his back to the forest, feet resting on the edge of the drop as if he'd floated down from the sky. Which I guessed was exactly what he'd done.

Stumbling to a breathless halt, I grinned idiotically. "Connor."

He smiled back, teeth gleaming in the moonlight. "Ashala Wolf."

"Are you ... um, is everything OK?"

"I know who the traitor is."

Oh. There'd been a small, unrealistic part of me that had been hoping it would somehow turn out to be a horrible mistake, and I suddenly didn't want to hear the name, didn't want it to be made irrevocably real. "Don't tell me yet! I mean, Ember should be here soon. She's behind me somewhere."

"Then I suppose we had better wait to talk until she catches up with you."

"Yeah." I stared down at the ground, feeling awkward and uncomfortable. There had been no need for me to come running up here like a lunatic. He was fine.

"Ashala?" His voice had changed. Not so smooth, or so cold.

"Yes?" I asked hopefully.

"I ... I think of you. And the Firstwood. When things are bad."

My throat closed over, and I answered, "I know." And I did. That was *why* I'd been so worried these past weeks. Without even being conscious of it, I'd picked up on his loneliness, his extreme isolation, grown so much more acute now that I'd shown him what it was like to belong. The memory sharing had created a link between us, just as Ember had said it would. Taking a hesitant step closer, I said, "I can hear you, Connor. Even when you're not here. Even when you don't speak."

For a second, he was still. Then he moved towards me, or maybe we moved towards each other. I flung my arms around his neck, and he hugged me back, the two of us clinging together as if we could make everything else disappear if we held on tight enough. Resting my cheek against this shoulder, I whispered, "You're not alone."

He sighed raggedly, and pressed a kiss to the top of my head. Then he pushed me gently away. I clenched my hands into fists to stop myself from hanging on to him, watching as he took a step back, and another, and another, until he'd nearly run out of the cave.

"Ashala... I have ... there are things I have to tell you. There are some difficult decisions to be made. I still need... I cannot let go..."

He stopped, shaking his head in frustration at

not being able to get the words out. But I could fill in the blanks – *I still need Justin. I cannot let go of him yet.* He had to maintain the defence system that allowed him to survive in a Citizen's world, and he was worried that if he allowed himself to be completely Connor, the mask of Justin-the-enforcer would disappear for ever.

"It's all right. I get it."

He exhaled, and when he spoke again, I could hear the relief in his voice. "Yes. You would."

Ember arrived to find the two of us standing in total silence, a long way apart. She looked from him to me, and I could almost hear her mind ticking over.

But all she said was, "I've put a lamp in one of the smaller caves across the way. I didn't want to bring a light in here. I mean, I'm sure everyone's asleep..." Her voice trailed off, but she didn't need to say any more. We didn't want anyone looking up from the forest and spotting us, not when no one but Georgie knew about Connor.

I strode out jerkily, heading for the smaller cave and leaving Connor and Ember to follow. The three of us settled down in a loose circle on the floor, and Ember asked, "So, enforcer? Who's the traitor?"

He cast a concerned glance at me, and I knew that he'd realized I was dreading hearing a name. Bracing myself, I nodded at him, and he said, "Her name is Briony."

Bry? "It can't be!"

Ember sighed. "She was on the list, Ash."

Connor's brows drew together. "You made a list of the people who might betray you? Are there so many?"

"No," Em replied, "we made a list of anyone who could have left the forest to make contact with the government. Although Bry was a maybe, because she could only have done it if she's been lying about how strong her ability is."

Bewildered, I asked, *"Why* would she do this?"

"Because," Connor answered, "she wants an Exemption."

Ember shook her head in disbelief. "They'll never give an Exemption to a Runner!"

"No, they won't. But she doesn't know that. She's told them the names and abilities of everyone in the Tribe, and given them a description of each of you."

I gasped. "They know what we look like?"

"General descriptions aren't photos, Ash," Ember said soothingly. "It'd be hard for anyone to pick us out in a crowd without more than that."

"They could pick *you* out."

"Yes, but you know I can fix my eyes."

She could too. Ember had a special contact lens that her dad had given her, which made her blue eye as brown as the other one. But that didn't make me feel a whole lot better. "It's still bad, Em."

"Believe me, I know." Turning to Connor, she said, "Some of the Tribe are still in contact with their relatives. If the government starts investigating them—"

"They aren't, yet. Briony knows you by your forest names. Ashala Wolf, Ember Crow and so on. It'll take time to match first names and descriptions against all the records of runaways."

I drew my knees up to my chest. "Neville found *me* quick enough. He gave you my file."

Connor's eyes darkened. "You weren't hard to locate because Briony knew your sister had been killed in Gull City four years ago. Besides, he isn't even trying to track the rest of you down."

"Why not?"

His mouth twisted as if he'd tasted something bad. "I'm afraid the Chief Administrator has made the Tribe

284

his own personal project. He's hoarding information about you, keeping it away from the rest of the government."

There was a small silence as Ember and I absorbed the level of Neville's unwelcome interest in us. Then Connor said, "There's something I must know. Does Briony possess any information of importance, other than what she's already told them?"

I felt very grateful for Ember's circles of secrets. "No. She's passed on everything she knows. Why does that matter?"

"Because she's going to be told to introduce me to you. I think it would be best to let her continue betraying the Tribe long enough to do it."

"What?"

"Neville doesn't consider Briony to be very reliable," he explained, "so he wants someone he trusts to make contact. The idea is that I will pose as a clerk seeking help for an Illegal relative."

Ember looked thoughtful. "That could be useful. It would put you in a position to cast doubt on everything Bry has already told them."

"Connor, that's too big a risk for you!" I objected. "Besides, now that we know who the traitor is, you're coming to live with us."

But he shook his head. There was an odd expression on his face that I hadn't seen before, and couldn't place. *Is he ... afraid?* I felt cold all over, wondering what could possibly scare Connor.

"Ashala," he said, "Neville has promised Briony an Exemption if she delivers *you*. He is sending me to the Tribe to get to you. And the best way for me to protect you, is to be by his side."

Dismayed, I asked, "What does he want with me?"

"I believe he thinks capturing you will break the Tribe, and he *has* to break the Tribe. He can't risk having free Illegals so close to things he is trying to hide. Chief Administrator Neville Rose is a man with a lot of secrets."

"The rumours are true?" Ember demanded. "About Doctor Grey and her interrogation machine?"

"It's supposed to read memories. Not unlike your ability."

"Because," I said bleakly, "they probably experimented on someone like Ember to develop it."

"It's possible," he agreed. "And there's more. I've seen the machine, and it's a small electronic device, a box about so big." He measured a space in the air with his hands, and Ember let out a strangled sound.

"You're sure that's it?"

"Unfortunately, yes."

The size and shape of the machine clearly had some significance to the two of them that had escaped me. "I don't get it! What does it matter what it looks like?"

It was Ember who answered, sounding shaken. "Ash, do you remember me telling you about those little, powerful electronic boxes, the ones that are used to run stuff like the Rail system, and the recyclers, and the solar generators? Computers?"

"Yeah, but what does that have to ... hang on, you think the machine is a *computer*? It can't be!" Computers were advanced technology, and as every schoolkid knew, advanced tech was restricted to projects of public good, and then only if the Council of Primes determined the potential good to the Balance outweighed the harm. "You're telling me the Primes approved—"

Connor and Ember shook their heads. "We would have heard," Ember said, "if the Council had allowed a computer to be developed for something like this.

So if that machine is a computer, then Neville is breaking the Benign Technology Accords."

I tried to get my mind around this latest disturbing piece of information. It seemed impossible. I mean, *everyone* knew the dangers of advanced tech. It had isolated the people of the old world from nature, shielding them from the consequences of imbalance, and yet they'd believed, right up until the very end, that it would save them. But as Hoffman himself said, advances in technology could never compensate for failures in empathy. That was one of the reasons why we *had* Benign Technology Accords, to stop us from making the same mistakes.

"I'm afraid," Connor said, "that what Neville's doing doesn't end with the machine. He has something going on in the Steeps, too, only I don't know what yet. It seems to me that there is one sure way to deal with the threat he represents. I can kill him."

Ember straightened in sudden interest, but I snapped, "No!"

"There wouldn't be much danger of being caught. With my ability, it would be easy enough to make it seem like an accident—"

"Absolutely not, Connor!"

He seemed taken aback by my reaction. "Why not?"

I couldn't believe he was even asking why it would bother me to tell him to kill. "Because I am not your father."

He seemed surprised. "Ashala. It wouldn't be the same."

"It would feel the same. To me." *And to you, even if you don't know it.*

His brow creased, as if I'd presented his quick mind with a puzzle he couldn't solve, and I knew he still didn't understand. *Because you're not used to anybody caring, Connor. Caring if you succeed or fail, yes. But not caring about you.* I don't know what he read in my face, but his expression changed, growing softer. I longed to reach out to him, but I couldn't do that without breaching the boundaries he'd set between us, so I stared at him instead, willing him to feel what I was feeling. After a moment, his lips curved faintly into a smile, and I smiled back.

Ember cleared her throat. When Connor and I didn't react she did it again, a bit louder.

We both looked at her this time. "There's a better way to get to Neville than killing him," she told us. "We can *expose* him."

"For breaking the Tech Accords?" I asked.

"And whatever else he's up to in that place. I don't think we even want him dead, because he's not doing this alone. Grey might just carry on without him. If he was exposed, though..."

Connor seemed intrigued by the idea. "There'd be an inquiry for certain, and they might even shut down the centre temporarily. There's talk of an Inspectorate visit being scheduled soon after the centre opens. We might be able to use that."

Happy with any notion that didn't involve Connor assassinating somebody, I put in brightly, "I think this is a terrific idea. We'll just have to come up with a plan. One of your twisty plots, Em, to catch Neville out. Maybe rescue some detainees, too?"

She laughed. "I'm afraid it would have to be some amazing plan to do all that." Then her face grew serious. "Have you thought about how this ends, Ash? With Briony, I mean?"

I frowned, and she continued, "I take it we're agreed that it would be best to let her introduce Connor to us. And we couldn't expose her as a traitor immediately after that, either, because Neville would wonder if we suspected Connor too. There'll come a time, though, when we won't have to pretend any more, and I guess what I'm asking is, are you prepared to forgive her?"

Connor glared at Em. "You can't possibly think Ashala should forgive her."

"No," she replied tartly, "I don't. If it was up to me, Briony would be fed to the saurs. However, I am not the leader of the Tribe."

The two of them turned their attention to me. I didn't say anything, and Connor snapped, "She betrayed you! She put you in danger!"

"I *know* that. But she's still Tribe. So I need time to think, OK? Both of you, just give me time to think."

He and Ember exchanged glances, united in their common desire to have Briony consumed by giant lizards. I absently picked up some pebbles, and scattered them across the floor, trying to sort things out in my head. It wasn't like we could even do anything about Bry yet, but Ember was right – I had to consider how this ended. We might have to act fast, and it was my job to decide what happened when somebody broke an important rule. It was awful to sit in judgement on someone you loved, but on the other hand, I wouldn't have wanted anyone who didn't care for Briony to do it. At least I could try to understand.

I thought through all the things I valued about Bry. Her smile. The way she was always so bubbly and happy, and how intensely she believed in her dreams for the future. But she'd done something terrible to make those dreams come true. Knowing Bry, she'd thought it was a bit of a game when she started, but after what happened to Jaz, she must have realized how serious it was. Only she hadn't stopped, and she'd told the government everything she knew. She'd been prepared to put everyone at risk, and all to grasp at an illusion, a fantasy of family life that didn't exist outside her head. I loved her, and I always would. But I could never trust her again.

"Exile," I said heavily. "We exile her. Everyone gets told what she did, and she's never allowed to come back here." It was the worst fate I could imagine, and I felt close to tears at inflicting it on Briony, even after everything she'd done.

Ember beamed her approval. "It's the right decision, Ash."

Connor looked relieved, and a little confused. I knew he'd be trying to work out later why I was so upset over someone who'd betrayed me. I thought, feeling tired and sick, *It's simple, Connor. Family is family.*

After a moment's silence, he said reluctantly, "I'm afraid that I must get back."

I jumped. "So soon?"

"It's going to take me some time to return to the city, and none of us can afford for me to be missed."

Ember gave him a cheerful wave. "Bye, then, Connor."

He responded with such perfect courtesy, it was clearly meant to be sarcastic. "Goodbye, Ember."

Right, so these two aren't going to be best friends any time soon. I scrambled to my feet. "Come on, Connor. I'll, um, show you the way out."

He followed me into the gloom of the tunnel, and Ember called after us, "The Serpent, Ash!"

"OK, Em, I'll tell him." I said to Connor, "We kind of accidentally invented an Illegal, and we were wondering if you could help us make him more believable."

Sounding amused, he asked, "How do you 'accidentally' invent an Illegal?"

I explained, "Ember told this story to the Tribe one night, a really ancient story from the old world about a giant snake that created everything there is – all the plants and animals and people and so on.

Not all of the Tribe were there to hear it, so people must have told it to each other, and somehow it got garbled. The next thing we knew, there was this rumour going around the Tribe that there was some special Illegal with the power to make a new world."

"Named the Serpent?"

"Yep. Anyhow, this was months ago. But when you came and told us that someone was informing on the Tribe, Em revived the rumour because she thought it would be a good idea to give the government someone else to chase. And she added details, like the Serpent covers up his face so no one knows who he is, and that he won't work with the Tribe. We thought you could maybe spread a few rumours about him in the city."

"A good idea, although I won't need to begin any rumours. I'll simply report that I've *heard* some, which will have precisely the same effect. That, combined with the information Neville will get from Briony, might convince them there's something to the story. And if not..." He shrugged. "It was still worth a try."

"Ember thinks they'll be concerned, because a few years back there *was* someone trying to organize resistance to the government who always kept his face hidden. He wasn't actually an Illegal, but everyone thought he was."

"Someone Ember knew, I take it?"

"Um, yeah. He died." It was a part of Ember's father's story that she'd told us later, how her dad had insisted on exploring the tunnels, even though he'd known he was sick, and had died there. "It's complicated, but no one knows he's dead, so..."

Connor finished the thought: "The Serpent could still be him, or else a copycat. That will definitely give it more substance."

The two of us had reached the big cavern now, and were approaching the opening to the forest. My steps grew slower and slower as we neared it, until I stopped altogether in the middle of the cave. Connor stopped too, and shifted to face me.

"Connor..." I said huskily. "Don't lose yourself out there."

"Oh, Ashala." I could hear the smile in his voice. "You need not fear that. I am always here, now. With you. The girl who hears me, even when I do not speak."

I couldn't answer without crying, so I nodded instead. He turned, moving rapidly to the opening. When he reached it, he paused, balancing on the edge with his body outlined in moonlight, and glanced back over his shoulder.

"Ashala. Think of me."

Then he was gone, swooping over the treetops and melting into the night.

I walked until I was standing almost where he had stood, staring out over the silvery, shadowy forest.

And I thought of him.

FIVE DAYS AGO

I peered around at the stacks of containers. It was night outside, and *really* dark in here. The tiny portable solar lamp I was holding wasn't very strong, but it would have to be enough. We couldn't risk anyone seeing light through the windows, and wondering what people were doing in the warehouse. The last thing we needed was for things to go wrong now.

Over the past weeks, Connor had continued to pass on information about Neville, the Steeps and the workings of the centre. We'd introduced Connor to the Tribe as the administrator he was pretending to be, while Ember had worked on an increasingly complex plan to ensure Neville's downfall. Then, seven days ago, we'd begun to put our scheme into action. Daniel – who now knew everything – had pretended to spot Connor outside the centre in enforcer black. Naturally, Briony had been shocked to find the administrator she'd brought to me was no administrator at all. She'd said over and over how astonished she was, before reporting our "discovery" to Connor himself. In turn, Connor had asked Bry to let him know the instant I left the security of the grasslands. Which was exactly what she should be on her way to do now.

I could imagine how everything would have unfolded back in the Firstwood tonight, so much so that it was almost like I'd seen it for myself. The way Daniel would have loped into summer camp to lie about how he'd just met Ember, newly arrived back from the grasslands. He'd have told the Tribe that Em was furious because I'd taken off to Cambergull instead of helping her spy on the centre from afar. He might even have acted out her bad mood, and since he was an excellent mimic, everyone would've roared with laughter. Briony would have laughed too. And then, as soon as she could, she would have slipped away. *She'll be halfway to the centre by now.*

There was movement in the gloom behind me, and Ember spoke. "We should probably begin soon, Ash."

I held out my light, pacing through the darkness towards her. She'd laid out a collection of objects on top of one of the containers – a flask that contained the sleepy herb mix, an aromatic pouch tied to a piece of fishing line, and a river stone strung on to a cord.

"I wish you didn't have to be here, Em. If they search the town tomorrow..."

"They won't. They've no reason to. Bry thinks I'm still in the Firstwood and you're here alone." She sighed, and added, "Ash, are you *sure* about this? I mean, one hundred per cent sure? Do me a favour and think about it, OK?"

I put the lamp down on a container and shoved my hands in my pockets, knowing that I'd have to go all quiet and contemplative for a while to make her happy. And I did think about what was going to happen, although for me, the first part would be relatively easy. I would go to sleep, then wake not quite myself. Ember would be the one who had to mess with my memories, which would take a while. Then she would prop my unconscious body against one of the containers and hang the stone around my neck, before climbing up the stack above to conceal herself next to one of the windows. If she opened it a crack, she'd hear the vehicle motoring onto the nearby main street in the morning, especially since there was going to be a helpful breeze blowing the sound in this direction. Since all vehicles belonged to the government, and the only ones around here belonged to the centre, there was no chance of the approaching truck being anyone except Connor and the enforcers.

Once the truck stopped, Ember would dangle the salts under my nose. I'd wake up convinced that I had just been chatting to the Serpent, and head out of town. Which was when I'd run into Connor, waiting outside the Bureau of Citizenship office.

Everything that followed afterwards would be horrible. Painful. *Necessary.*

"I'm not stupid, Em. I know things could go wrong. But yes, I'm sure I have to do this. And, if I don't make it—"

She interrupted me, indignant and a little desperate. "You'll make it."

"*Listen* to me. If I don't, then you're in charge. I've told Daniel, Georgie and the saurs. I even told the Firstwood. You're the new leader of the Tribe."

She didn't answer, but I heard a distinct sobbing sound. *She's crying?* Ember never cried! "I won't let you down, Ash. You know I won't. Please come back."

"That's what I'm planning to do."

"At least," she sniffed, "Connor will be there to take care of you."

"I thought you didn't like him."

"He's dangerous." I opened my mouth to protest, and she shook her head at me. "Don't tell me he isn't, because he is. Only, after hearing the way he says your name, I've decided that he's not dangerous to *you*."

"How does he say my name?"

"Slowly!" She laughed at my puzzled expression. "Don't worry, you'll get it yourself eventually."

"So you're OK with Connor?"

"Yes, I suppose I am."

"Good." I knew it was silly to be so pleased to hear that. All things considered, I had much bigger problems than Connor and Ember not getting along. Still, it was reassuring to know those two would be all right. I wanted everything to be all right between the people I loved.

There was a sudden noise outside the warehouse

door. Ember jabbed at the button for the light, putting it out, and the two of us huddled down behind a container. We listened as someone came inside, shutting the door behind them.

"Ashala?"

I sagged in relief. It was Connor. *And my name just sounds like my name to me.* Em switched the light back on, and I made my way to where he was standing. "I thought you might be the government! What are you doing here?"

"I had to see you."

Ember arrived beside me, lamp in hand. "Has something gone wrong?"

Connor shook his head and looked at her pleadingly. He didn't say anything, but she seemed to understand what he was asking, because she put the lamp down on the nearest container and walked away, vanishing into the depths of the warehouse.

Feeling confused, I asked, "If nothing's wrong, then why did you have to see me?"

"Ashala, I..." He paused, took a breath and started again. "I have been asked to do difficult things before. Terrible things. You *know* that. But what you are asking of me, to stand by while you are at risk... I'm not sure I can do it."

He sounded strained, and I knew he must be almost at breaking point to come here. I searched around for the right words to say to him, the ones that would explain what he meant to me, and what I needed him to be.

"Georgie once told me," I said softly, "that in any given moment, there are thousands of futures. But I don't believe there is a single one in which we didn't find each other."

He smiled at that. "I don't believe there is either."

"I sometimes wonder if there was a future where my sister didn't die, and your mother didn't. So you and I, we just ran into each other someplace. I was walking on the beach, and you were fishing, or something."

"If my mother had not died, I probably would have been an artist. She was an artist. Perhaps I painted your picture."

I liked that idea. Only I couldn't let myself imagine it, not now. "Except, Connor, that's not the world we live in. In this world, Neville is coming for the Tribe."

He shifted, and I knew he didn't like the turn the conversation had taken, but I pressed on. "Do you remember when I showed you how I came to the Firstwood and touched the trees?"

"Of course I remember."

"I'd always heard about the Balance before that. But that was the first time I actually felt it. That was when I knew that there was something greater than all of us. Those trees, and the Tribe, and even the saurs – that's the heart of me. The essence of who I am. And Neville is trying to destroy it."

He ran a hand through his hair, saying nothing, but I could sense his distress. "So," I concluded, "I guess what I'm trying to tell you is that in that other future, the one where you were an artist, I would have trusted you with my life. But in *this* future – Connor, in this future, I'm trusting you with my soul."

There was a long silence. Finally, he said, "I understand." And I knew, from the desolation in his voice, that he'd heard the words I didn't speak. *I'm asking you to protect the part of me that continues for ever. Even if it costs me my life.*

He reached out, putting his hands on either side of my face and leaning down until his forehead touched mine.

"You will not know it," he said in a low, intense

tone, "but I will be with you, Ashala."

I didn't move, knowing that if I so much as leaned towards him, he'd never be able to let go of me, and I wasn't certain I'd be able to let go of him. For the space of three heartbeats, we stood together. Then he turned away, rushing past the containers and out of the warehouse. It wasn't until the door closed behind him that I let the tears slide down my cheeks.

I whispered, "Connor. In my heart, I will know."

DAY FOUR
THE FIRESTARTER

I gradually came back to myself. I was sitting, curled up against someone, my head resting against soft fabric through which I could hear a steady heartbeat. My entire body ached, and there were stabbing pains at so many different points on my skull that it felt like my brain had been taken apart and put back together again. *Which I guess it sort of has.* Everything still seemed to be shifting around in my mind, with everything I'd experienced at the centre and everything that had happened before I came here settling into its proper place. It wasn't just the four sets of "key events" memories either. There were a bunch of other, smaller moments that were integrating into my consciousness, a thousand tiny interactions with Jaz, the saurs, Daniel, Connor, Georgie and Ember. Now that I had all my hidden experiences back, I could see how my previous recollections of the recent past – especially the ones of Connor-the-traitor! – had been flimsy, lacking in colour and depth. Exactly as Ember had said, my mind had gathered up a bunch of fragmented experiences and pieces of knowledge, and arranged them into a pattern that made sense. Except that pattern had formed a flawed picture of reality, and I was incredibly glad that none of it had been quite true.

"Ashala? You need to wake up."

Connor. He pressed a flask to my lips, and I gulped at the syrupy liquid. Wentworth's magic concoction slid down my throat, radiating outwards, and I opened my eyes to bright daylight. Connor spoke again. "Are you … yourself?"

He sounded worried, and very serious. I couldn't be serious, not right now. Because I was happy. Gloriously, overwhelmingly happy. *Jaz is alive. Connor didn't betray me.* I could have shouted, or sung, or danced. What I actually did was tip my head back to gaze up at him and say, "I think everything went well, don't you?"

It was quite something to see the lightning flashing

306

across his face. "You almost died. Twice!"

"Yeah, but only *almost*."

He glared at me, and I grinned back at him. An answering smile began to tug at the corner of his lips, and I snuggled in close, thinking I'd be content to stay where I was for a while. "Ashala..." He sighed. "We need to move to the window to wait for Jaz. The detainees will be having their afternoon nap soon."

I pulled away a little. "Afternoon?" I'd lost a night and most of a day! "Don't we need to get to..." But then I took in my surroundings. We were sitting on a narrow bed. Opposite us was a set of drawers with a slim white case resting on top, and on the far wall there was a wide window with a long storage box beneath. The blind was closed, so I couldn't see out, but I knew where we had to be. "We're already inside the empty detainee house?"

He brushed a strand of hair back from my face, his fingers lingering against my skin. "Yes, and we have to go to the window so that Jaz can see you when he looks in. I doubt he'll come over, otherwise."

That got me moving. I shifted away, swinging my feet to the floor and perching on the edge of the bed. Connor stood beside me, putting an arm around my waist, and I leaned against him as we walked to the window. More heavily than I needed to, since Wentworth's medicine had once again done its job and I was feeling much better. Only I wasn't willing to give up being near to him yet. "How'd I even get here from the cell? What have you been doing, carrying me around the centre?"

"Yes."

"I hope no one saw you!"

"I'm *supposed* to shift you around to places where the Inspectorate won't stumble across you, and they've already been through the housing. But," he added, as he eased me onto the storage box, "I agree it would be better if no one was sure of where we are, so I made sure nobody saw us. It wasn't difficult. Without the enforcers, this place is almost deserted."

"The plan worked, then?"

"Oh yes. Neville spent the night moving every enforcer he could spare into the Steeps."

We exchanged glances of fierce satisfaction. Then he straightened, lifting the side of the blind. I leaned back to find myself looking out at another window in a house exactly like this one, across a thin strip of land. "Is that where they're keeping Jaz?"

Connor nodded. "Their blind is still up, which means

they haven't locked the detainees in their bedrooms for the afternoon nap. We'll have to wait a while longer."

He settled onto the opposite end of the box. I took the chance to examine him, noting the small signs of exhaustion – the faint carelessness of his movements, the grim set to his mouth and the way his skin was even paler than usual. He'd been pushed to the limits of his endurance and beyond, and I was guiltily aware that I was the one that had done the pushing. The last four days had to have been almost as terrible for him as they'd been for me, or maybe even worse. Because, surely, it *was* worse to watch something bad happening to someone you cared about, rather than to have it happen to you. Trying to see how it had been from his perspective, I replayed events in my head, thinking about the bad times, like when he'd first put me in the chair and I'd wanted to ask him to save me – no, I realized, in moments of extreme stress, I'd felt what he was feeling. He'd *wanted* me to ask him to save me. And in return, I hadn't been very nice.

"Connor? I'm sorry for all the horrible things I said to you. And for trying to punch you."

"I wish I could have let you. It would have made me feel better."

309

"To be *hit*?"

"I haven't liked myself very much recently."

"You were doing what I asked you to do."

He looked out the window again, and then back into the room, bowing his head. "I failed you, Ashala."

"You did not."

"I let you be injured, twice over—"

"I threw myself onto that sword the first time—"

"I should have considered the possibility that you might do something like that! I didn't react fast enough."

"Connor, you weren't responsible for me trying to kill myself. In fact..." I paused, remembering something. The too-quick way that enforcer had drawn her arm back, so the sword didn't bite as deep as I'd wanted it to. And how I'd felt something pressing on the wound, even as I was falling, long before anyone reached me. "You stopped the enforcer, didn't you? And put pressure on the wound with air. You're lucky you weren't caught!"

"*I* was in no danger. The others were all too concerned about what Neville would do to them if you died to notice anything wrong. Besides, even with my ability, I couldn't prevent you from being hurt. Not then, or with Briony." He shook his head angrily. "That knife was confiscated when she first arrived. Evan must have given it back to her. I should have made sure she was searched again."

"You couldn't control everything."

He didn't reply, and I stretched my hand out across the space between us, holding it there until he took it. Winding my fingers around his, I said, "Connor. For the last three days, I have walked among pain and madness ... and..." I tried to find the right word to describe what I'd seen in Neville's eyes that last time on the machine. Eventually, I whispered, "Evil." I took a shuddering breath, and continued, "Except I didn't walk into any of it alone, because you were always with me. Connor, you were the angel standing at my shoulder. And the reason you didn't fly me away was because I wouldn't let you."

He let out a choked laugh. "I told you, there's no such thing as angels."

"You're *so* wrong about that."

He didn't answer, but the bleakness left his face. For a while after that the two of us just sat there, leaning back against the wall and holding hands, neither of us speaking and neither of us needing to. We both knew that we were still in the middle of a detention centre, in terrible danger, surrounded by enemies and too far from the tuarts. But somehow, everything bad that had happened, and everything that might be going to happen, seemed to fade away, vanishing into the past or the future. For now, I was myself again. We were together. And this small measure of time was ours alone.

Eventually Connor stirred, checking outside again. "The blind's gone down. It won't be long now." He stood, rolling up our blind and unlocking the catch on the window.

I looked out at the other house, but nothing was happening yet. "Are you sure he can open his window?"

"I hid a master key near the climbing frame this morning. Jaz should have collected it when the administrators took them out for playtime."

"Was that what you were telling him when you spoke to him at the park?"

"Yes, and I tried to let him know that you were here on purpose. I was worried he might do something rash."

I grinned at him. "Rash? Jaz? Surely not!"

There was sudden movement in the house opposite, and a small, worried face appeared. I gave Jaz a cheerful wave. He unlocked his window with the purloined key and slithered out, scrambling across the space between us. Connor opened our own window, and I bent down to help Jaz inside. The second he was on his feet in the room, he flung his arms around me, and I hugged him back. We broke apart, and both spoke at once: "Are you OK?"

"I'm fine, Jaz. Are you?"

"'Course!"

I stared anxiously at him. He was thinner, maybe, but other than that he did seem all right. Still... "Are you sure they haven't hurt you?"

"It's going to take more than detention to get the better of me. Besides, I knew you'd come."

He said that last part with such complete faith that I wasn't sure whether to laugh or cry. I'd had so many worries in the weeks leading up to coming here, continually waking up in the night beset by nagging fears and secret doubts, but apparently my incorrigible Firestarter hadn't been a bit concerned.

Standing up, I drew Jaz over to the bed where we could sit comfortably next to each other. Connor pulled the blind down over our now-closed window and sat down on the box, going still and silent. I cast a grateful look at him, knowing he was retreating from the room in the only way he could, to give me time with Jaz.

I tried to think of all the stuff that Jaz needed to know, and started with what I thought he'd want to hear most. "We got Pepper. The saurs are taking care of her."

I'd expected him to be happy, to smile his toothy smile. Except he just glowered at Connor. I said quickly, "Connor's on our side, Jaz. I told you about him ages ago, remember?"

"He didn't seem like he was on our side in the park."

"That was – I mean, wasn't – it's kind of a long story. He's with us, though, promise. I'll prove it. He's going to take your collar off."

At my words, Connor rose and moved to the bed, leaning over to enter in the code to the band around Jaz's neck, before shifting across to undo mine. Jaz felt at his neck as Connor took the collars away, and exclaimed, "It's gone! It's actually gone."

"Jaz, we need to—"

He interrupted me, "Ash, you know I can't go yet, right?"

"Why not?"

"Because of the others. Can you believe, until I came

along, none of them knew anything about resisting the government? They need me."

I couldn't believe it – was this my careless Jaz, taking responsibility for other human beings? I remembered the clever way those kids had shown me their abilities, and how I'd thought they were Tribe in their hearts. *Jaz is their ... leader?* It seemed such a strange word to apply to him, and yet it was the right one. "Um, you don't need to worry, Jaz. We're taking them all with us."

"What about the traitor? Is she still in here somewhere? 'Cause I think we should let the government keep her, if she is."

Oh yeah, he saw Briony at the park too. "I'm afraid that Bry – she died."

His face lit up. "Excellent! Did you kill her?"

"No!"

He patted my leg. "Never mind, Ash. The important thing is that she's gone."

Disconcerted, I asked, "Aren't you sorry that she's dead?"

Jaz sniffed. "She didn't keep faith with the pack. You can't feel sorry for people like that." His attention shifted to Connor, who was opening the case that sat on the drawers. "Is that another collar? What's it for?" he asked.

"I'm afraid you have to wear it. But," I reassured him, as Connor handed the collar to me, "it's OK, because it doesn't work."

"What do you mean, it doesn't work?"

"It's a government secret. When an Illegal has a collar on for years and years, it wears out. Let me get this on you, and I'll prove it."

He seemed doubtful, but held himself still as I put it around his neck. It felt awful to do this to him, but I reminded myself that it wasn't a real collar as I clipped it into place. "OK, let's test it. Can you make fire?"

His brow furrowed in concentration, and Connor let out a startled yelp, leaping backwards to escape the flames that had flared up around his feet.

"Jaz!" I growled.

The fire vanished as fast as it had appeared.

"You *told* me to use my ability, Ash," Jaz said in a familiar tone of injured innocence.

"I didn't mean like that, and you know it!"

Connor was checking the soles of his boots, making sure they hadn't burned.

"Are you all right?" I asked.

He nodded, his lips twitching like he was trying not to laugh. I glared at Jaz, who was holding out his hand

316

and making tiny flames dance along the tops of his fingers. I knew I had no time to be mad at him now.

"Listen, I need to explain some things to you. Later tonight, Connor is going to start a fire—"

The flames winked out. "You don't need him for that. I can start it."

"No," I told him patiently, "you can't. We need it to be in a very specific place, and you won't be able to set it that accurately, because you'll be too far away. So Connor will light it and you'll ... encourage it."

He was clearly unhappy at not having the fire-lighting job. "What exactly do you mean by 'encourage it'?"

"Once you feel it start, count to a hundred, and then make it go big. Very, *very* big. This is super important, Jaz. Everything else depends on it. Can you do it?"

"Of course! Only," he added in a disgusted tone, "this place is built out of composite, which is totally fire-retardant. So if you're trying to burn it all down..."

I shook my head. "We're not. The fire's to get people to evacuate, and to act as a distraction."

"A distraction from what?"

"I'll tell you in a second. I just need you to test out one more thing first. Can you try to mindspeak me?"

317

Jaz went pale, casting a horrified glance at Connor. "Ash!"

I rolled my eyes. "It's OK. The saurs let me tell him all about mindspeaking. He has to know, because it's part of the plan."

"Oh. I guess that's OK then." He shifted closer, and confessed in a low voice, "Ash, I've been trying to contact the saurs for days, and you too, in the park. No one hears me."

"That was probably because of the collars. The saurs haven't been able to reach you either. Em thinks maybe rhondarite interferes with mindspeaking same as it does with abilities."

His black eyes gleamed, and within a few seconds, words appeared in my head.

ASH! CAN YOU HEAR ME?

I winced, and mind-answered him, *Yes, and you don't have to shout! Can you hear me?*

Yep!

Good! Now, can you reach the saurs, too?

His face went distant as he focused on the lizards. "I can hear Hatches! She's so happy I'm OK. She says they're ready for the escape." He bounced in place. "How are we going to bust out, Ash? Are you gonna

318

Sleepwalk? Because you could smash the walls with a fist of power and then—"

"I'm not Sleepwalking, Jaz."

He looked disappointed "You're not?"

"Nope. It's way too unpredictable. Besides, the whole idea is to do this so no one knows anyone from the Tribe was involved. I guess you could say we're kind of playing a trick on the government."

"A trick? Is that all?"

"A really good trick." Drawing in a long breath, I explained the plan, laying it out carefully to make sure he understood everything.

When I reached the end, he said, in an awed tone, "That is the best trick *ever*."

"Yeah, I think so too."

Connor cleared his throat, jerking his head towards the window. I understood. There wasn't anything left to tell Jaz now, and we couldn't risk anyone noticing a detainee was missing. "I'm afraid you have to go, Jaz."

"I've got heaps of time! The house administrator won't check on me for ages."

"They check in thirty-five minute intervals," I told him. "Believe it or not, there's a rule about it."

"About afternoon sleeps?"

"About *everything*."

Jaz slid off the bed, and I did too, bending down to give him one last hug. It was surprisingly hard to let go. I struggled with a crazy impulse to take him and run, to forget everything and everyone else and save this one precious life. My eyes met Connor's over Jaz's head, and I could see he knew what I was thinking. He shrugged, as if to say, *If that's what you want…* And, for a second, I considered it. Only I knew it wouldn't be right, even if Jaz would leave without the other detainees. Besides, there was no safety anywhere if we couldn't stop Neville.

I made myself release Jaz. Connor let him out the window, and he hurried across the gap into the other house. Once he was inside he waved happily at us, before pulling down his blind and vanishing from sight. I took a sharp breath as he disappeared, and another, finding it suddenly difficult to get air around the tightness in my chest. *I can't keep saying goodbye to Jaz. I can't!*

"Connor! Tell me that we'll save him."

He smiled at me.

"Ashala Wolf. We will save them all."

DAY FOUR

THE INSPECTORATE

I was alone, and waiting, in yet another warehouse –
this time a featureless white building that was used for
storage in Detention Centre 3. I'd positioned myself
on the upper level of the structure, an open half-floor
filled with containers, and was lying flat so I could
peer through the railing into the gloom below. Except
the only thing to see right now was the faint outlines
of more containers. Connor had left a while back to
get ready for his part in tonight's events, and it felt like
he'd been gone *for ever*. I'd changed into the enforcer
uniform he'd left for me, and all I'd had to do while
the afternoon rolled into night was torture myself by

imagining all the ways in which things could go wrong. I'd done a good job of that too, so much so that I was now twitching with anxiety. Finally, I heard a long, piercing siren, then another. The fire alarm, at last!

I spent a few happy minutes dwelling on the image of all Neville's records about the Tribe – which was what Connor had used to start the fire – going up in flames. Then I focused on what would be happening outside, imagining how Neville and the remaining enforcers would be scrambling to locate the blaze. Everyone else would hurry through the centre to the designated emergency gathering point outside the front entrance, and if things went right for us, the Inspectorate wouldn't arrive there with the others. Because Connor would be waiting along the evacuation route, dressed in administrator beige so that he could mingle with the crowd. He'd draw the Inspectorate away with promises of revealing Neville's secrets, and bring them here.

Time dragged on endlessly, and no one came. I was starting to worry when the door below swung open. The downstairs lights flicked on, and I exhaled in relief at seeing Connor ushering the two members of the Inspectorate into the warehouse.

I examined the Inspectorate. *Jeremy Duoro and Belle*

Willis. Both were dressed in standard issue Gull-City-blue shirts and pants, but other than that they seemed nothing alike. He was short, thin and dark-haired, while she was tall, stout and blonde, and the differences between them didn't end there. Duoro was youngish, maybe mid-twenties, and his bright gaze darted all over the place as he shifted from foot to foot. Willis, on the other hand, was a lot older, and she moved with a purposeful energy, scanning her surroundings in a single glance. They were each wearing small badges on their sleeves with some kind of symbol printed on them, and I had to clap my hand over my mouth to hold back a giggle when I realized I was looking at red question marks. *They wore Question pins into a detention centre? Neville must have been furious!*

Willis spoke in a low, powerful voice that seemed to roll out across the warehouse. "This appears to be nothing more than a storage area. What exactly are we doing here?"

"I'll show you," Connor answered, walking over to a big crate and pulling back the canvas cloth covering the top. The Inspectorate hurried after him, staring down at the mottled chunks of rock inside the crate. When I'd first seen the stuff, I hadn't known what it was. It took a lot of time and effort to transform raw rhondarite into the smooth white material that the collars were made from.

Belle Willis picked up one of the pieces, weighing it in her hand. "What could Chief Administrator Rose possibly want with unprocessed rhondarite?"

"It's not just that it's unprocessed," Connor explained. "That rhondarite does not come from any of the mines allowed under the Three Mines Accords." He clasped his hands behind his back, drawing out the moment before delivering the terrible truth: "The Chief Administrator has built a secret rhondarite mine in the Steeps."

The Inspectorate looked every bit as appalled as I'd been when Connor first told me.

"But," Duoro said in a stunned voice, "what about the Balance? We all know what a disaster the exhaustion of the earth's resources was for the old world!"

"I'm afraid the Chief Administrator believes almost anything is justified to stop the Illegal threat."

Belle Willis subjected Connor to a searching stare. "I can't imagine this is common knowledge. How did you find out about it?"

Connor pulled open the top buttons of his administrator robes to show the black uniform beneath. "I found out because I'm an enforcer." Duoro made an astonished noise, and Connor continued, doing a good job of sounding genuinely troubled. "It's the enforcers who mine and process the rhondarite. They were all personally recruited by Neville Rose himself, including me. However, I simply *cannot* condone what he is doing."

"I should think not!" Duoro spluttered. "The man is even more of a raving fanatic than Prime Talbot was." Waving an arm at the rhondarite, he demanded, "What does he even imagine he's going to do with all this?"

"Reserves," Connor replied. "He thinks we need much more than we have. Because rhondarite wears out."

Interestingly, that information didn't seem to be news to the Inspectorate. Neither of them looked particularly surprised. "We'd heard rumours about that," Willis said, "although it's good to have it confirmed."

"Except," Duoro put in, "according to our sources, it takes years for a collar to become ineffective, and the government's stockpiled more than enough rhondarite to compensate for it."

Connor nodded. "At the current rate of detentions, yes. Only Rose wants to increase detentions threefold

– random assessments, more enforcer patrols and fewer Exemptions. If he wins the Prime election, he's going to start putting those measures into place."

Willis and Duoro exchanged worried glances, and I thought, *Good.* They were reacting pretty much as we'd expected them to. They seemed to have no difficulty either in believing that Connor was a rebel enforcer betraying Neville for the sake of the Balance. Which was just as well, because we were hardly going to let them in on all our secrets.

I was feeling quite smug until I noticed something coming down the side of one of the boxes to my right.

Spider!

I leaned to my left, trying to get away from the thing without making any noise, as Duoro's voice floated upwards.

"We've heard other things about Rose. Rumours of an interrogation device, and something about a girl being killed in Cambergull a few days ago?"

My pulse skyrocketed. I swung my attention back to what was happening below. It was not part of our plan to have the Inspectorate go chasing after the machine, or me.

"I've heard about the device too," Connor told them,

"but I've never seen it. As to Cambergull, I don't know. There was a prisoner here, a member of the group of runaways living in the Firstwood. She was shot while trying to escape." The Inspectorate seemed to accept that artful mixture of truth and lie, and I relaxed.

Then something furry brushed against my hand.

Before I could stop myself, I scooted backwards, knees scraping against the floor.

Willis spoke sharply. "What was that?"

I forced myself to be still, staring at the spider which was meandering towards me, and wondered if I could try to flick it away. Was that a yellow mark on its back? I couldn't be sure in the dark, but if it was a yellow-back, the thing was deadly poisonous. *Which means coming into contact with it isn't a good idea...*

Connor answered Willis dismissively. "We've got an ongoing problem with rats. You needn't be afraid, they rarely come out into the light."

"I wasn't—"

"And," he interrupted, "there is something else you need to see here."

I let out a breath as I heard Connor striding towards the front of the warehouse and the Inspectorate following along behind. The spider was getting closer, but I didn't dare move, not while everything was so quiet. Except it was almost upon me. *A few seconds more and it...* From below, there was the sound of a lid being taken off a container. Now!

I rolled to the side until I was well away from the spider, any noise I made more than covered by the Inspectorate's gasps of dismay.

"There must be a hundred streakers in there!" Duoro exclaimed. "There's only supposed to be fifty in existence anywhere. That's all the Council of Primes approved!"

"Yes," Willis agreed, "and since anyone who produces more is in violation of the Advanced Weaponry Accords, it begs the question, how did Rose even get these manufactured?"

The spider went scuttling past, unaware of the disaster it had almost caused. Connor imparted the conclusion that we had all reached weeks ago: "I don't believe the Chief Administrator is doing this alone. He must have allies, similarly minded people who are also willing to break Accords."

There was shocked silence. It was broken by Duoro pronouncing excitedly, "I *knew* there were conspiracies in the government! Didn't I tell you, Belle? Didn't I?"

"Yes, you did, and it seems that you were right. Although I have to believe it's the work of a few malcontents. Surely there couldn't be that many Citizens willing to risk endangering the Balance."

The spider disappeared into the dark beyond me. I started to creep forwards, wanting to see what was happening, as Connor spoke again: "What I'm worried about is what the Chief Administrator and his friends might do with these weapons if he *doesn't* win the Prime election. There's a chance he might try to take over the government by force."

"It would never work!" Duoro objected. "The people would not stand for it."

"If the circumstances were right," Willis responded thoughtfully, "the people might not even notice it was happening. Do you remember a few months back, when the whole of Gull City panicked over those snake-shaped clouds?"

"Yes, and it was ridiculous. They were just clouds!"

"Jeremy, there were enforcers everywhere for those few weeks, and no one made a fuss because everyone wanted to be protected from the Serpent. If Rose could manufacture some looming Illegal threat, Citizens would beg him to bring his enforcers to the city to protect them. Once he was there, it might prove very difficult to get him to leave again."

Wow. She'd put that scenario together as quickly as Ember had when we'd first learned of the weapons stash. I reached the railing in time to see Duoro start to pace back and forth. "We *have* to find a way to stop him, Belle!"

"If you took a piece of rhondarite back to the city," Connor said, offering them the suggestion we'd worked out beforehand, "a simple composition test would show it didn't come from any of the mines allowed under the Three Mines Accords. That should be enough to prove some of what's going on here."

"It's a good start," Willis agreed. "But if Neville's got allies in the government who could cover this up, we might need more. Some publicity would be useful. I think Friends of Detainees would help, don't you, Jeremy?"

He stopped pacing, his face lighting up. "Yes, and the smaller groups too. We'll contact them all – Citizens against Detention, Mothers of Illegals, Free the Children – by the time we're through, there'll be such an outcry that the government will *have* to take action against Rose." Turning to Connor, he added,

"You can come with us. Let people know what you've seen in this place."

No, he can't! But Connor was already shaking his head. "I can't be seen with you tonight. I'll make my own way out once you're gone. Before then, Neville must have no reason to suspect that anyone has given you any information."

Willis frowned. "He's sure to know something's wrong. We've been missing for a while now."

"Yes, but it would have been very difficult for you to stumble across any of this on your own, and provided his suspicions are not raised, the Chief Administrator is going to be anxious to evacuate you before you ask questions about the source of the fire." Willis looked questioningly at Connor, and he said, "It started in the rhondarite processing plant."

A delighted smile spread across Jeremy Duoro's face. "In *that* case, he'll hustle us back to Cambergull as quickly as he can. All we need to do is act dumb. Fortunately, I'm quite good at that."

Belle Willis stifled a laugh and held out her hand to Connor. "Thank you."

He shook it firmly, while Duoro clapped him on the shoulder. "Come and find us once you get out of here."

"I will," Connor lied.

The little group broke apart. Willis walked over to the rhondarite, grabbing a small piece and concealing it in her pocket before making her way to the door with Duoro beside her. Connor was the last to leave, and before he followed the Inspectorate out, he paused, staring up at where he knew I was hidden. I reached through the railing to give him a quick thumbs-up signal, letting him know I was OK.

He nodded in relieved acknowledgement. Then he shut the door, and I was alone.

DAY FOUR

THE DOCTOR

I counted to two hundred, giving Connor time to get the Inspectorate out of the area. Then I ran downstairs, pausing to take a streaker from the tub. I hated the things, but I'd promised Connor not to go out unarmed. So, exactly like he'd showed me, I checked the safety switch was on, making sure the weapon couldn't go off by accident, before shoving it into my pocket and slipping into the night.

Outside was another world, one of eerily empty spaces, hazy air and the far-off screeches of saurs. The sky was all lit up with the angry glow of the fire, and I could smell the acrid tang of the smoke. It had a nasty odour to it, which was no doubt due to the small store of chemicals in the processing plant. Ember had warned us that some of them were toxic, though she said they shouldn't hurt us, not in low quantities. Still, it was making me feel queasy, and I tried to take shallow breaths as I hurried through the centre. The composite buildings around me seemed to shine faintly orange, reflecting the flames, and that, plus the soft night lighting, was the only illumination I had to guide me. But I'd spent weeks memorizing the plans of this place, and I moved without hesitation, darting from one shadow to the next.

It felt strange to be drifting around here without being collared and watched. I had a sudden, insane desire to do something silly, like go running into open space and twirl in circles, just because I could. Instead, I skulked onwards, until I was entering a familiar building. My chest immediately went tight and my mouth dry, as if my body remembered I'd suffered in this place. *Stop it, Ash! You put yourself into that chair.* That didn't seem to make any difference, so I tried to focus on what I had to do.

We'd always planned to take the machine, both to prevent it from being used on anyone else and because

Ember wanted to take it apart to see how it worked. Except that had been before I knew the machine was really a dog, and I had other plans now. It was terrible to think of a dog-spirit being confined to a motionless box. Ember had made Georgie a mechanical spider once, which was still clicking creepily around the caves somewhere, so I didn't see why she couldn't build a mechanical canine body to match a canine soul. *I think I'll call him Blackie. Or maybe Howler. Or Tooth?*

Reaching the machine room, I gave the box a reassuring pat and pulled out the cords that shackled it to the silver hoop and the screen. I hugged it to me as I raced back through the building, feeling giddy with relief to be leaving this part of the centre behind me for ever.

Then I rounded a corner, and came face to face with Miriam Grey.

For an airless second, the two of us stared at each other. She spotted the box, and her face went red with rage. "That's mine!" Grey leaped, grabbing hold of the machine and trying to wrest it from my grasp. I clung on, and we struggled wildly, careening back and forth across the corridor. She shoved me against the wall, and I shoved right back, jerking the box sideways to shake her loose. Something went clattering across the floor. The streaker! We both lunged for it. But I'd had to drop the box, putting me a precious second behind her, and Grey reached it first. She snatched it up, flicking the safety switch off, swinging around to point it at my head. I froze, gazing into her empty green eyes as she hissed in her high-pitched, whiny voice, "You tried to *steal* my machine!" She sounded like a kid who'd had her toy taken away, and I knew that without Neville here to control her, she was unstable enough to be capable of anything.

This woman is crazy and I am dead.

Somebody came barrelling down the corridor behind her. Grey started to turn towards the approaching footsteps, and I saw my chance. Charging forwards, I grabbed hold of her wrist, just as the new person wrapped their arms around her shoulders. Grey collapsed, and I tore the weapon from her unfeeling fingers, scuttling backwards and pointing it at – *Wentworth!*

I stared, gaping in astonished disbelief as Rae Wentworth lowered an unconscious Miriam Grey to the ground.

"What…" I stuttered. "I mean, how … what did you *do* to her?"

"I used my ability to make her sleep."

"I didn't know Menders could do that!"

Wentworth shrugged. She wasn't looking so good – her nut-brown complexion was sallow, and her dark eyes had lost their cheery sparkle. "I don't know if all Menders can do it, either," she answered. "But I can Mend whatever requires healing, short of death. And you'll find that almost everyone needs more sleep." Her gaze dropped to the streaker. "Are you going to shoot me, Ashala?"

I hadn't even realized I was still pointing the thing in her direction, and I let my arm fall. I wasn't going to kill Wentworth, and I couldn't see how threatening her would solve anything either, especially since she'd be in trouble herself over this. Grey wasn't going to take too kindly to being knocked out, and the reason Wentworth had done it was to save my life. *Again.*

"No, I'm not going to shoot you."

"I wouldn't blame you if you did," she said bleakly. "I know you were telling me the truth."

"Um, you do?"

"There was an enforcer in the hospital. He told me

everything. About how you were being tortured on the machine, and how they'd already killed one Illegal and wouldn't hesitate to kill another. He said they'd kill him too for what he knew."

Evan. Briony's enforcer. What was it Connor had said, that Evan had gone a little crazy and had to be sedated? It sounded like he'd woken up just as nutty as when they'd knocked him out, if he'd spilled all that stuff to Wentworth. Only I didn't have time to waste on thinking about Evan now, not when I had more urgent problems. It was becoming rapidly clear that there were a worrying number of people running about the centre, and Connor was out there somewhere with the Inspectorate.

Flicking the safety switch back on the streaker, I pushed it into my pocket. "Is Neville still with the enforcers? Fighting the fire?"

"Yes, as far as I know."

"And who else is inside? Besides you?"

Wentworth looked puzzled by the question. "A couple of my staff. We wanted to fetch some medical supplies, in case anyone needed treatment."

"Is that all?"

It seemed to dawn on her why I might be concerned.

Her brow cleared as she replied, "Yes, that's all. There's no one to stop you from, ah, getting away. Everyone is outside the gates, and they're supposed to stay there."

That was a relief. Although Wentworth and her staff had broken the rules, and they weren't the only ones. She must have been thinking the same thing, because she added, "I don't know what Miriam was doing. That's why I followed her when I saw her in the centre. After everything that enforcer told me, it seemed suspicious."

Grey was worried her precious machine would get all burned up. I opened my mouth to ask how long we had until Grey woke up. Before I could get a word out, Wentworth said, "I helped that enforcer. I gave him a doctor's robe and let him go. It would have been easy for him to slip out the gates."

Wow. Maybe Evan hadn't been so crazy to talk to her.

"I should've have helped you too," she told me remorsefully. "I'm sorry, Ashala! I didn't know what was happening, I swear I didn't know."

Yeah, but you should have. Except she did seem genuinely sorry. Plus, if her haggard appearance was anything to go by, she was punishing herself pretty hard for not acting sooner.

"Well, you've saved my life three times now. I guess that makes us OK." Then I thought of all the other Illegals who might one day need her help. "Don't be fooled by someone like Neville Rose again."

"I promise you," she answered, a determined glint in her eyes, "I won't. And you've got to *go*, get out of this place while you can."

"Grey's seen me, and she probably saw you too, by the way. If she wakes up…"

Wentworth shook her head. "She'll sleep for a while yet, but you're right. We can't have her telling anyone you're escaping." She gazed down at the unconscious doctor. "There's a drug I can administer. Harmless, but it'll keep her out until tomorrow, and her memory will be very foggy when she wakes up."

Seemed like a plan. "OK. Won't you have to get her to the hospital, though? Or I guess you could bring the drug and give it to her here, no one would find her until the morning."

"We can't leave her in this place, not with the fire!"

Well, I could, but I wasn't going to argue the point. Besides, Neville would probably start a search if he discovered Grey was missed.

"We can drag her out of the building," Wentworth

suggested, "and I'll fetch my people from the hospital. We'll take it from there."

"How are you going to explain her being unconscious in the first place?"

She grinned, some of her former brightness returning. "I'll say she was overcome by the smoke."

I had to admit, I was impressed. *She's good at this, for a beginner.* Wentworth bent over Grey, keen to get started on her scheme. I grabbed the box, tucking it under one arm so I could help Wentworth drag Grey with the other.

"That box is something to do with the machine, isn't it?" Wentworth asked, as we began to manoeuvre the unconscious woman down the corridor. "Some vital component?"

Uh-oh. I wanted to deny it, or make up a story, but I couldn't think of anything fast enough, and anyway, I wasn't sure how much she'd heard of what Grey had said. Apparently, though, Wentworth had constructed a story of her own.

"You were escaping, but you came back for the machine. To make sure it could never be used on anyone else."

Not exactly, but it sounded good. "Yes. I'm going

to" – *build him a body and name him Fang* – "destroy it."

She nodded, as if she'd expected no other answer, and we continued on.

"You know," I told her, "there'll be questions tomorrow, especially about how that enforcer got out of the hospital. You should think about leaving too."

We'd reached the end of the corridor, and she straightened. "There's a *fire*, Ashala. People might need a doctor. And the detainees – I have to try to protect them. To put things right."

After tonight there aren't going to be any detainees here. But I couldn't tell her that. "The best thing you can do for those detainees is to expose what Neville's done, and to do that you have to go somewhere he can't shut you up."

I could tell by the stubborn set of her mouth that she didn't agree. She didn't bother arguing, though, just held out her hand to me. I shook it, remembering how Connor had shaken Belle Willis's hand back in the warehouse. *Citizens and Illegals and Exempts shaking hands.* The world was upside down tonight, in more ways than one.

"I'm glad to have known you, Ashala Wolf."

A panicked expression came over her face, and she added hastily, "I mean, I'm not glad that you were imprisoned and tortured, or anything—"

I laughed. "I get it. I'm glad to have met you too, Rae Wentworth. And you know, if you ever need help, you can come to the Tribe."

For some reason that offer really seemed to mean something to her. She sniffed, her eyes glistening with tears. "Thank you. And, Ashala – *run*. Run, and don't look back."

"Believe me, I'm going."

I let go of Wentworth's hand and went to the door, taking a moment to be sure there was no one outside. When I was satisfied it was deserted, I headed outside, sprinting away with the dog-box clutched securely to my chest.

And I didn't look back.

DAY FOUR

THE SAURS

I flitted through the centre, making my way to where I was supposed to meet Connor. But I wasn't even halfway there when he came tearing out of the night, dressed once again in enforcer black.

Seizing hold of my shoulders, he demanded, "Are you all right? Ashala, are you all right?"

"I'm fine—"

"You were afraid! Why were you afraid?"

I forgot sometimes that the connection between us wasn't one-way. In moments of extreme emotion, he picked up on my feelings too. And I *had* been terrified when Miriam Grey had pointed that weapon at my head. "Connor, I'm totally OK. You can see that, right?" He nodded, and I added, "Except – and don't freak out now – I did run into Grey, and Wentworth."

"You *what*?"

"Let me explain."

And I did, going rapidly over what had happened. When I'd finished, he drew in a long breath, and asked, "You're sure Wentworth won't tell that she's seen you?"

"Positive," I answered firmly. "We're good, Connor. Let's go save them all!"

He laughed shakily, and released me. The two of us raced side by side through the smoky air, the shrill cries of saurs getting louder as we neared the front of the centre. Connor tried to take the weight of the box, but I shook my head, holding on to the dog as we made our way past endless white structures.

He stopped beside one of the centre's tall office blocks. "This rooftop will do. Are you ready?"

"Just let me find a place for the d— I mean, the machine." Glancing around, I spotted a small gap between two buildings and darted over to conceal the box deep in the shadowed space. When I was sure it was completely hidden, I turned back to Connor, only to find he was staring in the direction of the far-off blaze. "What is it?" I asked.

"There's a north-easterly moving in from the Steeps."

It took me a second to make sense of his words. *The wind.* It was going to start blowing the flames through the centre, and while composite was fire-retardant, it wasn't fireproof. This place was going to burn, and we could be in trouble if the blaze spread too far while we were still in here. "You can divert the wind, though, right?"

"I can encourage it in the other direction for a while. But we'd best get this done, and get *out.*"

The air pressed in around me, and we rose upwards until we landed on the pitch of the roof. I flattened myself against the slope, crawling forwards on my elbows to peer over the ridge. Connor did the same. We perched, shoulder to shoulder, looking down at the scene below. The area around the outer wall of the centre was lit up by a series of floodlights, and my gaze went to the two vehicles parked by the side of the road that led to Cambergull. I skipped over the sedan that was probably meant for the Inspectorate, and stared at the bus beside it, heaving a sigh of relief when I made out the shapes of small heads through its windows. The

347

detainees were ready to be evacuated if the fire couldn't be extinguished, exactly as the "Detention Centre 3, Emergency Procedures in the Case of Fire" required. And their four administrator guardians were standing several paces away, chatting amongst themselves. Close, but not close enough to be a problem for us.

Everyone else was waiting outside the gates, with red-robed medical staff organizing some kind of first-aid station, and beige-robed administrators milling about. So far as I could tell, Wentworth hadn't returned yet. But someone else had, and I frowned, just as Connor said, "Neville."

"Yeah, I see him."

The Chief Administrator was involved in some kind of discussion with the Inspectorate, and from the way Jeremy Duoro was waving his arms around, it seemed pretty intense. A smile spread over my face as snatches of what the Inspectorate were saying drifted upwards:

"… deserve an explanation … still burning …"

"… entirely within our powers to investigate …"

Then Neville's voice, coming through clearly as he raised it to speak over the top of both of them. "I am responsible for your safety, and I'm afraid I must insist you evacuate to Cambergull. You'll be free to continue your inspection once I'm satisfied the danger has passed."

Willis and Duoro began to raise objections, as if going to Cambergull was the last thing they wanted to do, and I relaxed. They knew what they were doing.

Feeling increasingly euphoric, I cast my gaze outwards, past the road and over the long stretch of ground to the rolling grasslands beyond. The light ended some distance before the edge of the grasses, but I could make out the movements of large scaly bodies in the dark and, more importantly, a distinctive pale shape that wasn't moving at all. Hatches-with-Stars appeared to be standing absolutely still, although I was willing to bet she was quivering with excitement. *I know how she feels.*

"Connor? We can start, right?"

"Yes. Tell Jaz they can begin."

I reached for his hand, gripping it as I sent my thoughts outwards. *Jaz. JAZ?*

Right here, Ash!

We're ready to go.

His presence disappeared from my mind. Moments later, there was a sudden cacophony of screeches, and a single saur charged out of the dark, skittering to a halt just inside the reach of the floodlights. There were cries of terror and dismay, and Neville shouted, "Nobody move! If you run the saur will chase you!"

The great black beast began to stalk back and forth, head held high and scales gleaming in the light. He swished his tail – once, twice, three times – sending pebbles flying in all directions. Then he rose up to balance on his hind legs, throwing back his head to let out a long, eerie wail.

Wanders-too-Far was really hamming it up.

For a few precious minutes, no one moved and no one looked away from Wanders, who was standing in the opposite direction from where the vehicles were parked. It took a pleasingly long time before someone called out, "The bus!"

There was a collective intake of breath as everyone realized the bus containing the detainees was rolling towards the grasslands, and then a confused babble of shouts.

"The detainees have got control of the bus!"

"They're heading for the saurs…"

"Nobody move, or that beast will come after us!"

Except someone *was* moving. Rae Wentworth was coming through the main gates, and following her were two red-robed staff, bearing a stretcher that contained the unconscious Miriam Grey. A few people hissed a warning at them. The stretcher-bearers stopped dead. But Wentworth raced forwards. "We have to help the children!" Worse still, her reckless behaviour jolted others into action. Some of the crowd began running too, including the Inspectorate. And – the biggest potential disaster of all – Belle Willis did the smart thing and headed for the sedan, yelling, "We can catch them in the car."

I gasped. *"Connor."*

He replied through gritted teeth, "I know."

The bus picked up speed, barrelling over the rocky ground as if it was being pushed along by the wind itself – which, of course, it was. Wanders reacted almost as fast as Connor had, crashing down onto all fours and pounding towards the crowd. He stopped before he reached them, but he was close enough to be even more terrifying than he had been before as he stomped one clawed foot on the ground, hissing threateningly. Everyone froze again. Well, almost everyone – Wentworth and Duoro were both inching forwards. I muttered angrily, "Stop *helping*, you idiots!"

But they were too late. The bus careened into the grasses, rolling to a halt near that pale shape in the dark. Connor exhaled, leaning against me as the saurs converged on the vehicle, stampeding around it until it was hidden from view. There was simply no way, now, for anyone to see the sixteen detainees scurrying out of the bus and through the long grasses to freedom.

I nudged Connor. "We did it!"

He replied softly, "Not quite yet. And I think you may have broken my hand."

Oh. I *had* been clinging on tight. Feeling guilty, I started to release him, but he caught hold of my fingers, murmuring, "I didn't say let go."

A goofy grin spread over my face. "Connor..." I got no further before the wind brought a sudden gust of unpleasant-smelling smoke wafting over the rooftops. We both ducked our heads, coughing.

"Sorry. I couldn't hold the wind and the detainees."

I glanced over my shoulder to find the sky was lit up with a far brighter glow than it had been before. "It's spread, all right. And that *smell*!"

"They must have been storing more chemicals in this place than we thought. I'll try to blow it away from us."

352

We've started some kind of toxic blaze? "We've got to get out of here."

I tried to breathe as shallowly as possible, thinking at Jaz, *Hurry up, hurry up.* I wasn't sure if he could hear me from this distance, but the saurs seemed to be rushing along anyway.

There was a high-pitched, squealing noise of metal being ripped to shreds as they started to attack the bus. Wanders-too-Far let out a last fearsome screech, and ran back to the grasslands. Soon after, another sound began to echo through the night, a series of sharp, popping snaps – *crunch, crunch!* And again, *crunch!*

To my disappointment, everyone below was silent, not realizing what they were hearing. *Come on, it's not that hard to work out…* Finally, Jeremy Duoro pointed one trembling finger towards the grasslands. "That sound – it's *bones*. They're eating the children!"

A groan of dismay swept through the people below, and I chortled gleefully as the gruesome noises continued.

Crunch! Snap! Crunch! It all sounded convincingly realistic, which wasn't surprising since the saurs really were chewing on bones. The big lizards had spent the past few nights shifting Gnaws-the-Bones's entire personal stash onto the grasslands, scattering them around the area where Hatches had been standing to mark the way for us.

The crunching gradually slowed, then stopped. The screeching died down too, and the saurs began to disperse, drifting into the grasslands. I focused my attention on the crowd. Wentworth had sunk to her knees, putting her head in her hands. Willis had wrapped her arms around herself, and Duoro was reeling on his feet. Some of the administrators burst into tears, while others clung on to each other. And standing in the middle of it all was Neville Rose, who, for once, didn't seem to have anything to say.

Every last one of the many witnesses below clearly believed that they'd just seen the horrible end of sixteen detainees.

Which meant that after four days, three near-death experiences and a whole lot of pain, Connor and I could finally get out of Detention Centre 3.

I grinned at Connor, but he didn't grin back, and my smile faded. I'd been so absorbed in what was going on below, I hadn't noticed that his shoulder was rigid with tension against mine. He looked at me, and said hoarsely, "Ashala. There's something wrong with my ability."

THE ESCAPE
THE OVERTHROW

"What? How…" I gasped.

"It's the smoke. I don't think it's chemicals burning. I think it's rhondarite."

Rhondarite? No wonder the haze had made me feel queasy before! None of us had considered the possibility that rhondarite could burn, and maybe it couldn't, in an ordinary fire. Only we'd made a Firestarter fire, which was a lot hotter.

"Can you use your ability at all?" I asked.

"It isn't gone, but I can't control it as well as normal, and I can't hold back the wind. Also," he admitted, "I'm not sure I can fly us out of here."

And that, I knew, was what was truly worrying him. The notion that he might not be able to get me out of the centre the way we'd planned, the prospect of somehow failing me. *Connor. As if you ever could.*

"So we don't fly," I told him. "We walk, we run – it doesn't matter, let's go."

The two of us began to slither backwards down the roof. We hadn't even made it halfway when Belle Willis shouted, "Chief Administrator Neville Rose, in the name of the Balance, I am relieving you of command of this centre."

Connor groaned. "She's going to get herself killed!"

We scrambled back up to find that Willis was striding towards Neville, her head and shoulders thrown back like a warrior going into battle. *The woman's gone crazy.* Although she hadn't, not quite. She must have read the shocked horror and bewilderment of the crowd, just as I had done, and understood how vulnerable they were. That, in addition to the lack of enforcers among them, had clearly made her think she had an opportunity to seize control.

I knew she'd underestimated Neville Rose.

Willis came to a halt in front of Neville, but the wily Chief Administrator refused to respond to her aggressive posture with anger of his own. He shook his head reprovingly, and spoke in a clear, carrying voice. "Belle, you have no power to relieve me of command, and you know it. I fear you are somewhat overwrought. Let's get you evacuated to Cambergull, and we'll forget all about this, shall we?"

Some of the anxiety amongst the people below evaporated as they reacted to his familiar, soothing tones. From up here, I could spot all the small movements that showed their trust in him – the way heads turned towards the sound of his voice, and bodies repositioned themselves to angle in his direction. I silently urged Willis to see what I saw, and to let it alone. Duoro came charging over to her side, gesturing to the grasslands and calling to the crowd, "You all witnessed what happened to those children. Ask yourselves, what was it that made them so terrified that they chose to run into such danger? What has been happening in this place?"

I bit back a scream of frustration, furious Duoro would even hint at wrongdoing in the centre before the Inspectorate was safely away.

Neville drew himself up in righteous indignation. "It is outrageous to imply that I had anything to do with the tragic deaths of those children. I fear you have

357

overstepped your authority here, Mr Duoro." He spun on his heel, pointing to some administrators. "You, you and you – come here. I must ask you to watch over the Inspectorate, until I can report their misconduct to the appropriate authorities."

He's suspicious. Or maybe he was simply reacting to the events of the night, wanting to stop things spiralling out of his control further than they already had. Either way, Duoro and Willis were in serious trouble. Connor and I exchanged despairing glances, and I tried to think of something that might help us fix the situation. There didn't seem to be any way for me to intervene, or Connor either, not without a blatant use of his ability, which would expose the presence of Illegals in the area – the last thing we wanted. There seemed to be nothing left to do, no paths left to take. Until a new voice rang out: "Chief Administrator, there's no need for this."

Everybody looked at Rae Wentworth, who was standing on the rocky earth where she'd been kneeling before. "Surely," she continued briskly, "you can see these people are traumatized? I'm quite certain they hardly know what they're saying. They need treatment."

Willis and Duoro both protested that they were

perfectly fine. But the three administrators came to an uncertain halt, and Neville was quiet, seeming to be considering Wentworth's words. It didn't take a genius to realize that he'd love to attribute any accusations the Inspectorate made to being the result of shock. On the other hand, he'd seen Wentworth come out of the centre with Grey, so he was probably suspicious of her as well. *Except,* I thought with rising excitement, *he can't possibly be suspicious enough.* Because he had no idea what she could do with her ability.

I'd thought that I was out of options. But I wasn't out of allies.

"I believe," Neville said, a hint of smugness in his voice, "that you're right, Doctor. Perhaps this is a matter for the medical staff."

This time it was Connor who reached for *my* hand as Wentworth approached the Chief Administrator. We both knew she was the Inspectorate's best chance, and I hoped she understood that she couldn't shield them from Neville simply by making them her patients. Had she grasped how much of a monster he was? Willis and Duoro were in as much danger from Neville now as I'd been from Miriam Grey when she'd pointed a weapon at my head. *Don't be fooled again, Rae...*

I leaned forwards for a better view as Wentworth strode towards the Inspectorate. She grasped hold of Neville's arm as she brushed past him, just for an instant, before hurrying on. She got one pace away from him. Two...

Neville staggered, and collapsed.

People cried out, and Wentworth swung around with an artistic gasp, leaping to half-catch the Chief Administrator as he toppled over. I was filled with a wild joy at the sight of him falling, even though I knew he was sleeping. I'd never expected to see Neville defeated, at least not tonight, and I was surprised by how much it meant to me.

"You see, Neville?" I whispered in a raw, angry snarl. "*I carry my friends with me*, you bastard."

Connor tore his hand from mine to fling his arm around my shoulders, pulling me against him. I pressed my face into his shirt, feeling shaky and on the verge of tears.

Below us, there was a moment's tense silence. Then Jeremy Duoro roared, "The Chief Administrator has been struck down by the Balance!"

I choked back an astonished giggle. *What utter nonsense!* Only, when I stared down at what was happening,

I saw that no one seemed to think it was nonsense. Neville's mysterious collapse, following on the end of everything else that had happened tonight, seemed to have left them all willing to believe almost anything. Frightened murmurs rose up, a hubbub of anxiety and confusion. And Belle Willis seized her moment.

"We have all been given a message today," she shouted, her powerful voice rolling out across the yard. "The Balance has spoken, and it has spoken to *us*. There are monstrous things happening inside that centre. But we have a chance to put them right. Who among you will help me?"

Wentworth responded instantly, yelling, "I will!"

Others followed her lead, a bit slow at first, and then faster and faster – "I will!" "I will!" "I will!" The three administrators who Neville had sent after the Inspectorate joined in the shouting too, attempting to mingle with the larger group. Everyone else edged away, leaving them standing in circles of space. The whole scene suddenly struck me as hilarious, and I began to laugh. Connor did too, and pretty soon we were both almost hysterical with mirth, clinging to each other and trying not to make too much noise.

Belle Willis began to issue orders to her newly

converted followers, and Connor whispered against my ear, "I think we can leave now."

I smothered another giggle. "I think we can too!"

We slid back down the roof for the second and final time and floated unsteadily to the ground. I retrieved the box, and the two of us began to run, even faster than we had before. The smoke was making me dizzy and ill, but I didn't slacken my pace, and nor did Connor. On we went until we reached the southern side of the centre. He sprinted up the stairs that led to the walkway on the top of the boundary wall, and I followed a step behind. Catching my breath, I leaned on the edge. There were floodlights here too, and I mentally traced our route – across the bare ground that surrounded the centre, into the trees and then turn right. If we kept going, we'd eventually come to the road to Cambergull. Once we were over it, there was only a bit more forest before we reached the grasslands, and, beyond that, the Firstwood. *I'm coming home, my tuarts.*

"So what now?" I asked Connor. "Float down the wall and then run?" He was staring down at the ground, and I knew he was imagining how visible we'd be, running across that long distance in the glare of the lights. "We'll be fine. There's no one here to see us," I assured him.

He shook his head. "Things keep going *wrong*. And I don't want to take any more risks. Not with you."

"It's not that big a risk! And your ability…"

"I can handle my ability. We have to fly, Ashala. Just until we're over the gravel and into the cover of the trees."

I wanted to ask if he was sure he'd be able to do it, but that would sound like I doubted him, and I didn't. In fact, I didn't really think that there was anything Connor couldn't do. Taking a tighter grip on the box, I said, "OK. We fly."

He grinned at me. And then I was pulled off my feet, and flung into the sky at his side.

THE ESCAPE
THE FALL

I went hurtling through the air so fast that it felt like the skin was being pushed back from my bones. I clung on to the box as Connor and I careered onwards, weaving shakily from side to side as we left the gravelly, floodlit earth behind. We plunged over the forest and slowed, beginning to descend.

Zap! Something bright and hot streaked upwards through the night.

Suddenly I was falling, faster and faster, as if the air itself was trying to drag me downwards. I couldn't see Connor, couldn't see anything except brief, frightening impressions of the world as I tumbled through the trees. Small branches and leaves scratched and tore at me, but I somehow managed to miss the large ones that could have really done some damage. I stopped right before hitting the ground, and floated downwards to rest among the leaves, still clutching the box. I had an instant to realize that there'd been some sort of danger, and Connor had saved my life.

Then he came crashing through the trees to slam into the ground, and I heard the terrible sound of his body breaking.

I stumbled over to his side. "Connor? Connor?" Dropping to my knees, I felt for a pulse at his neck. But his heartbeat was weak and erratic, and when he took a breath, I could hear a dreadful rattling sound. I was gasping for air myself, and I didn't know if it was his pain or my own that I was feeling. In the dark, I couldn't see exactly where he was hurt, but it was obvious that it was bad. He spoke, a single word, "Ashala."

And, for the very first time, I heard what Ember heard when he said my name. The way he drew it out over three syllables, two short and one long. *Ashala. A-shay-la. I love you.*

Tears started to leak out of my eyes. "Connor, I'll go

366

and get Wentworth, bring her here. You have to hang on..."

"No, Ashala." His hand twitched, and I clasped it in mine as he rasped, "Shot."

Shot? That made no sense – there'd been something in the sky, but it had come from the forest, not the centre! Footsteps came rushing through the trees in our direction. I looked up in alarm, and let out a cry of joy at the sight of red medical robes. A doctor or a nurse! "Help!" I called. "Please, we..." But the words died on my lips as the blond figure came closer, and I took in the weapon held steadily in his hand. I couldn't make out the details of his face in the gloom, but I didn't need to.

It was Evan, Briony's enforcer.

We hadn't been shot at from the centre. We'd been shot at from the trees, where Evan had been ... hiding? Running? I didn't know, and it didn't matter. The important thing was that I had to get away so I could find Wentworth and save Connor's life.

"You," Evan said with loathing, stopping a few paces away. "I knew it was you."

Swallowing, I stared up at him. I still had one hand on the pulse in Connor's neck, and I was frantically aware of his stuttering heartbeat as I tried to figure out what to do. Then I remembered I'd taken a streaker from the centre. Which pocket had it been in? *WHICH POCKET?* I began to feel for it, doing my best to seem as though I was just shifting in place.

"You're alive," Evan hissed, "and you're escaping. Going back to your Firstwood, are you? Do you know she died? Do you even care?"

It wasn't in the left-hand pocket, which meant I had to search the right. I answered quickly. "Of course I care—"

"Don't lie to me!" His hand was starting to tremble, and I shut up, recognizing the high, jagged edge of instability in his voice. This was the second time tonight I'd had a weapon pointed at me by someone less than sane, and Wentworth wasn't here to help this time. No one was, and Connor was relying on me, and *the streaker wasn't in my other pocket!* Oblivious to my panic, Evan snapped, "You didn't care. *I* was the one who cared about her."

Is that what you told him, Bry? "I did care," I said. "Briony was one of my Tribe, and I care about them all." Meanwhile, my eyes searched the area around me, because the weapon had to have fallen out when I descended.

Evan took a step closer. "Then why wouldn't you help her? All you had to do was cooperate, do one tiny thing, and he would have let her go. But no, you were too proud, too stubborn to bother trying to save her."

Neville never would have given her an Exemption! Only I didn't bother saying it out loud. Because something had happened that made Evan insignificant.

The heartbeat beneath my fingers had stopped.

I turned my head, dreading what I would see, and found myself staring into those beautiful blue eyes, the ones that could flash with lightning rage or sparkle like light over water. The ones that gazed at me as if I was all that mattered, and all that would ever matter. They were wide open, but I knew he'd never really look at me again.

Connor was dead.

The entire world shifted, breaking apart and leaving me falling into nothingness. Evan didn't seem to notice. He was still ranting. "You were willing to let her suffer. You were willing to let her die! Maybe I'll kill you, the way they killed her."

He paused, clearly expecting me to say something, to beg for my life maybe. I just sat there. Couldn't he see that it wasn't important what happened to me now?

After a moment, he realized something was wrong. "He's dead, isn't he?"

"Yes." My voice sounded strange to my own ears, hoarse and hesitant, as if I didn't quite know how to use it any more.

Evan continued excitedly, "And he's an Illegal. It was him that was flying, not you. Neville's golden boy, an Illegal! And you – you *cared* for him." A grin split his features. "It hurts, doesn't it, to lose him? Tell me that it hurts."

Oh yes, it hurts. Something hot and savage bloomed in my chest, spreading until my entire body felt like it was on fire with rage and hate and the overwhelming desire to strike back. "She. Didn't. Love. You."

He scowled. "You didn't know her."

I laughed at that, a crazy, angry laugh that splintered at the edges. "*I* didn't know her? She was using you, the same way she used everyone to get what she wanted."

"She didn't. She wasn't." I could hear the note of doubt in his voice, and my lip curled up in triumph. He wasn't sure if she'd loved him, although he longed to believe that she had. I had a way to get to him now.

I rose. He jabbed the streaker in my direction, but didn't fire it, and anyway, I wasn't afraid of it any more.

Everything was becoming very strange – the world was going all fluid, seeming to melt into a new, strange version of itself. I thought I was probably dying. It seemed only right that this was the one loss I could not survive. And I wanted to use the time I had left to inflict pain on Evan, the way he'd inflicted it on me.

"Briony told me about you, Evan," I lied. "How you used to follow her around when you were both kids. She said you were like an ugly dog that she couldn't get rid of no matter how hard she tried. She *laughed* at you."

"She didn't! That isn't true!"

The shapes were extending outwards now, the entire world morphing weirdly, but I kept my focus on him. "You remember her laugh? How pretty it was, like her smile? You kept her amused for *hours*. She could barely speak your name without giggling."

"She did not." He raised the weapon, aiming it straight at my heart, and said coldly, "You tell me the truth, or I will kill you."

"I *am* telling the truth. So go ahead and shoot." Except he didn't, and I knew why. He wanted to hear me take it back, to say it was all lies. I never would. He'd taken Connor from me, and I wanted him to pay for it.

The pieces of the world that hadn't yet transformed started to dissolve. Everything around me seemed to be turning into symbols of themselves in a way that was oddly familiar. Had this happened to me before? I thought somehow that it had, that there'd once been another time when grief and anger had thrown me into this strange state of being.

Evan whispered, "Your eyes…"

My surroundings disappeared for an instant, before winking back into being. I was standing in a forest of metal, one where the trees were all shining shapes and glinting edges, and I wasn't dead after all. Because I knew, with total certainty, that I was asleep. More than that, I knew I was dreaming.

And in my dreams, I could do whatever I wanted.

THE ESCAPE
THE CHOICE

There was a man in my forest, one who had blood-red skin and a box of lightning in his hand. He thrust the box towards me, and a bolt came flying out. I dived to the side. I'd intended to move fast, far too fast for even lightning to catch me, because I could be as quick as I liked in my own dream. Only something was wrong. My body was sluggish and clumsy, and the lightning skimmed across my shoulder, leaving searing pain in its wake.

With a roar, I grabbed hold of the red man's arm, struggling with him for the box. I wanted to tear it from his grasp, except I wasn't strong enough, even though

I knew I should be. There was poison in my body, some kind of foreign substance running through my veins and interfering with my power. Had the red man given me the poison? I didn't think so. It didn't matter anyway, because he'd done *something* terrible, and although I didn't remember exactly what, I was going to punish him for it. That was why I was here, and I'd do what I came to do, or die trying.

We staggered together through the forest. I tried to urge strength into my limbs, and a brief flare of power pulsed through my body. I pushed the red man into a tree so fast he almost tripped over his own feet, and slammed his wrist against the metal trunk, once, and again.

He howled, and the box tumbled from his grasp. Before I could grab it, the red man swung his other hand into my middle, driving the air out of my lungs. I stumbled back, wheezing, and he went for the weapon. Snarling, I brought my foot down on the box. Pain shot through my leg. I ignored it, stomping on the lightning thing over and over until it broke into pieces. The red man lunged, and the two of us went crashing to the ground. He punched my face, and agony exploded through my jaw.

This was *my* dream, and I could do anything I *wanted*!

Again the power came, not as strong as I knew it was supposed to be, but enough so that I could give the red man one almighty shove, sending him flying backwards through the air. He bounced along the ground a few times, and stopped, sprawled awkwardly among the metal trees. I jumped to my feet, yelling, "Giving up already?"

He still didn't move. I limped over to find that his head was lolling against a rock, and blood was leaking out of his skull. *He's dead.* I'd wanted to make him pay, and I had. I'd killed the red man.

It wasn't enough to quench the burning anger in my heart.

I searched for another enemy, and caught sight of something big and white through the trees. How could I have forgotten? There was a house outside the forest, one that was shiny and windowless and circled by a high wall. The red man had lived there once, even though the house didn't belong to him. It belonged to someone else. *Not a red man, but a bad man.* I couldn't remember the other man's name, or even his face, just that he'd done horrible things, like the red man had. He was someone

I could fight. Someone I could kill.

I moved towards the house, heedless of the pain in my foot and jaw. *I'm coming to get you, bad man...*

Suddenly, a little girl appeared in front of me. She was small and brown and perfect, and there was blue light rippling and sparkling around the edges of her being. *Cassie.* I loved her dearly, but she was in my way, so I tried to get around her. When I stepped to the right, she stepped to the right, and when I stepped to the left, she stepped to the left. Finally, I shouted, "Cassie, *move!*"

Cassie lifted a chubby arm, pointing behind me, and I was afraid. Because I knew that somewhere back there was the terrible thing that the red man had done, the thing that I didn't remember and didn't *want* to remember. I shook my head. Cassie frowned, pointing again.

"No!" I yelled.

She stayed exactly where she was with her arm stretched out, directing me towards something heartbreaking in the dark.

I stared over her curls, to the house of the bad man who I longed to fight. *I can push her out of the way...* I couldn't, though. Because this was my lost sister, who I loved and hadn't treated right. This was the one person who, if she asked me to do something, I had to obey. That was the way things were. I knew that, and so did she.

"Cassie, please don't make me ... please don't..." But I could see that she wasn't going to listen. She would stand there for ever, until I looked.

So I looked.

And saw the angel, lying on the ground.

A scream tore itself out of my throat, and I staggered over to the statue. He was cold, and made of stone, and that was *wrong*! The angel should speak and move and laugh. The angel should fly. I crouched over him, trying to turn his head, to make him smile. "Wake up, please wake up..." He didn't respond, and I called upon my power. *This is MY dream, and I can do ANYTHING I want.* Something came to life inside me, and I put my hand on the chest of the angel, commanding, "Live!"

There was a jolt, a jump, a twitch. I almost felt him take a breath. Then the momentary flicker faded away, and he remained stone.

I glanced around for Cassie but couldn't find her. "Cassie! I need help!" Nothing happened, there was no one else to help me. Wait ... there had been someone else, who'd said that he would help me if I needed him. Who had that been? It was so hard to think! Concentrating, I dredged up a dim recollection of an ancient, laughing being. Someone who lived in all worlds, and in the spaces between them.

Someone who had made life where there'd been none.

I called out, putting all my hope and desperation into a single anguished cry. "Grandfather, *help!*"

In response, there was a sound. But to call it that was too small a word, too tiny a description for such a vast thing. It rang out all around me, a long note that was part of a song and yet was somehow the whole song too. The song sank into my flesh, and I started to shiver, whimpering at the sheer power and complexity of it. Pain flared throughout my body, then faded quickly, and with it went all the hurts in my jaw and shoulder and foot. *I'm better?* Still the sound kept coming, until I felt as if I might fly apart, shattered by something that was too unearthly for my fragile being to contain. Finally, it stopped, and I was holding the entirety of that wonderful, wondrous music.

I bent to the angel, pressing my lips against his, and whispered, *"Live."*

The song poured into the word and the word poured into the song, and all of it poured out of me. It ran into the angel, leaving me feeling weak and empty, but I didn't mind. I'd give the whole of the song and the whole of myself too, if it would make the angel smile again. He remained cold and lifeless, and for a few terrifying seconds, I thought that even the music hadn't been enough. Then his lips softened beneath mine, and his arm came up around my neck, pulling me closer.

Electricity sparked between us, and I was burning, but not with rage this time. Everything seemed to vanish, until there was nothing except the feel and the taste of him, and the music pulsing through us both. The boundaries between his self and mine disappeared, and for a glorious moment I was the angel, and he was me, and the two of us together were the whole world.

The kiss finally ended, leaving me dizzy and disorientated. I glanced around woozily, and found myself surrounded by a forest of ordinary, non-metallic trees. There was an unmoving shape on the ground some distance away that had to be Evan. I knew I'd killed him, but I couldn't think about that right now. I couldn't think about anything other than Connor.

I put my hand to the pulse in his neck, rejoicing in the feel of a strong, steady heartbeat.

He blinked up at me, looking bewildered.

"Ashala? What happened?" he asked.

You were dead and now you're not. But that wasn't the most important thing to say. "I love you, Connor." I saw his lips curve in a delighted smile as I bent to press butterfly kisses on his cheek, his nose, his hair. "I love you, I love you, I love you…"

Connor laughed, and somewhere within the simple joy of it I heard the dim echo of the life-giving song. Then he propped himself up on one elbow, and reached to push my hair back from my face. He held my cheek cupped in his hand, wiping at a tear with his thumb, and I lifted my own hand to wrap around his.

And he said, "Ashala." *A-shay-la.* "Let's go home."

THE ESCAPE
THE AFTERMATH

Ember says you can tell that events are of great social and historical significance when people start referring to them in capital letters. That was how it was with some of the things that happened on that night, and in the days that followed.

It didn't take the Inspectorate long to seize total control of the centre, not after they'd armed their supporters with the streakers from the cache that we'd shown them. But it wasn't until the next day that the fire was out. Once the flames were extinguished, Duoro drove the small sedan into Cambergull, and made a speech that would later be called the Cambergull

Oration, which was a pretty fancy name for an address delivered in the town square atop an upturned apple crate. He spoke of the terrible things Neville Rose and Miriam Grey had done, and recounted every horrifying detail of the deaths of the detainees, who would for ever afterwards be known as the Grasslands Sixteen. And then he went back to the centre with as many people as could fit crammed inside that tiny car.

Others soon followed, a steady stream of people who'd heard the Oration, or had been told about it by someone else. They arrived on bicycles, horses, even in carts pulled by oxen, and those who couldn't find any other way of getting there put on a pair of boots and walked. It wasn't only reformer types either. Breaking Accords was enough to upset a whole bunch of Citizens, many of whom had never even asked the Question. Under the Inspectorate's direction, they went through the centre like a storm, opening every container, unlocking every door and meticulously recording everything they found. Then they went out to the mine and recorded everything that was there too. They called it the Citizens' Occupation, and it was enough to make sure that there was no chance of anyone in the government being able to conceal what had gone on in Detention Centre 3.

In between and around the Grasslands Sixteen, the Cambergull Oration and the Citizens' Occupation, other stuff happened too. Not things that would be spoken of on the streets of Cambergull or in Gull City. But things that were important to me.

On the morning after the fire, before the light came, Ember and Connor went out to dispose of a body. They both told me I'd done the right thing, that Evan would have killed me. I just nodded. Neither of them knew the full story of what had happened that night, because I hadn't told them, yet. They didn't realize how angry I'd been, or what it was like to feel that all-consuming desire to hurt another human being. I did, though. I remembered it all, this time, everything that had happened when I was Sleepwalking while awake. Some of those memories I treasured – the ones of Cassie, of the song and of Connor, coming back to life.

The rest of it, I wished I could forget.

On the third day after the fire, I went to the caves and found Georgie. The two of us wandered together through the Firstwood, down to the big deep lake, and as we went, I started talking. I told her everything – all about Grandfather-Serpent, and Briony. Killing Evan, and seeing Cassie, and the way Connor had died and lived again. I knew it would take me a long time to process it all, but I felt better for the telling of it, lighter in body and soul. By the time I'd finished, we were standing by the water, and I said quietly, "When I saw Cassie while I was Sleepwalking, it wasn't quite like it usually is. I think it was her, and not just my memory of her. Her spirit, or something."

There was one way to be certain, although I wasn't sure I even wanted to ask, in case I didn't like the answer. But I had to. That was why I'd come here, and why I'd brought Georgie with me, who'd known and loved my little sister. She was the only other person to have met Grandfather, I guessed, although she'd done it while she was dreaming.

Walking over to the lake's edge, I bent over to trail my hand in the water. "Grandfather?"

Bubbles started rising up from the centre of the lake, and I took a quick step back. His head didn't break the surface. But the sense of a *presence*, and a charged weight to the air, was enough to tell me he was there. "I need to ask about Cassie. Is she – is she with you?"

There was a rippling in the water, a movement of waves and light. It was almost like sunshine on the surface of the lake, only it gleamed a bright shade of blue, and it moved, flashing back and forth across the surface in patterns that somehow suggested a skipping step, a gurgle of laughter. *Cassie.*

Georgie clutched at my arm. "Ash, do you see?"

Blinking back tears, I answered, "Yeah, Georgie. I see."

"You know, you haven't remembered her right, Ash. Not in a long time. You've only remembered how she died." She waved her arm at the lake. "This, though – this is *life*."

Yes, it was, and I had my answer. It would never be the same as seeing my sister grow up. But I knew for certain she went on. She'd joined the song which, for an instant, I'd held within my body, and now seemed to hear everywhere.

The patterns faded, and I whispered, "Thank you, Grandfather. For Cassie. For Connor too."

The Serpent was silent, although I got the feeling he was grinning at me from somewhere in the deeps. "Um, do I owe you anything?" I asked awkwardly. "Do you want me to do something for you in exchange? I mean, you brought him back to life..." The wind picked up, swirling through the trees. After a while

I realized that the sounds it was making as it blew through the leaves were words, if you listened right. *My* words, spoken when I'd first come to the Firstwood – *If anyone ever comes for you with machines or saws or axes or anything, they'll have to get through me first.*

I murmured to Georgie, "I think maybe he helped me to help the trees."

"I think," she replied, "that maybe he helped you to help *you*. He's your grandpa, Ash, and a part of you was dying too when you lost Connor. On the inside, I mean."

Binary stars. It hadn't occurred to me before to wonder what happened to a binary system if one star fell from the sky, how hard it might be for the other one to create a stable orbit on its own. I frowned at the lake, wishing Grandfather would come out so I could speak to him properly. Maybe he didn't do that in this world. But he'd done something so immense for me, and it didn't seem like I could ever repay him for it. Watching over the Firstwood definitely didn't seem like enough, not when I'd do that anyway. Maybe he didn't realize that?

Clearing my throat, I said, "I always would've looked after the trees, you know, even if you hadn't done what you did. Are you sure there's not something else?"

A sense of amusement came emanating up from the water. Grandfather thought it was funny that I would waste time worrying when everything had worked out well. The wind picked up again, forming different words this time.

He lives. You live. We survive.

I turned into the breeze, inhaling the many scents of the forest in spring. "Yes, Grandfather. We do!"

On the fifteenth day after the fire, we had a picnic on the grasslands.

Nine of us were gathered together: two saurs and seven humans. Ember had stationed herself on one of the rocky hills, and kept scrambling up to the top to peer at the distant centre, in case anything interesting was happening. Jaz and Pepper sat at the base of the hill, bickering cheerfully, with Hatches and Wanders dozing near by. Georgie was wandering around staring at clouds while Daniel picked wildflowers to string into a necklace for her. And I sat in a large circle of grass that the saurs had helpfully flattened, Connor lounging at my side.

Ember came down from yet another trip to the top

of the hill. "I told you what Daniel heard in Cambergull, didn't I? That Belle Willis has put her name forward as a candidate to be Gull City Prime?"

"Yeah, you told me, Em."

"She might win, too. Especially since nobody will be voting for Neville now." She chuckled. "We've changed the world, Ash!"

I laughed back at her. "I guess we have."

Jaz said, in a disgruntled tone, "Did she tell you he *also* said Friends of Detainees think Detention Centre 3 should be made into a memorial museum? A museum, Ash! That means people will keep visiting it."

"Better a museum than a detention centre," I pointed out.

"I still think it would've been better if it'd burned down completely. If too many people start coming to that place, *my* Tribe might have to do something about it."

"Remember what we agreed, Jaz," I warned him. "The saur Tribe isn't to do anything outside the grasslands without speaking to me first."

My enterprising Firestarter had somehow persuaded the lizards to adopt the rest of the detainees, and Pepper too. Worrying about what crazy schemes those wild children might dream up was already causing me sleepless nights, and all I could really do was hope that the saurs would keep them in line.

Pepper nudged her brother, whispering something in his ear. He shook his head, and she whispered again, more urgently. Finally he said, "Ask him yourself!"

She beamed at Connor. "Can you make me fly? Ash *promised* she would, but she hasn't yet."

"Pepper!" I protested. "I've been a bit busy, you know."

Connor didn't say anything, but Pepper began to rise into the air. She circled over the top of us, giggling like crazy, while I glanced from her to Connor. He was dressed like a proper Tribe member now, in patched Gull-City-blue shirt and pants, the colour of his clothes making his eyes seem all the bluer beneath his rumpled hair. Personally, I thought he'd never looked more gorgeous.

Pepper came drifting down from the sky to land next to Jaz, calling out, "I flew! I flew, I flew, I flew!"

I reached over to brush a smudge of dirt off Connor's cheek. "If I could do what you do, I don't think I'd ever walk on the ground."

He smiled dazzlingly. "Stick with me and you'll never have to."

I grinned, and bent my head to kiss him, just because I wanted to and I could. It wasn't a bring-someone-back-from-death kiss. But it had its own wild magic, wrapping us up together and carrying us away into a space that was for ever ours. When it ended we were both shaking a little, and I leaned my forehead against his, resting my hand on his chest and enjoying being close to him. Until some grass hit me in the shoulder, and a disgusted voice complained, "Do you *have* to do that where people can see you?"

"I'm afraid you're going to have to get used to it, Jaz," I said. Then I noticed Georgie, and I let Connor go, jumping to my feet. She'd come right up to the edge of where we were all sitting, and was gazing blankly into the distance. Out on the grasslands, Daniel was standing still, holding a bunch of flowers in his hand. Like me, he wasn't sure whether there was something to be concerned about yet. Moving closer to her, I said quietly, "Georgie? Do you *see* something?"

For a second, she didn't respond. Then she focused on my face, and asked, very seriously, "Ash, is this the real world?"

I was so relieved I started to laugh. A moment later, I felt myself rising upwards into the air. Lifting my face to the sun, I stretched out my arms, turning slowly in space.

"Yes, Georgie!" I shouted joyfully. "This is the real world!"

AUTHOR'S NOTE

Where do you get your ideas?

This is a question that writers get asked all the time, and more often than not, the answer I give is "Everywhere!" Writers, at least in my experience, run short on time, money and energy; never on ideas. But when I am writing The Tribe series, I feel as though it is a story I discover more than one I create; it is as if the characters take me on their own journeys, which I interpret through the lens of my experiences. There has been so much interest in the parts of Ashala's story which are drawn from my own cultural background that I thought it was worth saying something about the source of these aspects of the novel.

Aboriginal people of Australia have the oldest continuous living culture on earth. We are not a single homogenous group; we are many nations, and we hail from diverse homelands. Some of us are rangeland people, some forest and some desert, some river and some salt water. We call our homelands our Countries. The Country of my people, the Palyku people, is dry, inland Country. But in case you are thinking of unending sand-dunes, that's not what it looks like; Palyku Country is a place of sharp contrasts and bright colours – red earth, yellow spinifex grass bleached white, purple hills, green gum trees and blue sky.

The world that Ashala occupies is not Australia, of course. There is no Australia in Ashala's time, and nowhere else that exists now either. The earth has torn itself apart, the tectonic plates have shifted and a single, entirely new continent is the only piece of land remaining on the planet. But every landscape I describe in The Tribe series is inspired by one of the many biodiverse regions of Australia. So there really are towering tuarts: they grow in the Country of the Nyoongah people, in the south-west of Western Australia, and are one of the rarest ecosystems on earth.

In Ashala's world, where people no longer distinguish themselves on the basis of race, the word "Aboriginal" would have no meaning. But Ashala carries that ancient bloodline, and has the same deep connection to the Firstwood that present-day Aboriginal people have to their Countries. For me, one of the most profound moments in *The Interrogation of Ashala Wolf* is when Ashala is being taken to the machine for the final time, thinking she is about to die, and the wind brings her the scent of eucalyptus from the faraway Firstwood. She has, or so she believes, no hope of escape; but she is not alone.

The best storytellers I know are Aboriginal Elders. So in writing about the Tribe, I thought about the way the Elders draw you into a tale that is always more than it first appears. I thought, too, about the generations of Palyku women who have gone before me, who have walked red earth and told the ancient tales of my people beneath the glittering stars of a desert night. Great storytellers, one and all. Their tales are like gifts that can continually be unwrapped, so filled with layers of meaning that you never reach the end of the wisdom or comfort that the story holds. And I tried to honour that tradition by writing a tale that was, first and foremost, a riveting tale – as their stories always are – but that asked bigger questions about what has been, what is and what will be.

My great-grandmother once described Australia as a place where everything lives and nothing dies. She was talking about a way of understanding the world as a web of living, interconnected beings; where everything is born from, and eventually goes back to, the greater pattern of life itself. The oldest of our stories tell us that our Countries began with the creative Ancestors, in what is often called the Dreaming. These Ancestors came in many shapes – magpie and kangaroo, butterfly and serpent, sun and moon – and through their songs, dances and travels, the world was made.

In such a world, the fact that we humans may not always understand the voices of other beings – the cry of Crow, the murmurings of Rain or Wind, or the slow rumble of Rock – does not mean those voices do not exist. And it is through sustaining caring relationships with other shapes of life that we give substance and meaning to our own existence. When seen in the context of this greater pattern, all our actions and interactions with the world take on a larger significance. It is this idea which is captured, in much simpler terms, in the concept of the Balance – that there is an inherent balance between all life, and the only way to preserve it is to live in harmony with ourselves, with each other, and with the earth.

In *The Interrogation of Ashala Wolf*, it is one of the clever old spirits of the earth who survives the destruction of everything else. He travels through the chaos, carrying scraps of life in his mouth, and arrives at what will become the Firstwood. Then, as he tells Ashala, he sings – to remind life of its shapes, strength and its many transformations. Until life remembers its nature, and grows.

To write a dystopia is to write of the end of the world. But in an animate, interconnected existence, where everything has consciousness and agency, life is not easily overcome. Its nature is always to adapt, to change, to make itself anew – and in so doing, to remake all else. This is the cry of the trees of the Firstwood: We live. You live. We survive!

Everything lives, and nothing dies.

ACKNOWLEDGEMENTS

No novel is ever written alone, and especially not this one. A heartfelt thanks must go to everyone at Walker Books, especially Sarah Foster, who believed in Ashala's story even when she only had one chapter of it; and Mary Verney, whose editorial input has brought out the world I saw in my head.

Beyond that, this book would not exist at all without the love and support of my family. Thanks go to Mum, who convinced me to keep writing when I wanted to quit; to Blaze, for the coolest title ever; and to Zeke, who twice intervened to put this story on the right path. Love you all.

ABOUT THE AUTHOR

Ambelin Kwaymullina loves reading science-fiction and fantasy novels, and has wanted to write a book since she was six years old. She comes from the Palyku people of the Pilbara region of Western Australia. When not writing or reading she works in cultural heritage, illustrates picture books and hangs out with her dogs. She has previously written a number of children's picture books, both alone and with other members of her family. *The Interrogation of Ashala Wolf* is her first novel. To find out more about Ambelin and the Tribe, visit www.thefirstwood.com.au.